BREAKING DOWN
HER WALLS

D0036282

By the Author

Falling into Her

Breaking Down Her Walls

Visit us at www.boldstrokesbooks.com

BREAKING DOWN HER WALLS

by
Erin Zak

2018

CREDITS
EDITOR: BARBARA ANN WRIGHT
PRODUCTION DESIGN: STACIA SEAMAN
COVER DESIGN BY MELODY POND

Acknowledgments

My heart belongs to Colorado. I grew up there. I experienced falling in love there, as well as my first heartbreak. It's where I figured myself out. Colorado has a soul, and fortunate people get to feel that soul. When I started writing this story, I was hoping the process would help me stop missing everything about living there, but all it did was remind me why I fell in love with Colorado's soul. I hope that I successfully made the mountains, the sky, the smells just as much a part of the story as the main characters, because for me? All of those things are why this story works to begin with.

I want to thank Radclyffe, Sandy Lowe, and the Bold Strokes Books team for taking another chance on me and my words. This entire experience has been so incredible, and I am honored that anyone thinks my stories are worth telling. So, thank you.

I also would like to thank my friends (writer friends included!) and family. For putting up with me when I had a deadline, for encouraging me when I was stuck in a rut, and for having a beer with me when I was so discouraged. The support and love I receive on a daily basis is so important, and I love every second, even when it might not seem that way.

Of course, I want to thank my amazing editor, Barbara. Your humor, wit, offerings of cake, and knowledge are so wonderful, and I thank the higher powers that I'm fortunate enough to have you on my side. Let's saddle up those unicorns and head into the sunset.

Also, I would like to thank my beta readers. Without either one of you, this would never have been what it is today. And I love you both for helping and encouraging and for rooting for these insanely flawed characters, especially for Julia, because she may be more like me than any other character I've ever created.

And I always save the best for last…I want to thank my readers. I never thought I'd ever be able to say that! But I do have some and it makes me so happy. I can't even describe the happiness, and I'm a writer! I should be able to explain things! The excitement you all had for *Falling Into Her*, and now for *Breaking Down Her Walls*, is so amazing and wonderful and unexpected. Thank you, thank you, thank you, from the bottom of my heart.

For anyone who has felt worthless…
You're worth it. You're always worth it.

CHAPTER ONE

Julia Finch's lime green '75 Dodge Dart stutters to a stop, clearly just as tired from the long drive as she is. She's been pushing her trusty friend hard for the past three days and is surprised the car has made it this far. Julia figured it'd crap out somewhere in Kansas. Hell, or ten feet away from her rundown studio apartment in Chicago. Now she's hoping to God it doesn't die on her in this small Colorado town that she was detoured to. She didn't pay much attention to the Falling Rocks signs, but when the highway was closed due to a rock slide, she realized maybe she should have heeded their warning.

She glances around the empty parking lot of the general store from the safety of her vehicle and wonders if she has stumbled into another realm. The town is straight from what she imagines the 1950s may have looked like. She hopes to God no one sees her and tries to be cordial. Julia always runs into someone somewhere who wants to learn more, ask more, look more than she wants or needs. And this place seems like just the spot where the people may have nothing better to do than ask questions.

Julia is angry about the detour. She just wants to drive and get away from Chicago, but now she's in this wide spot in the road for who knows how long? She takes a couple breaths and tells herself to calm down. She's farther along in her travels than she thought she'd be with only a couple days' travel. She needs a shower and a good night's sleep with clean sheets, so maybe this is the perfect opportunity.

When Julia stands, her knees ache, and she dreads the thought of getting back in her car for even another second. The temperature outside is warm, probably high eighties, and the sun is shining high and bright in the sky. Rocky, snowcapped peaks surround the town with a striking blue backdrop. Julia's not sure if she's ever seen a sky that color blue before. The colors are so vivid and beautiful that they practically take her breath away. She'd been so engrossed in driving and so pissed off about the detour that she didn't even bother looking at the scenery.

Julia looks up and down the main drag before hastily yanking her long blond hair back into a ponytail. She's hot and irritated, and this Podunk town is doing nothing for her mood. The street is littered with normal small-town staples: a pharmacy, a hardware store, a rinky-dink restaurant, a post office, and a Sinclair gas station with a giant green dinosaur in front of it. Quite a few people are walking from store to store, waving their hellos to each other, probably asking how the family is doing, how are the kids, how is little Suzie's ear infection.

"Try not to stick out like a sore thumb," Julia mumbles. She grabs a grocery basket on her way through the squeaky store door, slips the arm of her sunglasses over the neck of her black tank top, and tries to take her own advice. There's an older woman with very short gray hair toward the back working in the deli and a younger woman by the cash registers dressed like she's ready for a night on the town—certainly not *this* town. But another, more amazing town that actually *has* a nightlife. Julia nods a greeting toward the woman behind the deli counter and starts down the first aisle.

Julia grabs a few necessities (Doritos, bananas, a loaf of bread, Little Debbie snack cakes, three large bottles of water) and stops by the deli counter, where she receives a gentle nod from the older woman. Her name tag says "Agnes." Julia smiles. "Can I get a half pound of the smoked turkey?" she asks. Agnes peers at her from over a pair of glasses that have seen better days. The right arm is being held together with a piece of duct tape, and for some reason, Julia finds it ridiculously adorable.

"Sure thing, miss." Agnes goes to work, slapping cold cuts onto the scale, occasionally looking up and glaring from over the top of the rickety glasses. "Just the turkey?" she asks, nodding toward Julia.

Julia crosses her arms and adjusts her stance. "Yes. Unless you have a suggestion on some of these salads."

"Well," Agnes says as she bags the cold cuts and slides the plastic baggie across the cooler, "I made them, so they're all good."

"You made them? Like, from scratch?" Julia is shocked. When

was the last time she was in a grocery store where a single, solitary person just whipped up the pasta salad?

Agnes nods and when she does so, the extra skin under her neck nods along. She points to a couple of the salads. "This one here is good. I'm a fan of the broccoli raisin salad here." And then her finger from behind the glass lands on one. "The potato salad is the best, though. My great-granny's recipe. I'd get yourself some of that."

"Okay, then," Julia says, clearing her throat. "I'll take a quarter pound."

"Better take a half pound. You won't be disappointed."

"Well, all right." A smile comes to Julia's lips. "Thank you."

"Is that all?"

Julia nods and picks up the bag of turkey. "Maybe you could," she says and worries her bottom lip with her teeth, "tell me where I could get a room for a few days. Since, y'know, I'm not from around here."

Agnes lets out a low chuckle, one that says *obviously you aren't from around here.* She wipes her hands on her apron before saying, "There's a motel a couple blocks down on your left. Should have some accommodations for your type."

Your type? "Thanks," Julia says after furrowing her brow. *What the hell is that supposed to mean? My type?* She makes her way up to the checkout line to pay. The young, leggy brunette running the cash register is helping a guy who's wearing a long-sleeved shirt, blue jeans, and a cowboy hat. The girl is pretty in a way that screams for attention, especially considering the way she's dressed, but she's also plain in a way that is so small town that it almost makes Julia sad. It's not like Julia's much older than the girl. In fact, they may be the same age. Twenty-six, twenty-seven, but damn, Julia instantly feels like she's lived a lifetime compared to this girl.

Julia hears the pretty clerk ask the cowboy if he's hired a new ranch hand yet. He takes his hat off, wipes his mouth with the back of his hand, and laughs. When he answers that it's not easy to find someone who will work for nothing, his voice is as smooth as silk with a country twang. Julia agrees; it sounds like a horrible gig.

When it's Julia's turn, the clerk eyes her suspiciously as she takes out each item from the basket and types in the numbers of the prices with ease. Julia feels uncomfortable and notices her palms are sweating.

"You're not from around here. Where'd you blow in from?" the pretty clerk asks, a smile spreading across her bright red lips.

"You don't miss a beat, do you?" Julia rubs her palms on her cut-off shorts and smiles.

"Don't get a lot of tourists. You in town for long?"

"Not sure. Just until they can clear that rockslide," Julia answers as she holds out a twenty-dollar bill to pay for the groceries.

"That'll take a day or so," the clerk says. "Those are very common, but dammit if they don't act like it's the first frickin' time it's ever happened."

"Great." Julia sighs. "I heard there's a motel a couple blocks down?"

"The Hide-A-Way Inn." The clerk narrows her eyes. "You don't exactly look like the type that stays in one spot for long."

Julia smiles, then glances around the general store. "You might be right about that." She looks back at the brunette and nods. "Of course, people do change."

"Not around here they don't," the clerk replies. "Name's Toni, by the way."

"Toni?"

"Well, Antoinette. But I hate the formality of it. So, Toni."

Julia introduces herself and watches as the newly named Toni bags the last of her groceries. After a thank you and a "It's nice to meet you," Toni rips off a piece of receipt paper and scribbles a number onto it. "If you stay for longer, give me a call. We'll go get a drink together. The Main Street Tap is a hole in the wall, but the bartender pours a mean beer. And you're gonna need it. Those temps out there can be real unforgiving."

Julia nods and shrugs. "We'll see," she says as she grabs her bags and heads outside, the temperature rising and rising.

❖

Toni is absolutely right. The Main Street Tap is a complete hole in the wall. But it is right next to the Hide-A-Way Inn, which is a nice bonus. The bar is the epitome of an old dive bar on the outside—and surprise, surprise, that is exactly what it is on the inside. Dark, dingy, smelling like old beer and cigarettes. A sign behind the bar reads, "We reserve the right to refuse service to anyone, no matter who you are, who you think you are, or who your daddy is."

"Can I get a Jack on the rocks and an ice water?" Julia asks over the dull roar of a twangy country music tune after she settles onto a stool toward the end of the bar.

The bartender, who looks like he's about the same age as Julia, looks up from washing glasses, then down the bar top at her. He turns around, wipes his hands on a towel, and grabs the neck of the bottle of Jack Daniel's. As he pours the dark liquid, the ice cracks in the fresh glass. He glances up again at Julia. "Anything else, Blondie?"

"An ice water?" she asks again.

"Like, with no alcohol in it?"

"Yeah, like, water. With ice." Julia hopes her face isn't showing that she thinks this guy is a complete moron. She watches him shake his head as he pours water over a glassful of ice.

"That'll be four dollars."

"That's it?"

"*Yeah*, four dollars."

Julia can't hide the shocked expression on her face. "Jack Daniel's, right?"

"Look, Blondie, I gave you what you asked for."

"Okay, okay. Geez." Julia slides a five-dollar bill over the bar top to the man. He slams his hand onto the money and moves it closer to him. Julia stares at the glass of Jack in front of her. She tries to hide her eagerness to down the liquid but fails as she swipes the glass from the counter and downs the entire glass. She notices the bartender watching her. He's rubbing his stubble, a look in his eyes that is both strange and scary. He places both of his palms on the bar top. His hair is a dusty blond, and he has deep blue eyes and honestly, he is really cute. If she was in the mood for sloppy sex with a man, she'd probably entertain whatever ideas are going through his head. She doesn't turn down sex these days, regardless of who's on the giving end. Equal opportunities, she likes to tell herself, when really all it means is she doesn't want to be connected to anyone for any amount of time if she can help it.

Normally, she can help it.

"You need another?" the bartender asks.

She nods, he delivers, and she pays. It's a beautiful dance, and she's pretty sure that if she could afford it, she would sit here all day and drink herself into a deep, dark hole.

Julia ducks her head as she reaches for the glass, then looks at her phone. She's been tapping at the screen trying to track how far she's off the beaten path now that this detour has happened. The map keeps loading and loading, showing nothing but a spinning refresh wheel. She looks up at the bartender as she swirls the liquid in the glass, the ice cubes clinking against each other. "Am I not going to get a signal here?"

"Not really. If you wanted a signal, you should have stayed near whatever city that accent hails from."

"Awesome," Julia breathes. She slips her phone back into the back pocket of her cut-offs. "Do you think you could tell me how far the highway is from here? I'm trying to look it up on the maps app, but…"

He laughs. "Blondie, you're pretty far off your path. You headed west?"

Julia tilts her head. It's none of his business where the hell she's headed. "Something like that." She hears the bartender huff. What is it with these people? Why are they all so interested? When she glances around, she notices a man at the end of the bar top; his cowboy hat is sitting on the counter in front of him, and a small woman with dark hair and a pixie haircut is next to him. Julia overhears the man say something about a ranch hand and if he doesn't find one soon, "Bennett is gonna have his head."

"Wait a second," Julia mumbles, making it obvious that she's eavesdropping. It's the same guy from earlier that day in the general store. "Hey," she shouts at the bartender; he lifts his head and walks closer to her area. "What's up with this guy?" She jerks her thumb toward the couple.

"Elijah?" the bartender asks. "He's the lead rancher in charge of recruitment at the Bennett Ranch. Needs another ranch hand or Bennett is not going to be happy."

"Recruitment?" Julia asks, a laugh escaping from her throat. "It's not a college, for Christ's sake."

The bartender purses his lips and shakes his head. "You obviously do not know how perfect Bennett wants everything. And I mean *everything.*"

"Yeah, probably not, since I'm not from around here." The sarcasm is dripping from her words. "Why do they need another one so bad? Someone die?"

"Good *gravy*," the bartender says, his voice low. "You need to watch your tongue, Blondie, unless you like enemies."

Julia gulps and waves her hand. "I'm sorry."

"No, just," the bartender leans forward, "a lot of drama there. Not one to gossip, so you'll have to ask someone else."

"A bartender that doesn't like to gossip? Where the hell am I?" Julia asks before lifting her glass.

He pushes off the bar top and starts to walk away. "You don't need to worry about that since I'm sure you won't be sticking around long."

Julia rolls her eyes and downs the rest of her whiskey. "You're right about that."

❖

"Oh, no, no, no," Julia pleads when she tries to start her car for the tenth time. She keeps pumping the gas, praying, and cursing, and she's getting the same result. She cannot afford this right now. Not at all. The last thing she needs is for this car to do exactly what she has been dreading. She bangs her forehead on the steering wheel and groans. "This isn't happening. This isn't happening."

"It seems to me that it is happenin', City Girl."

Julia rolls her eyes, keeps her head on the steering wheel, and says, "I'm pretty sure she's dead."

"Well, that's a real shame."

Julia raises her head and is taken back by who is standing there. "You?"

"Huh?"

"You. You were in the bar. And the grocery store."

The man slides his thumbs through the belt loops of his jeans and makes a clicking sound with his mouth. "Look, do you need help or what?"

Julia watches as the woman he was at the bar with strides up behind him. "Elijah, honey, what's going on? Who is this?" She points nonchalantly as if she's trying to be coy.

"Young woman here's got a busted Dodge. I think we should get ol' Ray to help her out." He motions toward a car shop that's literally right next door. Julia isn't sure if she's annoyed at the convenience or impressed.

"I can handle it." Julia stands from the car and places her hand on the roof of the green beast. "I honestly don't even know if I can afford whatever's wrong with her."

"No, no." Elijah waves a hand at Julia. "Caroline, go get Ray. We'll get this taken care of for you."

Julia's shoulders fall after Caroline jogs over to Ray's Autobody. She disappears inside, and within seconds, an old man that looks a lot like Clint Eastwood is following her, wiping his hands on a dirty red cloth as he walks. When he gets closer, the first thing Julia notices are the deep wrinkles in his face. He has a very worn Colorado Rockies ball cap on, which he adjusts upward before he reaches out to shake Julia's hand. "I'm Ray, ma'am. What seems to be the problem?"

"She won't start."

"Did you flood her?"

"No. I didn't flood her," she says, complete with an eye roll. At least Julia hopes she didn't flood her. She's going to feel like an idiot if that's it.

He smiles, showing off some pretty gnarly teeth, but there's something about the twinkle in his eye that nudges the judgmental chip off Julia's shoulder just slightly. "So, she's just not turning over? Can I get in and see?"

Julia moves to the side and offers him full access to the car. She watches him get in, try to do what she had been trying, then get out quickly, and pop the hood. He's moving very well, considering how old he looks. She's surprised. *Not impressed.* Just surprised.

He works quickly under the hood, checking fluids and looking at sparkplugs, before he emerges. "I think it's just the alternator. But I'd like to get it over to my shop to be sure. Elijah? Can you help me push it? Ma'am, get in here and steer."

Julia does as he asks, throws the car in neutral, and in the rearview sees Elijah and Ray start pushing. She steers the car toward the auto body shop. She hears Ray shout to steer it right into one of the open garage doors. She puts the brakes on when they get into the spot in the garage and climbs out. "So—"

"Now, even if it's just the alternator, it'll be about a week to get the part. I don't have one to fit this. But I can get one. It just takes some time here." He motions to their surroundings. She had a bad feeling he was going to say something like that. "But if more is wrong that just that…" His voice trails off, and he folds his arms across his chest. "Just prepare yourself for the worst."

"And that is?"

"She might be going to that big car farm in the sky."

Elijah chuckles and stops immediately when Julia snaps her head toward him. "What do you mean? Like, you might not be able to fix her?"

"Uh, no, ma'am. I can fix her. But if it's an alternator, it'll be anywhere between three and four hundred dollars. If it's not the alternator and it's something else entirely, do you have a couple thousand dollars? Because it could get pricey."

Julia's stomach falls to her ass, and she gulps.

"I didn't think so." Ray puts his hand on her shoulder and squeezes. "Don't worry. I'll keep in touch here with Elijah and let him know what's going on with her. Deal?"

"I don't even know these people," Julia says. She realizes that she's whining, but she doesn't care.

"Well, looks like you're going to get to know them."

Julia walks out of the garage with a dark gray cloud hanging over her head. She wants to cry. Now what is she supposed to do? She was only going to dip into her stash for one night, but there's no way she'll be able to afford fixing her car. That cash was supposed to get her to… Well, somewhere farther away than this one-horse town. That's for sure. She was hoping to just barter with ol' Ray, but that's probably not going to happen. Her stomach is in knots. She cannot fucking believe this is happening.

"City Girl?"

Julia stops and sighs. "What?"

"I was just thinkin'…"

"Don't hurt yourself, cowboy," Julia mumbles.

"Easy there, killer," Caroline says with a voice that is much higher than earlier. She sounds a little like a cat in a fight.

"Look, I'm just tryin' to help you." Elijah moves so he's standing in front of Julia. "Why don't you come back to the ranch with me? I have a feeling you're going to need to make some money."

"I thought the pay was nothing."

"It is," Elijah says. "But I can always help you out with the car if you work hard. Are you a hard worker?"

Julia looks at his eyes, at the way he's standing and how he's handling this entire exchange. He's uncomfortable, and so is Caroline, who's perched right behind him. Julia's mind flashes back to her past, to the things she's had to do, how hard she's had to actually work sometimes, and she knows this guy has no idea what she's been through. She nods and finds a way to not glare at them both and their holier than thou attitudes.

"Then come with us. We aren't gonna hurt you."

Jesus, Julia hadn't even *thought* about that.

"Caroline, let's help get her things."

Caroline watches Elijah walk away before she looks at Julia. "Listen, I don't think this is a good idea any more than you do. But the ranch is safe and free, and we both know you can't afford to stay anywhere else. Just take our help. And stop looking at me like I'm some sort of horrible person." She takes off toward the garage, leaving Julia standing there, dumbfounded and, sadly, a little embarrassed.

❖

Julia feels like she's been in Elijah's old Ford pickup forever when she finally sees the road they're on coming to an end. She has no idea why she decided to accept the help these people were offering, but the longer she sits in the passenger seat with Caroline squished between her and Elijah, the more she feels as if maybe she is doing the wrong thing.

Of course, most of her life she's done the wrong thing. At least according to her birth parents, who sought her out and ridiculed every single thing she had ever done to survive. Her mind flashes back to their disappointed faces, to her mother's eerily similar blond hair, and how she said, so calmly and with no emotion, "I'm so glad we gave you up." And her father's simple nod and eyes that were hers and chin dimple that she hated she inherited from him. The memory of the encounter makes bile rise in her throat. She tastes it in her mouth; she wants to hang her head out the window, but any movement and she'll throw up. She closes her eyes, breathes in deep, and presses the feeling out of her mind, body, and soul.

Who cares if she doesn't always choose the right path? Honestly, she can't stay forever in this town, so maybe this will pan out in the end. She's gotta keep going. Where to? She doesn't really know—just knows where she doesn't want to be anymore. But this? Heading up to a ranch with a random cowboy and his cowgirl in the middle of East Jesus Nowhere, Colorado?

What the fuck is she doing?

She has no real clue, aside from hopefully being able to get her car fixed and escape, but the reality of having no other option and the fact that this is actually happening is starting to seep in as she sees the giant wooden overhang with an ornate metal *Bennett Ranch* sign proudly displayed.

Chapter Two

Julia hates admitting it, but the mountains are absolutely breathtaking. The higher she gets, the bigger they get. It's an odd phenomenon she isn't sure she understands. They stretch forever, though, surrounding her, making her feel a lot safer than she counted on and in a way she never thought nature could. They extend so high into the sky. She looks out the rolled-down passenger window of the truck at the snow-capped peaks. She breathes deep and takes the mountain air into her lungs. It's weird how the air almost has a familiar taste, like pine sap and cotton candy.

They follow the dirt road as it winds around, switchback after switchback, and climbs up and up, going through maple trees and then aspen trees and then pine trees. The road finally levels, and she wonders how far up the side of a mountain they've climbed because her ears need to pop from the change in altitude.

Julia checks the clock on the dusty truck dash and notices that it's taken almost an hour to get here from the town limit, and there is *still* nothing around, until all of a sudden, a log home sits in the distance. As they get closer, she sees a large, red barn off to the left and two circular horse corrals. There is a smaller, more run-down cabin to the right under a group of aspen trees that looks as if it's lived through quite the action. Storms, age, and lack of upkeep have made it look almost dilapidated.

They pull up to the side of the red barn and park next to two more Ford pickup trucks. As she emerges from the truck, she watches as Elijah helps Caroline out of the driver's side. The way Caroline smiles before she starts walking away toward the log home is sickening.

"So, City Girl," Elijah finally says as he approaches her.

"Y'know—" Julia says but is cut off when Elijah raises a hand to silence her.

"We need to get you a pair of gloves. You ready to start working?"

"Whoa there, *cowboy*," Julia says with a huff. "I have to start right this second?"

"Ain't no better time. Daylight's a burnin'." Elijah rocks on his heels and raises an eyebrow. "The quicker you start workin', the quicker you can get that car fixed, and the quicker you can run away like I'm sure you do best."

"Insulting me isn't exactly the way to get me to work hard." Julia is getting mad. *Who does this guy think he is?*

"Well, I reckon you don't have much of a choice. Am I right?" He studies Julia. "Unless you're curious?"

"The only thing I'm curious about is why you're helping me."

"Listen here." Elijah folds his arms across his chest. He looks as if he's kind, but his demeanor is completely the opposite. "Cut the chitchat, okay? I need the help. And I thought you were a hard worker?"

"I am."

"Then? What's the problem?"

"Nothing."

"You want that car back, don't you?"

"Of course I do. I just don't know if this is the job for me."

"Because all you're good at is running away?" Elijah drops his words and then turns to walk toward the barn, motioning for Julia to follow him.

"I'm not a *runaway*," Julia shouts, rushing up to help him slide the large barn door open. "Quit acting like you know anything about me."

"Okay, then," Elijah says over his shoulder.

"I'm too old to be a friggin' runaway."

"You sure shouldn't be in this town if you're trying to hide from someone."

"I'm not hiding." She's defiant in her tone and body, but her heart is racing because she *is* hiding, and she *is* running, and goddammit if she's going to start telling people here why. No one needs to know, especially this random cowboy in this random town. And he doesn't really want to know the sad, stupid details of her sad, stupid life. No one does.

Elijah stops what he's doing and looks over at her. He smiles a crooked little grin and asks, "Ain't ya, though?"

Julia folds her arms across her chest.

He takes a red handkerchief from his back pocket and wipes his brow. "Look, I don't have time to stand around yakkin'. You gonna help or not? I can get you back to town, and you can figure things out for yourself if you rather. I don't really give a good goddamn." He folds the red paisley material back into a square and pushes it into his pocket again.

Julia studies his face, his eyes, the way he seems so sturdy even though he's not much bigger than she is. He's definitely a dick, but there's a moment when this guy becomes endearing. "So, you promise this whole manual labor routine will help me get my car fixed? Because I swear to Christ, I am not about to do this for nothing."

Elijah nods. "And you can stay in the cabin over yonder. The car, free livin', and meals in exchange for hard work."

She looks away from Elijah, around the property, at her surroundings. The green of the trees is so vibrant against the blue of the sky. And the white trunks of the aspen trees remind her of the papier-mâché trees she used to make in high school drama club. The corral looks pretty run down, and it's in desperate need of some extra love and attention. She could actually help out around here. She knows she could. And she needs her car back desperately. That's non-negotiable. An inner voice tells her she should think twice before accepting the offer. In true Julia Finch style, though, she shakes Elijah's hand and ignores the inner voice. "You got a deal."

His eyes sparkle as he grabs her hand and shakes it hard.

Elijah then motions toward a wheelbarrow and a pitchfork. "Grab those tools there," he says. "First things first: muckin' the stalls."

"Shit. You, uh, you were serious about starting today?" she stammers, finding her bearings when she sees his irritated look and feels as if she's already in trouble. Julia catches a pair of leather gloves he throws at her face. "Just so you know," she says, trying to catch up while pushing the wheelbarrow. It almost falls over twice, and the pitchfork and shovel slide out and clang onto the ground. She picks them up, completely embarrassed by her inability to push a freaking wheelbarrow. How is she going to muck stalls and chuck hay bales? "I'm not real great with animals."

He wrinkles his nose. "Or people?"

She scoffs as they round a row of stalls. "You're a real comedian." The scent of manure and hay is so strong that it makes her stomach churn. Clearly the heat isn't good for the smell. She adapts, though, and breathes through her mouth. She remembers another time having to do this when she was younger. It had to do with a small car, vomit in a plastic 7-Eleven bag, and a hitchhiker.

The three horses hanging their heads over the stall doors start snorting loudly when they see Elijah approaching.

"We have a total of five horses. But we rotate the horses in the stalls from time to time, so you'll have to keep them all clean."

"Great," Julia responds.

He doesn't acknowledge her tone but instead carries on with, "Two horses are out now—Samwise, an American quarter horse, and Sweetie, a black Arabian. These others are Scout, he's a paint, and the pinto, Sully." His voice trails off as he goes over to a tall, white horse and lets it nuzzle his face. "And this…this is Jazz," Elijah murmurs while petting the side of the horse's face. "She's mine."

"She's beautiful," Julia says. "And huge." She cannot believe how tall the animal is. She feels like the shortest person alive standing next to it.

"Yeah, she's a white Arabian. Pretty big for her breed, about seventeen hands."

"What the hell's a 'hand'?" Julia asks, transfixed by the giant animal.

Elijah's words echo through the barn when he turns and waves his hand. "This is, City Girl."

"You're a *real* comedian."

"It's a measurement," he finally answers, showing her on his hand. He gathers a leather strap on the side of the door to the stall. He unlatches the stall door and swings it open, revealing Jazz, who looks gigantic. She moves around her stall a bit before Elijah rubs his hand along her side. "Roughly about the size of a palm. It's four inches. So, Jazz is about six feet tall from the withers," he motions to the shoulder, "to the ground."

Julia is about a half second away from freaking out. How is she going to learn all of this? Should she be taking notes? She didn't even take notes in high school! But as she watches Elijah explain different parts of the horse and attach a lead rope to a halter, she's so mesmerized that it takes her by surprise. An hour ago, she was ready to slug this guy right square in the jaw for taunting her, and now she's listening as if there might be a quiz afterward.

"Now, come here."

"No way."

"You have to get to know the horses. It's part of the job. And stop acting scared. They can smell fear."

"Perfect," Julia mutters. Her heart is beating so loud she wonders if the horse can hear. Her knees are shaking, too. Not only is she freaking out, but she's also afraid of being scared now because the horse is going to smell it radiating off her. *Just great.* She steps closer to the horse, which instantly bows its head and tries to pickpocket her shorts. The horse picks its head up, and next thing she knows, there's a warm mouth gently nibbling the palm of her hand. "Hi, Jazz. My name is Julia," she says next to the horse's head. She gets a snort of air on her hand in return.

"So, you know something about horses."

"Yeah, a little."

"Okay." Elijah hands her the lead rope. "Now walk her."

"Uh…"

"Part of the job." His voice is not kind when he says it, and it's making her so self-conscious.

"Come on, Jazz," Julia whispers, her voice cracking. "Let's do this together." The horse instantly follows her when she pulls gently on the lead. "Where am I taking her?"

"The corral."

Julia leads the horse, who is now nudging Julia on the back of the arm. She smiles as they're walking, hearing the gentle clip-clop of the horse behind her. "Good job, Jazz," Julia says over her shoulder as they approach the corral. The gate is open, so she leads the horse in and unlatches the rope from the halter. When she turns to walk away, the horse continues to follow her, and she just laughs. "No, Jazz, you stay here." The horse stops, and Julia looks back at Elijah.

Elijah looks at Jazz, then at Julia. "If you respect the horse, the horse will respect you. It's all about respect. Don't forget that."

"I'll remember."

"By the way," Elijah reaches out his hand, "it's nice to meet you, *Julia.*"

"And here I thought you'd just keep calling me City Girl." She shakes his hand, and he smiles at her. An honest to God smile. It almost takes her breath away.

"I still might."

"Oh, *great.*"

"Now, let's go clean those stalls."

Dread washes over Julia at the idea of having to smell the manure and having to get dirty and having to chuck poop into a wheelbarrow. And now she has to find a way to remember all of this information? She still has time to quit and leave. It's not as if she signed a contract. She can just call a Lyft. A Lyft could totally find her, right? Of course, that would mean spending money she needs to save for the car. And it would mean continuing to run. Does she really want to keep driving and running? She's never tried the whole "staying in one place" thing, and she has always envied other people's ability to commit to a person, a place, a feeling. Would it be a bad thing to just not fight it? She's spent her whole life fighting everything and everyone. And life has always fought back. And won. Maybe now's the time to try her hand at winning.

❖

After mucking six of the eight stalls, Julia feels fairly sure that her whole pep talk about winning is biting her in the ass. Her arms are going to fall off her body. Drinking two doubles of Jack Daniel's before working in the blazing heat was not a good idea. And even though the gloves helped, she still developed a couple of blisters. She smells horrible, too—sweat, liquor, body odor, and manure. It's a scent cocktail she never expected to be privy to. Her hair is sweaty. Julia put it into a bun, but it hasn't helped keep her any cooler. There is dirt covering every inch of bare skin, especially her legs. She's understanding the concept of jeans, even though she's so hot she could burst into flames right now. She would hate to see herself in a mirror because she is sure she looks a little like a barbarian. Julia leans against the wall in Sully's stall—he belongs to Caroline—and takes a long drink from the water bottle Elijah had brought her. It's lukewarm now but feels and tastes amazing nonetheless.

Julia wipes her mouth with her dirty forearm and takes a deep breath. She can hear commotion on the other side of the barn, so she goes to check it out. It's Elijah and a woman with long, dark hair that's pulled into a ponytail at the base of her neck. Even though she's smaller than Elijah, the woman looks sturdy. She's dressed in the normal ranch attire, except she has an old, beat-up straw cowboy hat hanging from a string around her neck. The jeans she's wearing are hugging her body like a glove with a flare at the boots. Julia cannot help but notice the curve of her ass and the way her hand is shoved into her back pocket. She feels her mouth go dry when her eyes travel up the woman's waist to the swell of her breasts under the dingy, blue plaid button-down that is tucked into the jeans. Julia is instantly captivated and feels herself hanging on every word she can hear coming from this woman's mouth.

Julia's ears perk at the name Bennett, and the realization that this must be one of the owners of the ranch hits her in the chest. Great. This is the woman she's going to have to impress so she can get her car back? The woman is rubbing her temples, pointing her finger at Elijah, and crossing her arms. She's standing very straight, like an arrow, and her body language is saying anything but excited to meet the new ranch hand. This is not going to be easy for Julia. She has never been good with authority. And she can tell immediately from this woman's posture and tone of her voice that it will be no different with her. Her mind flashes back to years earlier and her inability to straighten up and fly right. Julia is immediately dreading the rest of her time at the ranch, and she doesn't even know for how long that time will be.

"Free? You call a living space and three-square meals *free*?" Julia hears the woman shout.

"No, no. That's not what I mean. She needs to get her car fixed. I figured we could let her work here, and I could work something out with Ray." Elijah fumbles with his hat in his hands and his head held high. "I need the help. I can't keep doin' this on my own."

"We can't just have strange people staying the night here, Elijah. You know that."

"I know, ma'am. I know. But she needed the help. You know I can't just leave someone stranded. It's not in my nature."

"Don't act like you aren't a hard-ass when you need to be."

Elijah chuckles. "I know."

The woman crosses her arms, then points her left index finger again at Elijah. "You're responsible for teaching her everything. You hear me?" Elijah nods. The woman scoffs. "Does she even know how to ride?"

Elijah places his hat back on and pulls it down a bit. "It can be taught."

"*Jesus*, Elijah!"

"She's been muckin' all day. You can even go check her work on the stalls."

Julia hurries and gets back to the stall where she was working. She slips the gloves back on, breathing in through clenched teeth when the leather rakes over her blisters. She fumbles with the pitchfork but gets back to work, spreading fresh hay on the stall floor. Her heart is in her throat. She knows this can't be good.

"Julia?" Elijah's voice is behind her now.

She stands straight, turns, and plasters a fake smile on her face. "Hi," she says with a crack in her voice. "I'm Julia."

"I've heard," the woman replies; her voice is hard but smooth, her lips are full and dark pink, and the way her mouth moves is intriguing in a way Julia had not anticipated. "And you have no experience."

"That is true," Julia responds, keeping her cool, but not very well. The woman's beauty is breathtaking and rather overwhelming, and it's taking everything in Julia to focus. From a distance, Julia couldn't determine her age, but up close, she can see creases at the corners of the woman's eyes, and tiny lines at the edges of her mouth, probably from that frown that hasn't left her face. She looks like she might be around forty-five. A really good forty-five, though. She wears her age well, like a badge of honor. Her eyes are unlike anything Julia has ever seen before, fierce yet tired. Julia wants to yell at herself for even giving this woman's eyes a second thought. But she looks sad, as if she's made it through a lot of heartache and pain. Her skin, although aged, looks so smooth, and the color is beautiful, a shade of light brown that resembles coffee with just enough creamer. There is dirt smudged on her left cheek and across her neck. Julia hates eye contact, but as she catches this woman's eyes and holds for the briefest of seconds, she notices a flash of something in them. Was it kindness? Was it the same feeling of intrigue? She has no idea, but she realizes their gaze has locked a second too long when the woman's left eyebrow arches the tiniest of bits. It causes the hairs on the back of Julia's neck to stand at attention. She needs to pull herself together, or she's going to come across as a bumbling fool. Julia goes to prop the pitchfork against the stall wall and fumbles it again, causing the handle to almost smack her in the face. She catches it but is so embarrassed that she can barely feel her legs. Once Julia has the tool safely stored away from her, she looks at Elijah. His forehead is in his hand, and she's not sure if he's laughing or crying. Either way, she is positive she wants to jump from one of those high cliffs and never see this woman standing in front of her again. Julia clears her throat. "But I am a quick learner. And I'm more than fine with working off what I owe for my car."

"And the living arrangements and food, too," Elijah attaches to the end of her sentence after he has composed himself.

"Yes, and that. Those." Julia feigns a smile, still so embarrassed she may as well just sleep with the horses in a manure pile. "I love food," she adds, instantly feeling like an asshole for saying it.

"I trust you'll come to work from now on dressed appropriately?"

"Yes, of course," Julia says as she shakes off the feeling of the woman's intense gaze. "I'm so sorry. I didn't realize—"

"I know you didn't. Because you don't have experience," the woman says, eyeing Elijah now.

"Mrs. Bennett—"

"Miss."

Julia shakes her head. "I'm sorry?"

"I am not married. It is Miss Bennett."

"Oh, my bad," Julia mutters. "I just assumed."

"Everyone does."

Julia struggles to find her bearings. As far as first meetings go, this one has been a total fucking disaster. "I just wanted to say that I am very excited about this opportunity. I promise." She's lying. She's not excited at all. In fact, after this meeting, her stomach is in knots, and she's wondering what the fuck she's doing and why she'd ever want this job. *It's still not too late to leave and figure something else out.*

The woman turns around and heads away from Elijah and Julia while shouting, "You'd better not disappoint me," over her shoulder.

"Is she talking to me or you?" Julia whispers to Elijah.

"Both." Elijah shakes his head before he opens his mouth to speak. "I am very sorry," he says, barely above a whisper.

"And to think I was scared of the horses," Julia says.

"Yeah, boy, were you wrong."

"Tell me about it," she replies, picking the pitchfork back up.

"Give that thing a break for a minute." Elijah grabs the tool from Julia and walks out of the stall. "Food."

❖

A delicious cheeseburger and potato chips wasn't exactly what Julia expected after working her ass off mucking stalls, but it is exactly what she got. And the best salad she had ever tasted. So, she decides she'll stay at least for a night for the food. *May as well.* She happily munches away as she sits next to Elijah at the picnic table in the backyard area of the log home.

"Who all works here?" Julia asks around a mouthful of burger.

"Well, there's me and you, of course."

"That's it?"

Elijah takes a drink from a water bottle, then sets it back on the table. "We just lost Penn."

Julia gasps. "Oh God, I'm so sorry."

"What? Oh! No! Wait! She's not *dead*. That's not it at all. She's still alive," Elijah explains with more of a drawl than she's heard from him before.

"She? Penn sounds like a guy's name."

Elijah shakes his head, "Ah, no. Definitely a woman. Her name is Penny, Penn for short. She's more accustomed to the ranch life than I am, though. Better with the horses, too. She just…" His voice trails off. "You know, it's not your business."

"You're not going to tell me what happened?"

"Nothing that concerns you and your position here, so probably best to not ask too many questions." Elijah devours his cheeseburger, glancing over at the back porch of the house every so often. "There's Ed, he helps Elena run the business side of the ranch. But he's on vacation until vaccinations."

"Elena?"

"*That's* Miss Bennett." Elijah's eyes are wide as if saying, *I can't believe you just asked that.*

"Geez, sorry. How was I supposed to know? It's not like she introduced herself."

"She probably never will." Elijah shoves the last bite of the burger into his mouth, chews, swallows, and watches as the door from inside opens onto the porch and Caroline steps outside. "And you met Caroline," he says, his voice all dreamy.

"Goodness, keep it in your pants, man."

Elijah blushes ten shades of red and pulls his gaze away from the dark-haired woman. "She, uh, she works with Cole. Homeschooling."

"Who's Cole?"

"I am," comes a voice from behind where they're seated.

Julia turns around and sees a young man standing in the grass with dirt smeared across his face. He's wearing a dirty and tattered Colorado State University baseball hat that has probably seen better days. There's a pin in the bill that says *Rock Star.* She notices that he's wearing an old Ramones T-shirt, which makes her smile widen. He's tall and lanky with the blackest hair she's ever seen. His skin is so tan that Julia looks like a bag of flour next to him. "Hi there." Julia smiles, offers her hand. "Nice to meet you."

He returns the smile, takes her hand, and shakes it firmly. "I'm Elena's son," he says as he walks over, grabs a plate, and piles it high with salad. "I'm so hungry."

Julia watches him start to eat the salad as if someone is going to take it away from him. "All you're eating is salad?"

"Well, it's a big salad," Cole says, his mouth full of greens.

Elijah jerks a thumb at Cole. "Might be one of the only vegetarians I've ever known."

Julia's impressed with this kid already. "Health reasons or…"

"If I say it's inhumane to the animals would you start a debate with me? Because I really don't want that."

Julia shakes her head. "Absolutely not."

"Then that's the reason. I mean, you know we don't go to the store and *buy* ground beef, right?"

Julia's eyes go wide, and she swallows the food in her mouth. "Does he mean…?"

Elijah smacks Cole across the arm with his cowboy hat. "Don't make me get the hose, Cole."

A hearty laugh laced with the signs of puberty cascades from Cole's mouth before he takes a long drink from a water bottle. He points at Julia. "Are you the new ranch hand?"

Julia nods, still trying to get over the fact that they're eating family cattle. Are they like pets? What the hell is going on? "You look like you're about twenty-five years old," she says with a joking tone before moving on from the burger to her own salad.

"I'm sixteen," he says around a mouthful of salad. "Where are you from?"

Elijah lets out a laugh, then answers, "She's from the city, little man."

"What city? There are a lot of them."

"Chicago."

"That's awesome!" Cole's smile fades, though when he finishes with, "I've never been out of Colorado. Not that there's anything wrong with that. I just," he takes a deep breath, "I've always wanted to see the world. Or at least somewhere other than this wide spot in the road."

"Sometimes, the world is rough, kid," Julia replies. "But I know what you mean."

Cole groans when his name is shouted from the barn door. He shouts over his shoulder, "What, Mom?"

"Did you finish fixing the fence on the back forty?" Elena yells. Julia looks over at her standing there with her hands on her hips, tapping her left foot on the gravel.

"Yes, I finished it," he yells back and then rolls his eyes. "Does she think I want to deal with her wrath?" he asks Elijah while leaning over his plate.

"Man, is she always like this?" Julia says out of the corner of her mouth toward Elijah.

"She was better before…" Cole looks as if he knows he shouldn't continue the sentence. He ends up clearing his throat and finishing with, "You just learn to not piss her off."

"Don't let your mother hear you say that word," Elijah says before he stands from the picnic table and stretches. "Okay, Julia, let's get back to work."

She reluctantly stands with her plate and starts to follow him. She's going to like this kid and his Elena Bennett insights. "See you later, Cole."

"Bye!" he says enthusiastically. "It was really nice meeting you!"

❖

Julia closes the door to the last stall and takes a deep breath. She's done! Finally! She's finished cleaning and mucking, and all she wants is a beer and more food. Maybe chicken this time?

"So," comes Elena Bennett's voice from a few stalls away. "Why are you here?"

Julia makes her way toward the voice in the stall that had been empty when she first started. Now it holds a beautiful brown and white horse—the American quarter horse, she presumes—and Elena is brushing its side. "Excuse me?"

"Why are you here? Colorado. This town. *My ranch*. Why?"

Julia opens her mouth to respond, and Elena cuts her off with, "And spare me the 'it's none of my business' routine. It is my business now that you work here."

"My car—"

"Not good enough." Elena's voice is as dry as a piece of toast.

Julia pauses and chooses her words wisely. She watches Elena, her hands, her tan, toned arms, the way she methodically brushes her horse. Everything about Elena is mesmerizing. "Well, I can't leave until it's fixed, so it's going to have to be good enough."

"Why were you passing through town? Drugs? Don't you dare bring drugs on this ranch."

"Jesus, lady, I'm not a drug smuggler. What the hell?"

"Then?"

"I was getting out of the Midwest, out of Chicago. And without that car you won't let me talk about, I can't really keep going," Julia finally answers.

"And where were you headed?"

"You don't strike me as the kind of person that *really* wants to know."

Elena's eyes stay glued to the horse's side, and she clears her throat. "I guess you're right. I don't really want to know."

Julia lets out a puff of air because of course she was right about this woman's inability to actually *be* interested.

"I hope you realize that as soon as that car is finished, you need to be on your way. Understand?"

"Yes," Julia answers and holds back an eye roll. She really wants to ask why she would want to stay in such inhospitable conditions, but she refrains.

A silence falls between the two women as Elena continues to brush the side of her horse. Her hair is still in a ponytail, secured at the base of her neck, but it's looser than it was earlier in the day, and there are wisps of hair that have snuck out, framing Elena's face. She has this intense expression that Julia is sure she has never seen on another human being before, and she's not sure what to do with the feeling it's causing in her stomach. She hates that she's letting this woman get under her skin, but it's clear this is how she functions with everyone. And while it may be irritating and intimidating—considering they barely know each other—Julia decides for once in her life it's best to not rock the boat.

Elena clears her throat and looks over Samwise's haunches at Julia. "What is your last name?"

It's not a strange question, but it's one that no one else has bothered to ask, and coupled with Elena's intense stare and dark eyes, it throws Julia off guard. "I'm sorry, what?"

"Your last name. You do have one, don't you? Don't tell me you're one of those millennials that decides to go by a single name like you're Madonna or Cher." Elena makes her way to the other side of her horse and looks directly at Julia, an eyebrow arched to her hairline.

Julia shakes her head and immediately feels like an asshole. "It's Finch. Sorry. I just, people don't typically care what my last name is."

"Finch?" Elena asks, still looking at Julia.

"Yes, like the bird."

"Are birds your *thing*, then?" The question is sarcastic, but there's something in Elena's eyes that makes Julia think maybe she really does want to know.

"Yeah, I mean, I guess," Julia replies.

"Any particular reason?"

"They're free." Julia's response is so quick and matter-of-fact that the look that washes over Elena's face is something Julia wants an explanation for. In that fleeting moment, Elena seemed like an actual person, and it was frightening. And insanely stimulating.

"Are you not *free*, Miss Finch?"

Julia doesn't think she should answer the question. Regardless of what this woman has said, it isn't any of her goddamn business. But she finds herself compelled to respond. She opens her mouth and answers with, "I am now." She waits a beat before bowing her head and slipping the gloves from her hands. "Thank you for this, for helping me out, Miss Bennett. I'll see you tomorrow."

And with that, she turns and heads away from the stall.

Chapter Three

Julia manages to open the door to the small cabin while carrying a box, a duffel bag with some of her belongings, and a bag full of cleaning supplies that Elijah gave to her. She kicks the door open with her foot, cringing as it slams into the wall behind. As she reaches around and tries to find a light switch, she's hit with an old, musty smell. The light comes on with a pop and a soft whirring as she walks completely into the cabin and takes in her surroundings. The entryway is small with hooks for hats and coats and a bench with space under for shoes. *Actually, probably for boots.* In the living area, all of the furniture is covered with white sheets except for a small table in what Julia assumes is the dining room off to the left. It looks a little like something out of *Little House on the Prairie*. Or something the Boxcar Children would have lived in.

The windows all have the shades drawn, and the light that is sneaking in through the small spaces is catching the dust particles in the air perfectly. She takes a few steps inside the living area and drops the box and her duffel bag, which causes a huge billow of dust to form. A coughing attack later and she's going around to all of the windows, pulling up the blinds, opening the windows, and pulling the sheets off the furniture.

Julia looks around the living area and forces a smile. She imagines what it would feel like if this were *her* house. What if this whole thing was what she's been running toward since she took off from Chicago? What if all of this has happened for a reason?

A laugh cascades out Julia's mouth.

Who the hell is she kidding? She will *never* feel as if this could be a place to stay or actually find a spot to belong.

It's not out of the realm of possibility, though. *Staying.* Putting down roots. Aside from the town being maybe the weirdest spot in America, people seem to be ready to help out. Julia's certainly never encountered that before.

She shakes her head as tears start to form, and she quickly gets back to unpacking. She goes over to another box she brought in and finds her laptop, flips it open, and connects it to her wireless speaker. Once her music is playing, she feels a little lighter, a little more like being productive instead of standing around moping about her shitty life and the shitty people who just pass through it.

There's a knock on her door, and before she can rush over from where she's at in the small kitchenette, she hears the screen door creak and open.

"Hello?"

Julia rounds the corner to the door and sees Cole standing there holding a box from her car. "Cole, hi! What are you doing here?"

"I just wanted to offer my assistance…Help you with your things," he says, handing over the box. He's so tall standing there in her doorway, his dark hair a mess and his clothes still dirty from the day's chores. "You travel pretty light, huh?"

"Thank you so much," Julia says as she plops the box on the floor. "Yeah, I didn't want to be too cramped in my car." It's not really the truth. The truth is sad and lame, and who wants to hear that those few boxes and duffel bag are everything she owns?

"Do you need help with anything? I'm done working the ranch for the day. I don't have any homework." Cole smiles. "I'm a real great help in the kitchen, too."

"Oh, are you now?" Julia takes off toward the kitchen and motions for him to follow. "Maybe you can help me clean up in here. Sweep the floor?"

Cole's face lights up. "I would love to do that!" He lets out a laugh, his voice cracking, again from puberty, but Julia just lets them both think it's from excitement. "Sorry, I guess that sounds pretty desperate, doesn't it? What teenager likes to clean?"

Julia tosses the broom she found in the small pantry to him, and he catches it with ease. "Don't apologize. I'm glad to have the company," she says. "It's been a while since I've had it."

"The company?" he asks, running the broom over the old, yellow linoleum.

"Yeah."

"Same here."

"What about Caroline? And Elijah? And Ed, when he's not on vacation? I haven't met him yet, but I heard he's nice."

"They're great. And even when Toni and Agnes stop by...It's all fine."

"And your mother."

"Of course. Yeah. Mom, too." Cole clears his throat. "So, your car broke down?"

Julia knows the subject change tactic all too well, so she goes along with it. "Yeah, and I'll tell you what? It's not really helping my situation."

"What situation is that?"

"Well...I don't really know? I mean, I just needed to get out of the city. And now I have to work off paying for my car. This whole thing has put a real big dent in my whole plan."

Cole stops sweeping. "You actually had a plan?"

"What's that supposed to mean?"

"You just don't seem like the type of person that has a plan. No offense."

Julia wants to take offense, but Cole is right. Her plan is normally to not have a plan, to fly by the seat of her pants, to not let anyone else run her life but herself. "Yeah, well, whatever." She shrugs. "I guess you have a point. Guess I should just go with the flow?"

"Duh," he says while laughing. "I feel like you get let down a lot less that way."

"You're absolutely right about that."

They fall into a gentle silence. The only sound in the room is the music coming from Julia's portable speaker. She kind of hates that this sixteen-year-old boy has a point. There's no use in fighting this. Her situation is what it is, and fighting it will only make her more miserable, right? "So, Cole, what's up with your mom?"

"Why?"

"I mean, she seems like she's kind of drill sergeant-ish, but I figure she has a good side, right?"

"I think she does. I haven't seen it in a while."

"Everyone has bad moods."

"That last for years?"

Julia isn't quite sure how to respond. She wants to ask what the hell Elena's problem is, but she knows it probably isn't a good idea to badmouth the boss in front of her son.

"It's just nice to have someone else around." He glances up at her again. "You know what I mean?"

"I actually do get it," Julia replies, because she really does, which makes her like him even more. "Speaking of your mom, though…"

"What?"

Julia continues to wipe the countertop when she says, "Is she always going to seem so, y'know, irritated with my general presence?"

"Probably. But it just means she kind of likes you."

"You are blind, kid. She absolutely does not like me."

"Yeah, but that's Mom. She doesn't really know how to be *super* nice." He stops sweeping and finishes his thought with, "I mean, she's not mean. But she's just—"

"Abrasive?" Julia says. "Bitchy? Rude?"

"*Passionate*," Cole comes back with, a finger in the air to denote his point. "She's *passionate*."

For some reason, and Julia wishes she could push it out of her system, the thought of Elena Bennett being passionate about anything makes her entire body warm up. "Yeah," she replies before grabbing another disinfectant and continuing to wipe down the countertops.

"You'll see." Cole kneels down to sweep the dirt into the dustpan and then looks up at Julia. "Do you have anything you're passionate about?"

"Oh, I don't even know anymore," she answers before she even has a moment to think. "I was passionate about getting the hell out of Chicago and writing a new chapter for myself. But it seems the higher powers have a different story for me in mind. I won't be passionate about this job. That's for sure."

"That's what my mom wants me to be passionate about. This place. The ranch." Cole sighs and dumps the dustpan into the trash can. "I wish I was."

"Not what you want to do for the rest of your life?" Julia leans against the countertop and watches Cole as his face changes from sad to something else entirely. He resembles his mother so much in this moment that Julia is finding it a little hard to look at him, but the expression on his face and the gleam in his eyes makes her hang on for what he's about to say.

"I want to go to school to do architecture. I've been reading all these books from the library, and oh, God, Julia, it all seems so cool. Y'know, when you told me that you're from Chicago I was so excited because the University of Illinois in downtown Chicago has one of the best programs, and the city has some of the coolest buildings. I mean, well, the pictures look really cool anyway. It's, like, my dream school."

"Well, yeah, they are pretty cool. They have this really awesome architectural river tour you can do."

"Shut up, for real?"

Julia laughs at Cole's excitement.

"Man. That's so awesome. The idea of being able to draw buildings and bridges and homes and then see them come to life. I can't even tell you how excited it makes me."

"You don't have to tell me. I can see it all over your face."

Cole's cheeks flush a deep red, and he ducks his head. "It's just a pipe dream, though. I'll never be able to leave the ranch. Mom's pretty particular about that. She's been saying it since I was old enough to remember."

"Hey, kid, things change," Julia says.

"Do they?"

Julia doesn't know what to say. She knows it's hard to see sometimes how quickly things can change, but boy does she get it now. She knows his circumstances might not change, but maybe, just maybe, they will. She smiles at his dark eyes that look so much like his mother's and his dimples, apparent even though he isn't smiling. "You never know. Don't forget, you still have time to help her see the good side."

"True."

"When are you done with school?"

"Soon. I need to start applying if I want to get in anywhere. But…"
His voice trails off.

"What?" Julia asks.

"I'd have to do it behind my mom's back. And I just can't do that."

Julia shrugs. "Taking risks is what living is all about, my friend."

Cole's eyes lock on to Julia's, and he smiles. "I guess you're right."

"Yeah, but if you ever say I was the one that told you to do it, I will deny it. All the way to my grave."

Cole's laugh is so deep and contagious that Julia finds herself laughing right along with him. She pushes herself off the counter, grabs the remote for the speaker, and turns up the Madonna song. "I think that calls for a dance break!" Cole laughs harder as Julia dances around the small area, wiping the countertops as she sings "Like a Prayer" at the top of her lungs. Julia spins around, lost in her own world, and sees Elena standing in the doorway watching. "Holy *fuck*!" she yells while clutching at her chest; she somehow finds the pause button on her remote control. "You scared the *shit* out of me."

"Miss Finch," Elena says, "do you think it's appropriate to curse like a sailor in front of my son?"

"Mom, I hear it all the time from Elijah—" Cole is cut off by a wave of Elena's hand.

"Cole, don't you have homework?" Elena asks, her eyes never leaving Julia's face.

"No, I finished it all. And I finished the work with Elijah earlier. I promise. I was just helping Julia." Cole clutches the broom.

Elena looks from Cole to the speaker and then to Julia. "Madonna?" She purses her lips.

Julia thinks she sees the beginning of a smile there, but it's gone before she can be too sure. "Well, I mean, it *is* the best way to unwind after a hard day on the ranch."

"I see," Elena replies. "When do you think you'll be able to go into town with Elijah to get different clothes?"

Julia looks down at her cut-off shorts and her dirty red Chucks. "I have no idea. I don't really have a lot of money to spend on new clothes." She leans against the counter. "I was perfectly fine *today*."

"Just wait until a horse steps on your foot in those. Or your foot slides through the stirrup." She motions to Julia's feet. "You won't be fine anymore." Elena folds her arms across her chest.

Julia glances back at Cole. "Is she always this much fun?"

Cole's eyes go wide, but he can't hide the smile that starts to form on his lips. "Yes," he says, still trying to not smile.

"Mm-hmm." Julia looks back at Elena. "You want to stay and help clean up in here, Miss Bennett?"

Elena's right eyebrow is arched to her hairline. Obviously, it's not normal for an employee to speak to her in such a manner, and Julia is feeding right off Elena's surprised expression. "No." Elena's tone matches her posture, straight-laced and harsh. "Don't be too late, Cole. You have lessons tomorrow with Caroline."

"Okay, Mom," he says, his voice shaking with excitement.

"What the hell?" Julia asks after hearing the front screen door slam shut.

"Don't say that around my mom." Cole laughs. "She's being super nice to you. Probably best to just go with it."

Julia glances at Cole. "*That* was super nice? I seriously almost peed down my leg. She hates me!"

"Jules, she does not hate you."

His familiarity with her and her name is something Julia didn't expect, but she kind of likes it. It suits her. "How can you think that?" Her voice is an octave higher than normal, and she realizes she's screeching. "You're crazy!"

Cole smiles at her as he pulls the remote for the speaker from her hand. "I know because she didn't make me leave." He smirks before he presses play on the remote. He starts to dance around, mimicking what Julia had been doing earlier. And even though Julia was inwardly obsessing about Elena's inability to be nice to her, she can't help but laugh at Cole's complete lack of rhythm.

CHAPTER FOUR

"Elijah!" Julia shouts from the corral. "Oh, fuck, fuck, *fuck*! Elijah!" Elijah comes running from inside the barn just as Sully and Scout are galloping at full speed out of the corral. "Oh man, what the hell happened?" he asks, his hands on his hips, pure irritation all over his face.

"I don't know!" Julia rushes over toward him, her Chucks skidding across the dirt when she comes to an abrupt stop before him. "I was getting ready to approach Sully to take him back to his stall when something spooked him. He started running around the corral, and the other gate swung open—which apparently wasn't locked properly, which I want to point out was not my fault—and he took off out of it. And, of course, Scout decided to join in on the fun."

Elijah chuckles and starts walking after the horses. "Don't worry. We'll find them."

Julia starts after Elijah, fear and worry filling her stomach. She's only been there for two weeks, and already she's fucked up. Is this going to come back and haunt her when it comes time to pay for her car? She has hardly heard anything about the repairs or the cost except that it wasn't *just* the alternator. It was also the transmission *and* the exhaust system. So she knows it's going to cost her an arm and a leg. She follows him through the trails that wind back behind the house and barn, back where Elijah takes the horses when they need extra attention. The brush is pretty dense, and Julia's first fear is rattlesnakes. Every western movie she has ever seen seems to have someone being bitten by a snake. "How far do you think they went?"

"Not far, I'm sure." Elijah whistles a high whistle when they come to a clearing. The sound echoes off the trees and mountains. It's such a beautiful day, and if it wasn't for the impending doom of being in trouble for losing the horses, Julia would be loving this weather right now. "They're probably over that ridge. Let's go."

Just as they're heading toward the north ridge, Elena comes through the clearing directly in front of them riding Samwise with Cole beside her on Sweetie. Julia is immediately thrown off guard at seeing Elena atop the beautiful quarter horse, her hat smashed onto her head, and her posture determined and stoic. "They're this way," Elena shouts, looking as displeased as ever. She turns her horse around and heads back the way she came. Cole does the same but not before shouting, "Hi!" at Julia, waving his hat from across the open field.

Julia takes off down the trail, following Elijah. Both of them are running now at full speed, jumping over the random stones in their way, and Julia can feel the sagebrush that lines the path scratching at her jeans. She's thanking the heavens above that she wore jeans today instead of risking it and throwing on another pair of shorts—just to piss people off. It's funny; she's pissed off people intentionally before, but now? Now she's scared shitless that she may actually have to deal with the repercussions.

"Elijah, I see Sully over there," Julia says through heavy breaths. It's a warm day in the mountains, and running around at the altitude is doing nothing good for her. "I bet Scout isn't too far behind. Those two are inseparable."

"I'm glad you picked that up about them. They're best friends." Elijah comes to a halt. "You go that way; I'll come around the flank."

Julia cuts through the field and sees Elena and Cole on their horses coming up behind Sully. Scout is on the east side of the field about twenty yards away, grazing, so Julia decides to take a chance and go get him. "Scout, buddy, let's go," she says softly as she approaches him from the side. He picks his head up from grazing and whinnies. Julia walks right up to him and attaches the lead Elijah had given her to his halter. She pulls on him, and he starts to follow her, nudging her on the back of the arm the entire time. "Good job, beautiful." Julia looks back at Scout before turning to make her way over toward Elena, Cole, and Elijah. It seems they're having a bit more trouble getting Sully to cooperate.

Elijah walks up to her, eyes darting between her and the horse. "How'd you do that?"

"I walked up and attached the lead." Julia shrugs. "Why?"

"Because he is never that easy to get."

"Really?"

"You've been here for a couple weeks, and you're already better with these horses than most of the ranch hands we've had." Elijah shakes his head, takes Scout from Julia, and then holds out the lead for Sully. "Go. Get Sully now."

"What? No. Sully doesn't like me like Scout does."

Elijah points. "Go get Sully."

Julia sighs as she takes Sully's lead from Elijah and makes her way over toward the pinto. He looks kind of crazed, which makes Julia's heartbeat quicken. She glances back at Elijah, then over toward Elena and Cole.

"Julia, you need to be careful." Cole's voice is calm when he adds, "He's spooked by something. Look at his ears."

Julia nods, then stops, looking at Sully. "Sullivan, boy, come on. Let's go home," she says softly. "Come on, handsome. Let's go."

"Miss Finch," Elena says.

Julia doesn't look away from the horse when she answers. "What?"

"I don't want to alarm you, but—"

"*Bennett*, I got it. I need to *be careful*. I got this."

Elena's voice raises an octave when she says, "No, *Finch*. There is a brown bear about two hundred yards from us. I can see it walking through the brush."

Julia's head snaps toward Elena, and she stops in her tracks. "What *the fuck* did you just say?" She keeps her voice a normal tone so as to not frighten the horse, but her pulse instantly picks up.

"A bear, Miss Finch." Elena's tone has a lot more urgency than before. "We need to get the horse and get the hell out of here." Elena slowly slides a rifle from the opposite side of her saddle and checks the chamber, all while safely atop her horse. "I need you to cowboy up and get that damn horse, Miss Finch. *Now*."

"Holy shit." Julia looks at Sully. "Come on, Sullivan. Let's do this." She takes a few more steps, and he goes to rear up, but Julia holds her hands out. "No, no, it's okay." She's not going to lie; it really isn't okay. She can barely feel her legs because of the adrenaline pumping through her veins, but she takes another couple of steps until Sully finally allows her to get right next to him. She attaches the lead to his halter while soothing him with gentle encouragements and takes a step, leading him toward Elijah.

When she hands over the lead, Elijah hops onto Scout's bare back and looks down at Julia. "Ride back with Elena. I'll take the horses."

"You don't have a saddle," Julia says, her voice shocked.

"I know. We'll be fine. Go with Elena." He takes off on Scout with Sully running alongside him.

Elena's eyes are still on the bear when she asks, "Do you even know how to get on a horse?"

"Yes, Elijah taught me." Julia grabs the leather attached to the stirrup of Elena's horse's saddle and shoves her Chucks into the stirrup before moving her hand to the side of the saddle. Her arm brushes Elena's leg, and the heat radiating from her jean-covered thigh makes Julia's mouth go dry. "I've not done it with another person, though."

Elena raises an eyebrow, rifle still pointed steadily in the direction of the bear, and looks down at her.

"Oh my God, I didn't mean it like that." Julia watches Elena slide the rifle back into the saddle holster. She reaches her right hand down to Julia, who eyes the hand, then glances at Elena. The adrenaline is coursing through her body, but she can't for the life of her figure out how to move so she can take Elena's outstretched hand.

"*Today*, Miss Finch."

Julia swallows before reaching out with her left hand. Elena wraps her hand around Julia's wrist and before she knows it, she's being pulled up. She pushes on the stirrup and quickly maneuvers her body to slide behind Elena. "Won't this hurt Samwise?"

"Not for a short distance." Elena's eyes are still locked on the bear. "Are you good?"

Julia glances over at Cole before she slides her arms around Elena's waist. "Yes."

Coles smiles at her, his eyebrow rising just like his mother's does. "You'd better hold on tighter than that. She's not going to trot home," he says with a wink as he pushes his hat down and shouts, "Yah!" making Sweetie take off.

Elena grabs the reins tighter, clicks her tongue, and Samwise leaps into action. Julia hears herself yelp and clamps her mouth shut tight.

She's only ever taken Jazz around the corral at a nice and easy trot; Elijah said that she was bouncing around too much like a sack of shit, to which she took offense, even though it was true. Now she's trying very hard to not bounce off the back of Samwise, and it's harder than she thought. The way that Elena has situated herself in the stirrups and the saddle make it so Julia's entire body is smashed against Elena's. And she is focusing entirely too hard on the feeling of Elena's back, Elena's ass, Elena's *everything* pressing into her. She buries her face into Elena's blue gingham shirt and breathes deep. Even her scent is intoxicating, like lavender and summer and happiness. Julia cannot handle this. She's unraveling, and now is certainly not the time.

When they come to the clearing right before the barn and corral, Elena slows the horse down with a gentle pull on the reins. Julia feels Elena take a deep breath before she says, "You realize that could have ended a lot differently."

Julia loosens her grip on Elena's waist and clears her throat. Her face is on fire, along with other areas of her body. "I know." Julia takes a breath, tries to steady herself and her voice. "I am so sorry. I don't know what happened. The corral gate on the other side wasn't latched, and I would never leave it unlatched, so I didn't realize it, and all of a sudden, Sully bolted, and Scout took off after him, and I don't know. I feel horrible about it. I really do. I am so, so, *so* sorry." She takes another deep breath and stops herself from continuing to ramble. "I understand if you want to fire me."

Elena glances over her shoulder at Julia. "I don't want to *fire* you," she replies calmly. "But I need you to start paying more attention to your surroundings. There are a lot of things up here that you wouldn't encounter in a big city. Bears, in particular, happen to be one of them. And right now, the population of bear is increasing, and they are roaming around more and more, getting closer and closer to the house. The last thing we need is to lose a horse to something like that."

"Okay," Julia whispers.

"You know how important a car is to a police officer?"

"I do."

"Then you know how important a horse is to a rancher." Elena looks away from Julia and stops Samwise completely. "I didn't want Elijah to hire someone without experience. It's *not* because I'm a giant bitch, although I'm sure that's what you've thought. It's because not only do we have to teach you how to handle the animals, but we have to teach you how to handle the ranch. And the ranch *life*. It's not just my home. It's my livelihood."

"I get it," Julia replies. "I really do. That's why I understand if you want to get rid of me."

Elena lets out an annoyed groan. "I don't want you to leave, okay? I already said that." She clicks her tongue, and Samwise starts to walk again. "I know I can be a hard-ass."

Julia wants to argue. *Hard-ass* is too kind a description, but she keeps her mouth shut.

"I'm stubborn, and I'm rarely wrong." Elena stops Samwise by the corral, and Julia manages to swing her leg over and slide off the horse without making a fool of herself. "You're doing fine, though. Just keep working hard. I don't want you to run."

Julia stops brushing her hands on her jeans and looks up at Elena. She isn't looking at Julia, but there's something about the gleam in her eyes that makes Julia's stomach clench. And just like that, the moment is over, and Elena is riding away on Samwise.

But the moment still happened, and Julia cannot stop thinking about it.

❖

Julia wraps her wet head in a towel and steps out of the shower. The bathroom is full of steam, and the mirror is completely covered with condensation. She takes her hand and smears it across the mirror, revealing very tired eyes and cheeks pink from the sun. She glances down at her hands, at the blisters on her thumbs and the start of calluses on her palms.

She never imagined that working here would be leaving so many marks on her body. She has a huge scrape on her left arm from running through the sagebrush after the horses, too. It seems every time she turns around, she's getting another scratch, bruise, blister, or mark.

After Julia gets dressed and throws her hair into a messy bun on top of her head, she heads out to the couch. She plops down on the love seat and promptly puts her feet up. It's the first time she's really been able to sit down and relax. Her mind immediately wanders to the events from earlier, to the bear, to Elena, to riding behind her and having to hold on for dear life.

"What the fuck," she mumbles. She cannot be feeling like this about this woman. There's no good that can come of it. All that will happen is heartache, and she'll cry, and she has sworn off tears. Never again will she cry over a dumb woman or anything else, for that matter.

There's a gentle knock at the screen door. A part of her doesn't want to get up and answer it. Who the hell could be at the door at this time of night anyway? She pulls herself up from the couch, groaning from her sore muscles, and heads toward the door. Her eyes go wide when she sees Elena standing there.

"Miss Finch." Elena is holding a reusable grocery bag, but her face is devoid of emotion. "I figured you needed some groceries. You haven't taken Elijah up on the offer to use the truck to go into town."

Julia is too shocked that Elena Bennett is standing at her door holding a bag full of groceries to respond.

"It's just some necessities."

"Um." Julia fumbles with the latch on the screen door to open it. Her hands are shaking, and her fingers are sore, and she feels like an idiot who doesn't know how to open a damn door.

"First time opening a door?"

The latch finally comes free, and Julia pushes the door open. "You'd think so, wouldn't you?" she manages to say, not making eye contact. Elena steps into the cabin past Julia, and she can smell her. Is Elena wearing perfume? This late at night?

"I can put these away for you." Elena beelines to the kitchen. She always moves with such determination that Julia doesn't even consider saying she can handle it herself. It's easier to not get in Elena's way. Ever. Julia watches from the doorway as Elena unpacks the supplies. Elena opens the refrigerator, eyes the six-pack of beer and cold cuts. She glances over her shoulder at Julia, and Julia feels self-conscious, as if she's been caught underage drinking or something. "Elijah's been keeping you stocked?"

Julia nods.

"He's the only person I know that actually likes Pabst Blue Ribbon and smoked turkey lunch meat."

Is Elena talking to her? Like a normal human being? And being *nice*?

"You live like a homeless person."

Spoke too soon. Julia wants to say that she's clearly not homeless since they're quite literally standing in her home, but she doesn't. This isn't her *home*. It never will be. But dammit, even if it was, why was this woman treating her like that? Elena really knows how to make her feel small and insignificant.

Elena turns after finding a spot for the groceries and looks Julia up and down. Her gaze makes Julia sweat. "So, your car is going to take a few months before it's paid off."

"What? How did you find that out?"

"Elijah just told me."

Julia wants to vomit. A few months? This is ridiculous! What the hell kind of place is this? "Are you serious, or are you just saying that to hold me captive?"

"I'm sorry?"

"How much is it? Am I working for, like, a dollar an hour or what? I can't believe this!" Julia is pissed. There's no way she's hanging around for that long. She'll just escape and go steal her car back. She knows how to hotwire cars. That's how she got the old Dart to begin with.

"I resent the implication that I'm a warden, Miss Finch. If you don't believe me about your precious car, please feel free to call Ray at the shop."

"You're not going to tell me how much it is?"

"You can ask Elijah. He's paying for it, after all."

"This is bullshit."

Elena's face is beet red now. She looks like she's going to blow a fuse at any moment. But Julia doesn't care. She is pissed off! And for good reason! Elena's hands are on her hips, and she squares her shoulders toward Julia. "You realize that you are allowed to live in this cabin because I said so, right? That doesn't have to continue. I can very easily kick you off my property, and you would be consigned to finding other work. Somewhere else. Where you don't get food and lodging for free."

The tone in Elena's voice is enough to make Julia shut her mouth. She knows better than to argue, so she folds her arms across her chest. This "straighten up and fly right" crap is a routine she has had to do since she was old enough to remember. "Fine."

"Fine?"

"Yes, Miss Bennett. *Fine.*"

Elena mimics Julia's stance. "You still haven't bought boots, am I right?"

"How could I? I don't have a car. *Remember?*" Julia knows she's standing on thin ice, but she does not care at all. She is done being talked to like she's an idiot.

Elena clenches her jaw. Julia notices the way her muscle flexes all the way down into her neck and curses herself for finding it sexy as hell. "Nine and a half?" Elena's voice is dripping with anger.

"Do you mean my shoe size?"

"Yes, Miss Finch, your shoe size, not your age."

Julia can practically taste the disdain. She rolls her eyes, though, because fuck her.

"Tomorrow is a big day. We're bringing in a new horse."

"Elijah mentioned it." Julia furrows her brow. "Why another one?"

"We need another one for herding season," Elena answers matter-of-factly. "Can't very well have a ranch hand that doesn't have a horse for cattle herding season."

Julia's mouth falls open. Her anger is dissipating now that Elena has implied that this horse will be Julia's. What the hell? Why would Elena buy her a horse? "What are you talking about? I don't need a horse." She lowers her head but not before locking eyes with Elena.

A sly smile spreads across Elena's face. "Now that you'll be staying for a couple months, you'll need one."

Julia cannot stand this woman and that gorgeous smile. "I almost fell off the back of yours, though. I don't think this is a good idea."

"You'll probably fall off this one. I'm sure one of us will try to teach you how to not be a bumbling idiot." Elena cocks a dark, perfectly shaped eyebrow before she breezes past Julia and walks out the screen door.

And if it wasn't for that stupid sly smile, Julia would have been really upset by the bumbling idiot remark.

Chapter Five

Julia sits bolt upright in her bed when the old alarm clock next to her starts buzzing. For half a minute, she can't remember where she is, and it makes her heart beat rapidly. And then she remembers. *The cabin...* It keeps happening, the not-knowing-where-she-is routine. It's from waking up in too many different homes throughout her life. It never gets easier. She calms herself down and slides out of bed, her bare feet hitting the uneven wooden slat floor. Even though it's not yet five o'clock in the morning, she feels fairly rested considering she was up half the night worrying about bears and thinking about Elena shooting that rifle.

And that thought alone causes a chill to course through her body. Elena and her dark, sad eyes and beautiful smile have really gotten into Julia's head. It's not what she wants or needs right now. That kind of attachment is not good for her at all.

She pads over to the window, her bare legs covered in goose bumps from the cooler morning air. The sun hasn't risen, but she can see from the very early light that there is not a cloud for miles. The last few stars are starting to disappear. The mountains are starting to glow with the beginning of the early morning sun.

"At least it's beautiful up here," she murmurs before she turns around and heads over to the dresser where she stored the few clothes she owns. As she's pulling on a pair of jeans, she hears a knock at her door. She curses to herself and yells, "Coming!" and flies through the small cabin, approaching the door at top speed. She peers out the small window in the old, wooden door and sees Elena standing there wearing a red plaid shirt and dark blue jeans. She has that damn straw cowboy hat hanging around her neck, and aside from the pissed off expression, Julia has never seen anyone look as sexy as Elena Bennett does in that moment. "Oh, no. I must be so late."

"I can hear you. And you're not late," Elena says before the door is even opened.

Julia unlocks the door and opens it slowly, embarrassment flooding her. She watches as Elena's eyes take in her attire, from her white tank top, and unfortunately no bra, to her jeans that she didn't even get buttoned yet. Her eyes rake back up Julia's form and then land on her eyes. "Yes?" Julia asks, slightly breathless and definitely more turned on by this display than she probably should be.

Elena clears her throat, "These are for you. I took the liberty of guessing your size in pants." She hands over a box that says Ariat on the side and two pairs of blue jeans.

"I have jeans." Julia takes the items from Elena.

"You have jeans that are not made for riding a horse." Elena has her arms crossed now, and she's speaking in that same tone she uses to talk down to Julia. "The inseam on these jeans is flat so it doesn't irritate your...You know what? I'm not explaining it. Let's just say if you don't change your jeans and put these boots on, you're going to regret pissing me off."

It's Julia's turn to use the pissed-off expression. "Fine."

Elena turns to leave. "We're taking off in twenty minutes."

"Wait, we're going to *pick up* the horse?"

"Yes, Miss Finch. Horses don't just find their way here or magically appear like this is Hogwarts," she shouts over her shoulder as she trots down the steps and away from the front door.

Honestly? Julia has rolled her eyes more in the last week than she has in her entire life.

❖

Julia pulls her hair up into a ponytail as she leaves the cabin, slamming the door behind her. She is clad in the Wranglers that fit like a dream, tight in all the right places, and boots that are ridiculously comfortable, and she's only slightly pissed off that Elena was right. But Julia will never tell her that. No way, no how! And just to make sure she keeps a hold on a little bit of herself, she decided to wear a black and white Ramones baseball T-shirt. She better never be told she can't even wear her T-shirts, or she will pitch a fit. She's carrying a Chicago Cubs baseball hat that she can throw on if need be, just in case she gets scolded for that, too, which she knows she will. She's so annoyed already, and the sun hasn't even risen yet.

Elijah is standing by a very nice, very beautiful, black Ford F-250 that has an empty horse trailer attached to the back. He's talking to Elena, saying something about staying and riding up to the west side of the ranch to check on the new fence. Elena mentions something about getting an accurate count because of the wildlife. Elena looks over at Julia as she approaches and does a double take. Julia feels her stomach bottom out and her palms turn clammy, and she wonders if Elena realizes at all how much emotion is held in her expressions.

"Good morning, City Girl," Elijah says. He lets out a low whistle. "Look at you. Boots *and* Wranglers? Who'd have thought we'd convert you so soon." He motions to the baseball cap. "Now we gotta get you a real hat."

"Yeah, well, I don't think I had much of a choice in the clothing," Julia says and then bites her lower lip as she glances at Elena.

"You'll admit that I'm right one day."

"Doubtful," Julia mumbles. "So, where are we headed?"

"I'm staying here today. It's just going to be you two that head out."

"Wait, what? Why?" Julia says. "I mean, don't you need a couple people that know what they're doing?"

"Nice recovery," Elena says. "I'm going to show you how it's done, Miss Finch. Now, if you're ready?"

Julia watches Elena walk away. The sight causes something to stir in the pit of her stomach. The jeans, the boots, the old straw cowboy hat, the way her hair isn't in a ponytail at the base of her skull like it has been every day since Julia got there—it makes her feel things between her legs and in her hands, and she wants to smack herself for even thinking that way about her bitchy boss. "What the hell, Elijah? You found out about my car and didn't even tell me?"

"Whoa, whoa, I just found out last night. What's wrong? Where is this coming from?"

"Elena fucking told me! She said a couple months of work! Are you kidding me? I cannot be here for that long!" Julia can barely speak without sounding shrill. "I will never survive."

"Settle down, Julia. Please," Elijah says as he puts his hands on her arms to stop them from flailing about. "It's parts related, too. We aren't holding you captive. Your car isn't exactly a brand new one. It takes some time here. Your car will get done, but look, it's gonna be about three grand. Two months of work? That's not bad."

"Three grand?" Julia's heart is hurting. That's so much money!

Elijah smiles. "Is it really that bad here?"

Julia shakes her head. "I hate you right now."

"I know you do."

"And you're going to make me go with her? Alone? She hates me! And now I doubly hate you!"

Elijah shrugs. "We don't have enough workers for me to go with. Elena said she wanted to do this with you."

"You mean so she can murder me and dump my body on the side of the road," Julia says as she looks back at the truck. "Please have some beers ready for me if I make it back alive. Or maybe bourbon? Moonshine?"

"I will." Elijah chuckles. "Just try not to be too *city*."

Julia looks over her shoulder as she walks to the truck. "So, don't be myself?"

"Exactly!" Elijah shouts over the roar of the diesel engine. He gives a thumbs-up as Julia gets inside the cab and buckles her seat belt.

❖

They've been on the road now for about an hour, and Julia hasn't said a word. And neither has Elena. All Julia can think about is her car and how much it's going to cost. The thought is nauseating. She's trying to not focus on it, but all she hears in her head is "three grand" and "a couple months," and it makes her want to start crying.

She's watching the scenery fly by, seeing more and more as the sun climbs in the blue sky. There is still so much snow on the mountains, something Julia isn't used to seeing in the summer months. It's breathtaking, really, the way the landscape moves and changes. And the sky…Julia has never seen anything so beautiful.

Except, of course, when she looks at Elena, which, along with the inevitability of being trapped on this fucking ranch, is scaring the living shit out of her. Julia cannot stand that every time she sees Elena, she notices something else about her that makes it hard to focus, something else to wonder about. It's not that she doesn't understand or appreciate beautiful women; it's that she doesn't really get what's going on inside her. She's not supposed to get attached to anyone but especially not Elena. Not even on a friendship level. As Julia watches her flip through the radio stations a couple times, going between music stations and AM talk shows, Julia wills herself not to notice Elena's hands. Or the way her fingers turn the volume up or how they nimbly press the buttons on the radio. Or her wrists and how slender they are with the old, beat-up gold watch that she wears every day.

Now the radio is on an AM station, and the announcer is talking about the stock prices of soybeans, corn, cattle, and pigs. And all Julia can do is keep glancing at Elena, her stoic expression behind her sunglasses as she drives, the way she grips the steering wheel and continues to check her blind spots. It's slightly calming how relaxed Elena seems to be, but Julia remembers that this woman next to her has made it very clear that, so far, she thinks Julia is pretty irrelevant. Or maybe *relevant* but a complete *idiot*. Either way, none of this is doing anything good for Julia's nerves, which this early in the morning, shouldn't already be shot.

Julia hears Elena clear her throat, breaking the silence in the truck cab that has gone on for what seems like an eternity. "We're headed to a ranch right outside of Winter Park," Elena says, her voice loud in the confined area.

Julia doesn't know what to say in response. She's such a fool.

"Winter Park is a ski town. And Dusty Hearts Dude Ranch is about forty miles from the outskirts. They breed and train a lot of horses. We purchased Cole's horse Sweetie from them."

Still silent.

"Sweetie was already trained. A dream to ride, especially for Cole, who was a novice when he started." Elena takes her sunglasses off and glances at Julia out of the corner of her eye.

Silence.

"Your horse will also be trained."

And still nothing.

Elena lets out a *very* exasperated sigh. "Are you going to respond at all, Miss Finch?"

Julia looks over at Elena just as Elena looks over at her. Their eyes lock; Julia feels her breath catch and wants to smack herself. "I'm sorry," Julia says. "I'm a little nervous." She watches as Elena's face softens just the tiniest of bits.

"What are you nervous about? Contrary to popular opinion, I don't bite," Elena replies with an air of sarcasm that, in a different circumstance, probably would have been funny.

But in this circumstance, it makes Julia's stomach bottom out. "That's not it, Miss Bennett. It's this whole thing. And how you, well…" She wants to finish with *you hate me*, but decides on, "You're getting me a *horse*."

"It's *just* a horse."

"Come on, Miss Bennett, it's not *just* a horse. And you know it."

Elena smiles. She honest to God smiles! "I suppose you're right," she says, the smile still on her face.

"What if it hates me?"

"Can't hate you forever."

Julia doesn't know how to respond to that except to offer a very small smile. "If you say so," she whispers and looks out the window. "It's not like you'll be the one teaching me."

"What do you mean? Why won't I be the one teaching you?"

"Because," Julia replies, crossing her arms tighter, wishing she could just open the truck door and roll right out the cab. "Just a hunch."

"If there's one thing I hate, it's when a person doesn't treat a horse properly." Elena adjusts her hands on the steering wheel. "So, if you want me to, I will be the one to teach you. I can teach you everything you need to know." Her voice trembles a bit at the end of her sentence, and Julia wonders why.

"Don't put yourself out."

"Miss Finch, if I'm offering, it means I want to do it. So, just take the help and stop being so stubborn."

Julia feels her face getting hotter and hotter. If there's one thing she hates, it's being called stubborn. And anyway, how the heck would

Elena Bennett know if she's stubborn or not? Elena doesn't even know her! And she certainly hasn't tried to get to know Julia. She clenches her jaw, looks straight ahead, and asks, "Are you always this *fucking* pushy?"

"Ah, there we go. There *is* a spark in there."

"What the hell is that supposed to mean?"

"You haven't said a word since we got into the truck. Don't act like I don't know you like to yammer on and on about whatever is in that head of yours. I've seen you with Elijah and even Cole."

Julia is definitely getting more and more angry. "Are you serious right now?"

"Yes," Elena answers, her tone so succinct it's almost frightening.

And that's all it takes for Julia to snap. "*Why* would I talk to you at all when you think I'm worthless?" Julia licks her lips and waits for an answer but notices that she may have stunned Elena into silence. "It's not like you've gone out of your way to be overly nice to me. You bringing me groceries or new pants and boots is not winning you any medals. You barely talk to me unless it's to tell me I'm not dressed properly. I realize we aren't supposed to be friends, but Jesus Christ, I figured you'd at least stop reminding me what a piece of shit you think I am."

Elena takes a few visible deep breaths and turns the truck blinker on. She checks her mirrors, then starts to pull off and steer them toward a clearing on the side of the road. When the truck comes to a stop, Elena takes her hands from the steering wheel and calmly looks over at Julia. "Do you realize that the other day when the horses got out, I was furious?" Her eyes roam over Julia's features. "I was two seconds away from kicking you off the ranch."

Julia breathes in deep through her nose and lets it out slowly. "So, why didn't you?" she asks through clenched teeth. At this point, Julia almost wishes Elena would have. "Just cut your losses?"

"Because," Elena says.

"Because *why*?" Julia can see the contemplation on Elena's face, how she's studying Julia's features. The look of fear in her eyes. The trepidation in the way she takes each breath. It's driving Julia nuts. And Elena's eyes are making it difficult for Julia to continue to stand her ground.

"You," Elena says, her voice catching. "You were wonderful that day."

Julia's eyes go wide, and she feels her mouth hanging open. Did Elena Bennett just call her *wonderful*?

"So, stop thinking that I hate you. Because I don't. Far from it, in fact."

All Julia can hear, aside from the thud of her heart beating, is the sound of the diesel engine of the truck whirring and whirring. She swallows the lump in her throat and closes her mouth before pulling her eyes from Elena's.

Elena applies pressure to the brake and shifts the truck back into drive, easing them forward and back onto the road after checking her blind spots.

Now what? Does Julia talk? Should she talk? All she wants to do is question Elena. Ask her everything all at once. For reasons Julia can't seem to understand, she feels this intense pull to get to know everything about this unbearable woman. "How long have you been a horse person?" Julia asks, unclenching her fists and taking another deep breath.

"We do *not* have to keep talking, Miss Finch."

"I asked you a question," Julia says. "Don't be rude."

Elena glances back at Julia. The look is quick before Elena's eyes are back on the road, but there was something there Julia can't quite put her finger on. "Since I was a child." Elena slides her sunglasses back on. Is it so she can hide some of the emotion that bubbled to the surface? Julia wonders how often Elena actually lets people see those emotions. "My parents owned this ranch first, and when they passed— my mother first and then my dad—I was given the responsibility to take care of it."

"I'm really sorry about your parents."

"Thank you." Elena shrugs. "My dad was always my favorite, so his death was harder than my mother's." She pauses. "I have no idea why I just told you that."

Julia wants to say she has no idea, either, but she keeps that thought to herself. "And you love the ranch life?"

"I do." Elena eyes flit up to the rearview mirror, then she checks her side mirror. It's so methodical. It's *just* driving, but God, the way Elena drives is so calming and easy and attractive. "It's really fun when things go right. When we're fully staffed and the herding goes as planned and stock prices continue to stay up."

"And Cole has been in the business with you since birth, then?"

Elena laughs. Julia isn't sure why, but it sounds amazing nevertheless. "No, I took a break from the business."

"Oh, really?"

"I moved to Miami for about five years."

"Whoa, whoa, whoa." Julia waves her hands and turns in the passenger seat. She instantly feels the weight between them starting to lift. "*You* were a city girl?"

Another full-bodied laugh comes out of Elena's mouth, and she rakes a hand through her dark brown hair. There's a natural wave to it that before now Julia hasn't really noticed. "Yes, I was." Elena pauses, licks her lips, then looks at Julia. "Cole happened when I was in Miami."

"Were you married or…" Julia's voice trails off when she notices Elena's hands and her white knuckles from gripping the wheel a little tighter.

"Not necessarily."

Julia watches Elena's eyes behind her sunglasses.

"Artificial insemination," Elena says.

"Oh, I got you. You just wanted a baby."

Elena smiles. "Well, we both did."

"Your boyfriend at the time?"

"Girlfriend," Elena says as she glances over at Julia and shrugs.

Julia's heart clenches in her chest. "Oh." *Elena Bennett likes girls?*

"She was hit by a drunk driver. We all were. It was late." Elena shakes her head. Julia feels her stomach fall. "It was raining, and the guy ran a red light. Cole was a toddler. He wasn't hurt, thank God. But they couldn't save her."

"What was her name?" Julia whispers.

"Gloria."

Julia hears Elena's voice crack, and, before she realizes what she's doing, she reaches over to place her hand on Elena's arm. Her warm skin feels so nice under Julia's hand. "I'm so sorry."

"It's not your fault." Elena quickly wipes a stray tear from behind her sunglasses; she clears her throat. "So, we moved back, Cole and me. And my father taught me the business. The rest is history."

"So," Julia says after letting a few moments of silence pass. She is trying to not seem shocked, even though she really is.

"It's general knowledge, just so you know. It's just not talked about."

"What isn't?"

"Me. My past. Cole knows about his other mother. It's not a secret."

After hearing all of this, Julia wants to know more. So, so, so much more. She feels the urge to start talking, ask questions, find out as much as she can about this fascinating woman. Were her parents okay with this? Is everyone else okay with it? How has she handled this all so well? Maybe it hasn't been so well… Julia blinks, breathes, and smiles before saying, "Thank you for sharing with me, though. Contrary to popular opinion, I don't gossip. I don't like it when people gossip about me, so I don't do it about other people."

"How chivalrous of you." Elena's smile is soft and kind when she flashes it at Julia, and for some ridiculous reason, Julia feels it in her throat.

"So, your turn," Elena says through a breath. "What did you do before you came to Colorado?"

Julia looks away from Elena and out the truck window. "I don't think you'd believe me if I told you," she says, her breath making a puff of condensation on the window.

"You think you're going to get out of talking to me that easily, eh?"

Julia smiles, still looking out the window. "Yes."

"Maybe one day you'll tell me." Elena glances over at Julia. "I'm not going to push you," she says before she looks back at the road.

"Thanks." Julia feels herself *wanting* to talk, wanting to tell Elena everything. About her birth parents and how horrible the foster system was and how she still has nightmares about the sound of metal bars clanging shut. It doesn't make sense to her, either. Why does she want to open up to Elena? She literally just started talking to her. She may not hate Julia, but there is no way Julia is going to mess that up and overstep boundaries. She doesn't share things, she doesn't share herself, and she certainly isn't going to start sharing with Elena Bennett. Especially when Julia isn't sure where she stands. And also, because she may just ruin everything.

❖

Pulling up to the dude ranch in Winter Park is oddly similar to pulling onto the Bennett Ranch. Large house, big barn, and a large, circular horse corral. The only difference is this place has fifteen small cabins instead of just the one like the Bennett Ranch.

"They rent those out to tourists. You can learn to ride here." Elena pulls into a parking spot. "Very lucrative business."

Julia eyes the workers as they all file out of the barn to greet them. "So, what do we do?"

"We meet the horse, get her into the trailer, then leave."

"That's it?"

Elena chuckles. "Yes, that's it."

Julia takes a few breaths as she opens her door and slides out of the truck cab. She walks over toward Elena, who now has her straw cowboy hat pulled down on her head. "How old is that thing?" Julia asks with a laugh. The hat looks like it's seen better days.

"Old." Elena looks at Julia as she puts on her ratty, fitted baseball cap. "How old is *that*?" She motions to the Cubs hat while handing Julia a lead rope.

"*Old*," Julia replies, smiling and lifting an eyebrow.

"Elena!" a young man shouts. He's dressed pretty much identical to every other cowboy Julia has seen except he's *very* clean. His shirt has been starched to the point that it looks like there's a hanger still inside it. And his brown cowboy hat looks like it's brand new. "You're right on schedule!"

"Jerry." Elena holds out her hand for him to shake but is instead pulled into a giant hug.

"You look splendid," Jerry says as he releases Elena. His accent is very strong, but it's British, which is throwing Julia off something fierce. "Are you holding up all right? I heard what happened." His voice is filled with sympathy. Julia wants to know so badly what he's talking about.

"I'm surviving. Thank you for asking." Elena motions to Julia, "This is my newest ranch hand, Julia Finch. The horse is for her."

"Hi," Julia says as she slips her hands in her back pockets.

"Cowboys either shake hands or hug," Jerry says, holding his hand out. "You decide."

Julia widens her eyes as she looks from Jerry to Elena and back to Jerry. She throws her hand out, and he grabs it, then pulls her into a hug anyway.

"It's nice to meet you, Julia!" Jerry shouts as he picks her up. Julia shrieks, and he laughs as he sets her down. "Now, let's go see this mare."

"What the hell? Did he just pick me up?" Julia straightens her shirt and adjusts her hat, completely flustered.

"You need to settle down. He's very important and is giving me a phenomenal deal."

"I know. I'm sorry. I don't know what's wrong with me. I'm excited and nervous and ugh, I don't even know. And I don't like being picked up," Julia says as she leans into Elena's space.

"It's natural to be excited and scared," Jerry says over his shoulder. "You're getting ready to meet an animal that could kill you if you don't know what you're doing."

"*Jerry!*" Elena shouts.

"Well, Elena, tell me I'm wrong." Jerry turns around and takes a few steps while walking backward. "Of course, horses have been known to sacrifice their lives for their owner, as well."

Elena rolls her eyes, then looks at Julia. "That's actually what he *should* lead with when making a sales pitch."

Julia talks herself down from the anxiety attack that is looming on the horizon as they round the barn and continue to walk toward a giant, open field. There's a lone horse about fifty yards in, standing in the middle of the wildflowers, sun shining on its coat, which is a very light brown. The tail and mane are jet black. "Whoa."

Elena folds her arms across her chest and nods toward the horse. "She's a buckskin."

"What's her name?"

"Leia," Jerry says, stepping up onto the bottom rung of the fence that surrounds the field. He folds his arms and props them on the top rung. All the rest of the workers mimic him. "She's four, completely trained, and one of the most beautiful, well-mannered horses we've ever had. She's going to be great to learn on."

Julia can't take her eyes from the horse. Her mouth is hanging slightly open, and her heartbeat is racing. She really is excited, and for the first time in forever, she feels like maybe she won't fuck this up. "*Leia*. Like from Star Wars?"

Elena and Jerry chuckle as he responds with a nod.

"Can I go meet her?"

Elena's face is filled with joy as she nods at Jerry. "What do you think, Jer?"

"Yes, go on in. She'll be fine."

"Are you coming with me?" Julia's eyes are still glued to the horse.

"No," Elena says. "This is an important moment. You need to do this on your own." She walks over to the gate with Julia and lays her hand on Julia's forearm. "Don't be scared. I saw you with Jazz the first time. And the other day with Scout and Sully. You are a natural with these animals. They understand you. And you understand them. So, don't even worry about it, okay?"

Julia takes her eyes from the horse and looks at Elena finally. "You were watching that first time with Jazz?"

Elena shrugs, clicks open the latch on the gate, and hands Julia a feed bag with grain inside. "Good luck," she says softly as Julia walks through, taking the bag with her. "Don't rush it. Let the horse come to you. I know it's tempting to rush it, but you simply cannot. Walk out there, find an area—"

"And wait. Right. I got it." Julia bends her head to each side, cracks her neck, and takes a deep breath. "Let her come to me."

After Elena closes the gate behind her, she steps onto the bottom rung of the wooden fence and watches intently. "Take your time," Elena says, and Julia nods.

Julia can feel Jerry's and Elena's eyes watching her. She doesn't want to screw up. She knows from the limited research she's done while at the ranch that this bonding moment is so special between a rider and a horse. She needs for this to go well, but she also doesn't want to spook the horse. She is standing completely still about twenty feet from Leia now. The horse's ears are perked, but she doesn't look nervous. Well, not as nervous as Julia still feels. Julia finds a cleared spot in the wildflowers and she kneels down. The moisture from the ground seeps into her jeans. She can smell the wet grass, the sweetness from the flowers. It's amazing how alert she is in this moment. The buzzing of the flies, the chirping of nearby birds, the gentle whir of the power lines, it's all music to her ears. Leia is watching with a careful eye. Julia can read the nervous curiosity on this horse's face, and as Julia relaxes, waiting patiently, the horse starts to move. Leia takes a few steps, stops, flips her tail to swat the flies away, then continues on the journey. It takes a bit more patience on Julia's part with the hot sun beating down on her. The sweat is running down her neck, but she knows this is all worth it.

Finally, Leia is within a couple feet of Julia. "Hi there, Leia," Julia says as she watches the horse's movements and smiles when the horse takes another step toward her. "Good girl." She can barely hide her excitement when the horse takes five more steps and is standing directly in front of her. Still on her knees, Julia reaches up when the horse bends her head down to get Julia's scent. Her soft muzzle on Julia's hand are enough for Julia to instantly fall in love with this animal. Julia empties some grain into her hand and holds it out for Leia, who hungrily starts to eat. "Hi," Julia whispers, her voice soft and low. "You're my girl now, hmm? Think you can handle that?" The horse perks her ears and then, as if she has been around Julia forever, slides her head underneath Julia's forearm and nudges her. And before she can stop herself, Julia is crying.

She has never even had a pet before, let alone a horse, and now she has this most perfect animal. Julia reaches up to wipe her eyes and nose. "Let's go, Leia," Julia says as she clips the lead rope she had over her shoulder to the halter, stands, and slowly starts to walk back. When she gets closer, she realizes that she's not the only person crying. Elena's sunglasses are pushed up onto her head, and her eyes are wet with tears. She has her hand on her heart and a smile on her lips. And Julia can't help but smile back.

❖

The two women are silent when they get back into the cab of the truck after loading Leia into the trailer. And this time, the silence feels just right. The AM radio station is playing music from the 70s now instead of constant talk about stock prices. Julia feels her fingers start to drum away to the ABBA tune until she hears soft singing coming from Elena's side of the cab. "*You* like ABBA?"

"Uh, yes. This is my generation's music. Why are you so shocked?"

"Because I figured you only listened to country and western music."

Elena sighs. "You honestly have so many stereotypes about cowboys."

"Oh, *really*? That's definitely the pot calling the kettle black." Julia laughs. "You know you judged me immediately when you found out I wasn't a certified cowgirl."

"Actually, no, I didn't."

"Lies!" Julia points her right index finger at Elena. "You are totally lying right now."

"I didn't judge you because you weren't a cowgirl. I judged you because I didn't know what to think about you." Elena glances at Julia. "There. Happy?"

"At least you admit that you judged me. But why did you before you even had a chance to get to know me?"

"Because." Elena shrugs. "But I am trying to get past all that. Aren't I?"

"I don't know. Are you?" Julia leans her head on the headrest. She watches Elena, the way her left fingertips are feeling the leather wrap on the steering wheel. Julia's mind wanders and before she knows it, she's imagining Elena's fingers roaming over her breasts and stomach. Her thoughts are interrupted by Elena clearing her throat.

"Yes, I am." Elena's tone is firm. "I promise."

"Good." Julia smirks. "But all you people listen to is country music, and that's a fact." Elena laughs a deep, hearty, sexy laugh, and Julia's heart lodges itself into her throat. "What?" she asks with an air of shock.

"Miss Finch, I don't even *like* country music."

"Don't you think you could start calling me Julia?"

"Not going to happen." Elena's response is quick. "My number one rule is that I have to keep it professional with my staff."

"You have never called Elijah 'Mr. Williams' in my presence." Julia has made sure to listen, if for no other reason than to have something to be angry about. "Just for the record, I wouldn't mind if you dropped the whole Miss Finch thing. It's not like calling me by my first name is going to change the fact that you still think I'm an idiot."

"We'll see," Elena says softly. Julia sees the smile Elena is trying to hide, though.

"I'll still call you Miss Bennett, of course." Julia sits upright and at attention. "I mean, I'm not saying I would disrespect you."

"You can stop trying to explain yourself."

"Okay." Julia can feel the heat in her cheeks, which makes her so uncomfortable. She's not exactly used to feeling so nervous and jumpy around another person. She's normally cool, composed, full of confidence. But Elena…She makes Julia forget how to breathe, how to communicate, and how to not sound like a fool. Silence once more falls between them as the sun gets ready to dip behind the mountains. Julia glances at the clock and for the first time realizes that they've actually been gone most of the day, and she is *starving*. "How much longer?"

Elena looks down at the clock, then back at the road. "About two hours. Have something you need to get back to?"

"Oh, yeah, hot date with my couch." Julia's words are iced with sarcasm. "I'm starving. Can we stop at the next town and eat something?"

"There's a town about ten miles ahead. We can find something there."

"Thank God. I'm wasting away over here." Julia sees Elena crack a smile, which pleases Julia in a way she still can't understand. But whatever it is, she's starting to like it.

CHAPTER SIX

Julia doesn't know what to expect from a restaurant called the Cowboy Corral, but it doesn't sound appetizing. Elena assures her it will be fine, but Julia is still skeptical.

The menu has a little bit of everything, from salads to burgers to Salisbury steak, and the "famous Cowboy Corral Rocky Mountain Oysters," which Julia has no idea about so steers clear immediately. The restaurant itself reminds her of the little ma-and-pop shops in some of the neighborhoods in Chicago except, of course, for the name. The bright fluorescent lighting and booth seats that are in bad need of reupholstering are just a couple of the reasons why.

When the grilled cheese sandwich and French fries she orders gets delivered and she takes her first bite, she decides she was very wrong to place judgment just because of the name. "Jesus, this is amazing," she says around a mouthful of sandwich. It is made with two pieces of thick-cut, homemade bread with, according to the menu, fresh cheese from the dairy farm in the next town over. And the fries! Julia can't get over how good the French fries are.

"I told you," Elena offers before she slides a forkful of salad into her mouth.

"I don't know whether I'm starving, or it's just *that* amazing." Julia takes another bite and washes it down with her root beer. "Either way, it's hitting all the spots."

"All of them, hmm?"

"Yes, every single one."

"Has anyone ever told you that you eat like a child?" Elena asks, eyeing the way Julia is leaning over her basket of fries and grilled cheese.

"Yes, I've been told that before. But thank you for pointing it out again. Maybe if you hadn't starved me today, I'd be a little more refined."

"I have a hard time believing that food is a magic elixir for you acting like a lady."

"Hey, I can act like a lady."

"Oh, *really?*"

"Yes, before this I used to wear dresses and heels, and I can even walk in them. So, to me, that's pretty ladylike. Not everyone can walk in heels."

"Are you finally going to tell me what you used to do?" Elena's eyebrows are raised, and she's leaning forward in the booth.

"It's not really anything big. I used to help one of my friends out… He was a private investigator. Sometimes he needed bait."

"Bait?"

Julia picks up a fry and nibbles on it. "Y'know, like, be the girl that gets hit on at the bar by the married man that's not supposed to be out cheating on his wife."

"I'm sorry, what?"

"Look, it's not a big deal. It was just a job."

"Miss Finch—"

"Please, call me Julia."

"Are you…I mean…are you okay?"

Julia fights the instinct to clam up and looks at Elena across the dingy booth table. Their eyes lock. It would be so easy to get lost in those dark eyes of Elena's and just let go of everything. "Keep it professional, Miss Bennett." The words come out how Julia intended, but she sounds so small, and it shocks her.

"Professional doesn't mean heartless."

"Doesn't it?" Julia can tell Elena is holding her breath. She sees the breath release through Elena's nose.

"I just don't want to get hurt."

"Why would you get hurt?" There's a shift in the air surrounding them. Julia needs Elena to answer the question, but she can feel Elena's tension, the way her shoulders have raised and her neck muscles have tightened. "Hey," Julia says quietly. Elena blinks, once then twice, and Julia smiles. "Can you walk in heels?" And just like that, Elena's shoulders visibly relax, and she releases the breath she was holding, and the air seems lighter once more.

"Well, yeah. But I haven't had to in a really long time."

"Haven't you been out or anything? Where you had to dress up?"

"In my life? Yes. Lately?" Elena shakes her head. "No."

Julia shoves a fry into her mouth when she sees that same tension sneak back into Elena's shoulders. "It's overrated anyway," she says, talking around the food in her mouth. "I mean, who wants to be all flawless and *clean*? Not me!"

"Don't get me wrong. I like being clean. I just never do much outside of the ranch."

Julia tries her hardest to not imagine Elena in something other than cowboy boots and jeans. She always looks like a cowgirl, with messy hair and dusty boots on, and now that straw hat. It's not a bad look. In fact, it's so attractive Julia has a hard time concentrating most of the time around Elena, but...A *dressed-up* Elena? Julia's cheeks burn at the thought, and the temperature in the diner feels like it's 110 degrees. "Well, maybe we can hang out one night outside the ranch," she finally replies.

"Oh? You think I'd want to do that?"

"I mean, no, probably not. But you could shower or something. You kind of smell."

The loud laughter that spills from Elena's mouth is so endearing that Julia's heart aches. Elena tilts her head. "There's a child trapped inside you, I just know it."

Julia laughs through the uncomfortable moment. "Duh." She watches Elena take a long drink of her water and continue eating, moving the lettuce around on her plate. Elena does not need to be eating a salad. Her figure is amazing, and as hard as she works, she probably burns more calories in a day than most people do in a week.

Elena lifts her head and eyes Julia's fries before looking at her. "Do you know that guy over there?" Elena points toward the back of the restaurant.

Julia swivels around without even thinking. "Where?"

"Oh, you must have missed him."

Julia turns back around and shakes her head when she sees Elena chewing rapidly and the fry basket definitely missing a couple fries. "Oh, really?"

"Yeah, strangest thing." Elena smiles and shrugs.

"And I'm the child?"

"If the boots fit."

Julia pushes her basket of fries toward the middle of the table, lifts her eyes to look at Elena's, and smiles. "Would you like some more?"

After her cheeks redden, Elena reaches over and takes a couple more. "Thanks," she says quietly before munching away.

Julia notices the easy way Elena moves, the softness of her skin, the tan line along her middle finger where a ring would reside. It's freaking Julia out slightly. Being taken aback by everything Elena does or says is becoming really hard to deal with. Even the way Elena breathes is intriguing. Julia did not want to get this tangled up with anyone in this godforsaken town. Especially her temperamental boss who is, of course, turning out to be a really nice person under that tough exterior. But now all Julia wants is more, more, more. The *want* is going to become a *need* unless Julia puts a stop to it. She normally spends every moment of her life avoiding conversation, dodging relationships, and refusing to settle down. But now? All she wants is to know why Elena's eyes are so sad, why that tension in her shoulders appeared, and what can she do to fix it all.

When the two women finish their meals and another basket of fries, Julia snatches up the bill on the table. Elena tries to protest, but Julia glares at her and mumbles about *a new horse* and *really?*

"I get to leave the tip, then," Elena says sternly. Julia relents when she sees the way Elena's eyes seem to say *don't fucking push me on this*.

"Fine."

The two women leave the restaurant. After checking on Leia, who seems more than comfortable in the very nice trailer, they hop into the truck and take off.

❖

Unloading and getting Leia acquainted with the stall that Elijah put the finishing touches on is a breeze. Elena comments more than once that this horse has been the easiest to transport since getting Sweetie. Apparently, Sully kicked the side of the old trailer so hard that they had to buy a new one. "He has some temperament issues that only Penn could deal with." Elena scrunches her face, and Julia is happy she can still see the expression in the light from the moon. "Kind of why we were shocked he let you approach him."

"So, you basically let me walk up to a horse that was spooked, and I could have died. *Awesome*."

"No better way to learn," Elena says with a tired smile. "And you did beautifully."

As they approach the sidewalk that leads up to Julia's cabin, she wonders if this shift in Elena's mood will be permanent or if tomorrow she'll go back to hating Julia. She glances over at Elena; her hat is off and around her neck with the string, and her shirt is unbuttoned farther now than it had been earlier, which makes Julia's stomach flip. "Thank you," Julia says. "It was an *amazing* day."

"Tomorrow, you ride. So, get some sleep. We will go check on the cattle." Elena extends her hand for Julia to shake. "Really great getting to know you today," she says and then adds, "*Julia*."

Julia's voice snags in her throat, and she feels her entire body start to burn. She smiles, takes Elena's hand, and shakes it. "Likewise, Miss Bennett."

"Elena."

Julia blinks rapidly in response as Elena smiles and shrugs.

"Might as well," Elena says.

Julia still hasn't let go of Elena's hand when she says, "It's nice to meet you, *Elena*."

"Go get some rest."

Julia watches Elena start to walk away, and their hands finally pull apart. She wants to keep watching, but she knows better than to stare for too long, so she heads up to the cabin. After she unlocks the door, she turns around and sees Elena glance back over her shoulder and throw up a hand to wave good-bye again.

"Jesus," Julia whispers when she gets inside the cabin. She leans against the door, closing it firmly, and sighs. The day went way better than it was supposed to. And now, when she closes her eyes, all she can see is Elena's teary-eyed smile and the way she was clutching at her own heart, and it makes Julia feel woozy in a way that has never happened before.

Does that mean what she thinks it's starting to mean?

She pushes off the door and walks into the kitchen, flipping on lights as she goes, when there's a faint knock at the door. "Who is it?" she yells as she rounds the corner and sees Elijah standing there with a six-pack of PBR and a smile. She opens the screen door and laughs.

"She didn't kill you." Elijah holds a beer up for Julia.

"No, she didn't," Julia says as she walks outside on the small porch with Elijah and graciously accepts the can of PBR. They both sit down on the wooden steps, sigh in unison, and crack open their beers.

"How was it?"

Julia takes a very long pull from her beer. She gathers her thoughts and then looks over at Elijah. "It was insanely weird."

"What? Why?" he asks, looking out at the ranch. He doesn't have his hat on, and his hair has seen better days. There's an obvious tan line on his forehead, and it makes Julia smile.

"I cried. Like a baby."

"Oh, that's normal." Elijah waves her off as if he's seen worse. "Julia, this horse will be the one you are responsible for. If you didn't feel a connection to it, then it's not the horse for you. Understand?"

"I know, but…" Julia's voice trails off. "I just, I've never even had a dog or a cat before. And now, now I have a horse! Every little girl dreams of getting a pony, and now I have one. It just feels so strange, like I don't deserve it."

Elijah glances over at Julia and nudges her with his elbow. "You know that's not weird at all. I'm glad you see how big this is. Elena doesn't share these moments with just anyone. That's why I'm so shocked that you think she hates you."

"I kind of don't think that anymore."

"Oh, *really*?"

"Yeah," Julia replies, ducking her head and trying to hide her excitement. "We talked today. A lot."

"And?"

Julia looks over at Elijah, then turns again to look across the property at the log cabin. The curiousness inside her is really revving itself up. The feeling sits on her chest. "She's deep, isn't she?"

Elijah chuckles and a simple *mm-hmm* comes out of him.

"I didn't realize how much pain is there." Julia waits a second before she says, "She brought up Gloria."

"Wow."

"Is that not normal?"

Elijah shakes his head. "She never talks about Gloria unless it's to Cole."

"Were she and Penn together?"

"City Girl, you're gonna have to ask Elena about that one eventually if you really want to know."

Julia sighs, looks up at the night sky, and asks, "Has she ever asked a worker to call her Elena?"

"Not that I know of, except for Caroline. And Caroline and she have known each other for years." Elijah leans into her briefly, nudging her. "Maybe now you can be positive that she likes you."

"Yeah, I guess."

Elijah goes to stand up but snaps another beer from the six-pack holder and looks at Julia. "She's obviously warming up to you, so take my advice and don't screw it up."

"Gee, thanks for the vote of confidence."

"Well, I saw it happen once before. Saw her get close to someone and then saw that person fuck it up. And the aftermath wasn't fun for anyone involved. Especially Elena."

"Why do I get the feeling that you're talking about Penn?"

Elijah sighs, takes a drink from his freshly opened beer, and wipes his mouth with the back of his hand. "Because." He glances over each shoulder. Is he checking to make sure no one snuck up behind him? Who knows? He looks back at Julia and lowers his voice to say, "I am talking about that asshole, so, Julia? Don't fuck it up."

Chills shoot up Julia's spine. "I won't."

"Good. Now go get some rest. I'm sure Elena will want you up and at 'em early."

"Okay, boss. I guess we're going to ride to see the cattle tomorrow."

"Well, then, go. Sleep. Your first day riding won't be easy." He walks away from her, kicking up dirt as he walks. "Don't forget to wear your boots, for shit's sake," he shouts and then laughs at himself.

"Funny!" Julia watches him walk away. She doesn't really know what to do with the information she just learned. The only thing she knows for sure is that she's already nervous to see Elena in the morning. How is she going to sleep with all the questions and thoughts running through her head? She honestly has no idea. And really? She's not sure she wants to know the answers right now.

CHAPTER SEVEN

Julia pops out of bed way before her alarm clock goes off in the morning. The sun hasn't risen yet, and the breeze flowing in the window she left cracked all night is cool and crisp. She slept like a rock, getting maybe the first great night's sleep since she was forced to stop in this town. She gets dressed quicker than she ever has in her life—except the time or two she stole away in the middle of the night after a one-night stand.

The decision is made fairly fast to wear the other pair of blue jeans that Elena gave her, thinking that the last thing she wants to do is start off on the wrong foot today. Julia still cannot get over how well the jeans fit as she turns and checks out her backside and wonders how in the world Elena guessed her size. She throws on an old Star Wars T-shirt with a TIE fighter shooting its blasters because it's fitting, considering Leia's name. She then pulls on a red plaid button-down flannel over the top. She's not settling into the country routine as much as it seems. It's just chilly out, and she doesn't want to get cold.

At least, that's what she keeps telling herself.

Julia slides across the living room hardwood in her socks and into the kitchen, grabbing a banana and a granola bar before she sits on the bench by the door and shoves her feet into her boots. She absolutely *hates* to admit it, but the damn things never gave her one bit of trouble the day before. Not even a blister, which she knows is rare. They're leather! They should take a time or two to break them in. But nope. They fit like the pants do—like a dream.

As she gets outside on the porch, stuffing her ball cap into her back pocket, she realizes she didn't even check her cell phone. And it strikes her that she hasn't really looked at it in the past couple of days, and shockingly, it's so freeing she can barely handle the feeling. It's been a long time since she wasn't obsessed with technology and being connected to the world. Surprisingly, it feels really, *really* good.

The barn door is locked so she fishes her key out of her pocket, unlocks the padlock, and slides the large door open. The smell of manure and hay and horses hits her hard, but it doesn't bother her like it did the first time. It kind of excites her now, especially knowing that one of the horses in there belongs to her.

Her very own horse. It still seems so crazy to have this animal all to herself.

"Leia," Julia says softly as she walks up to the horse's stall. She sees Scout and Jazz stick their heads over their doors, so Julia says hi to both. Leia turns in her stall and immediately puts her head over the door like the others. "Hello there, beautiful girl," Julia coos, petting along the horse's jawline and under the chin. Julia giggles like a little kid when Leia whinnies. It's then that she hears a scuff of boots approaching in the barn. She glances over and sees Elena in her jeans and boots and white button-down, sleeves rolled up as always, and her straw hat hanging from her neck again. Her hair isn't pulled back, just pushed behind her ears, and the waves look natural and soft. Julia definitely approves. She's carrying two travel mugs and some sort of baked good.

"Good morning," Elena says, her voice deeper than normal. "I brought you a coffee and a banana nut muffin."

Julia smiles and accepts the offerings. "Thank you," she says, eagerly biting into the muffin. "*And* that's the best muffin I've ever had." Her mouth is full, but she doesn't even care. She can't believe how good it is.

Elena cocks an eyebrow and says, "Of course it is. I made it."

"When the hell did you find time to bake?"

"Last night." Elena moves around to the other side of the stalls where the saddles are stored. "I don't sleep well."

"Ever?"

"Not in a very long time." Elena sets her mug down and leans against the stall wall. Her movements are so casual that it's making Julia a little less nervous, which she's so thankful for. "I typically bake to relieve stress."

"You're stressed, then?"

It takes Elena a moment to answer the question, then she motions toward the horse and simply says, "Not after how well this lady traveled."

"Then?" Julia doesn't look over, just continues to keep herself focused on anything *but* Elena. "Why the baking?"

"Maybe confused is a better reason than stressed," Elena says after another annoyingly long pause.

"Confused?"

Elena nods, never taking her eyes off Julia. She can feel Elena's gaze, and her body is so warm from it. Elena sighs, and just like that, the moment is over. "Let's feed the horses a snack, groom them, and then get a leg over them. Long day ahead of us."

Julia glances over at Elena after she hears the change in her tone. "Okay," she replies, following Elena toward the hay and wheelbarrows. It'll be the first time they've worked side by side, and Julia is kind of nervous. She hopes to God she doesn't do something stupid. The last thing she wants to do is prove Elijah right and fuck up.

❖

"Grooming a horse before riding is a must. The dirt can irritate their skin, and that is definitely not something we want. Keep in mind, grooming should never feel like a chore." Elena's voice is so smooth and sexy as she speaks. She is not only easy to look at but easy to listen to and learn from. Probably more because Julia hangs on Elena's every word. Either way, Julia does exactly as she's taught as they both brush down their horses. "You bond with your horse while grooming it. When they trust you, it's the greatest feeling in the entire world." Elena glances over at Julia where they're stationed in the grooming and saddling area in the barn. "And trust between you and your horse? You can't buy that."

Julia catches Elena's gaze, feels chill bumps spring up on her arms, and she quickly looks away as she continues to run the curry comb in circular motions over Leia's coat. She transitions from the comb to the stiff-bristled brush and flicks her wrist with ease after each pass, making sure to get any dirt out of the coat. Out of everything she has done on the ranch, grooming the horses has been the most relaxing. She really likes the solitude, being able to just talk to the horses and get to know their little personalities. Or in the case of Sully and Scout, their big personalities. The only horse she hasn't groomed is Samwise, but that's because Elena won't let anyone else do it.

They both inspect and clean out each hoof of their horses, gently picking away the dirt and avoiding the soft center of the hoof. "Leia, why is this spot called a frog, anyway?" Julia hears Elena chuckle at her question, and it warms her heart to know she is listening.

"It's because in German it's called a 'frosh.' And that means 'frog' in English."

Julia lifts her head at the sound of Elena's explanation. "Well, did you hear that, Leia? Miss Fancy Pants over there knows German." And she's delighted when she hears Elena laugh again.

When it's time to saddle the horses, Elena goes over each step on Samwise. She points out all the parts of the saddle, even though Julia told her Elijah did that already. "It doesn't matter," Elena says. "I want you to learn from me."

Elena explains the purpose of double rigging and how having two straps, one in the front and one in the back, helps secure the saddle to the horse. She tells Julia that it's important for both the rider and the horse to be comfortable, the horse especially. Julia listens to every word and watches every move with even more intensity. Elena's talking about the horse and the horse's spirit, and how the bond between a horse and its rider is *fragile* and *special* and something that a person can never take for granted. It's in these moments that Julia realizes that Cole was absolutely right about Elena—she's passionate in a way Julia didn't realize a person could be. Julia wants to listen to Elena explain everything to her. The way her lips move and the sound of her voice are so enchanting. How her hands work and the way she smooths her hand over Leia's coat after every motion, telling the horse how good she's being. All of this is meaning a lot more to her than it did when Elijah trained her.

Julia is a quick study and picks up the techniques that Elena shows her effortlessly. When it's her turn, she has the saddle on Leia and the stirrups at the correct length in a good amount of time. When Julia goes to check the rigging in the front, she feels Elena's hand land on hers. She instantly looks over at Elena, at the scar above her eye, at the tiny creases at the corners. It feels like days pass, but Julia knows it's only a couple of seconds before Elena tells her that it's better to pull the leather strap a little at a time, not tug all at once. Julia really hopes that's all Elena has said because she can't really hear her over the heartbeat echoing in her ears.

"Nice," Elena says to Julia, never making eye contact. She has her hat securely on her head now, so she pushes it up slightly when she asks, "Now, you've mounted Scout? Or Jazz?"

"I've taken Jazz out a bunch of times in the pasture. Elijah said I bounce too much."

"Like a 'sack of shit.' I heard." Elena looks as if she's holding back a chuckle.

"Gee, news travels fast on the ranch *and* the town, eh?"

Elena cracks a smile now as she looks over at Julia, her left eyebrow arched. "Well, at least I don't call you City Girl like everyone else does."

Julia rolls her eyes, shakes her head, and says with as much sarcasm as she can muster, "I guess I should thank you."

"Okay, now get on the horse."

"Wait." Julia freezes. "Just, like, *get on*?"

"Yes, Julia, *like*, get on the horse."

"Without you getting on first? What if she bucks me off?"

Elena folds her arms across her chest. "Julia Finch, get on the horse. *Now.*"

"Yikes," Julia says under her breath as she pulls her eyes off Elena and looks at Leia. "She's mean," she says to the horse, and she gets a gentle neigh in response. She can hear Elena's deep sigh as she takes a few steps backward away from Julia and Leia.

"I can be meaner," Elena says, her voice low.

"Oh, I've heard." Julia grabs a stirrup and pulls gently. "Okay, Leia, I'm gonna get on you now. So, work with me, okay? Just be calm." Leia turns her head, looks at Julia, and blinks like she understands. She stands toward the center of the horse, picks her left foot up, and slides it into the stirrup. She has the reins in her hand, reaches up and grabs on to the saddle horn, hops once, pulls herself up, and throws her leg over the horse. It's the smoothest mount she's had, and it makes her grin like an idiot as she looks down at Elena, who has literally no emotion on her face. Now it's time to *feel* like an idiot, not just smile like one. Elena moves around to the other side of the horse, arms still crossed.

"Where'd you learn that method?"

Julia blinks, securing the reins in her right hand. "What do you mean?"

"That's not what Elijah taught you. Where'd you learn that?"

"How do you know what Elijah taught me?"

"Because he tells me everything." Elena taps her boot on the dirt. "So?"

Julia takes a deep breath. Elijah had taught her this ridiculous way of flipping the stirrup around and standing backward toward the shoulders of the horse, and it made Julia feel uncomfortable, like she was going to fall over every time. "I learned it by watching you," Julia says. "I didn't like the way Elijah taught me. It made me feel like I was going to fall over—"

"You just taught yourself?" Elena's question isn't really a question as much as it's a statement.

Julia's slightly worried that she just pissed Elena off, but she pulls her shoulders back, sits straight, and nods.

A small smile comes to Elena's lips. "It was perfect."

Julia's face is burning up, but the relief she feels is palpable.

"Now, what all do you know when it comes to getting the horse to move?"

"I trotted with Jazz. And walked, of course. So, the basic commands."

"And, of course, you bounced around in the saddle."

"Yes, we've established that."

"Okay, I want you to take Leia around the corral, and this time, sit up straight and pull your belly button in toward your spine. You look like you're leaning over the horse too much right now."

"Straight like this?"

"Yes," Elena says, eyeing Julia as she straightens her spine. "Do you feel like you're sitting back too far?"

"Yes."

"Then you're perfect."

Julia gently moves her legs to indicate to the horse to go forward. Leia takes a few steps.

"Go a little faster," Elena says. Leia starts to trot, and instantly, Julia starts bouncing. "Okay, now stop trying to squeeze your thighs together like a vise. You don't need to hug the horse as if it's going to escape from underneath you."

"That doesn't make sense; won't I fall off?"

Elena shakes her head. "You won't fall off. Use the stirrups. Sit *hard* into the saddle, don't squeeze your thighs so much, and you'll be fine."

"Elijah told me to squeeze," Julia says over the sound of the horse.

"And I'm the one teaching you now," Elena shouts. "Stop squeezing and *sit the horse*."

Julia does what she is told. She sits, loosens the vise-like grip she has on the horse, feels the saddle beneath her, and of course, she stops bouncing. Her mouth falls open, and she looks over at Elena. "Holy shit!"

"I told you," Elena says with a smile. Julia spurs Leia on a little faster, almost a gallop now. She's not bouncing nearly as bad, which is good. After Julia has rounded the corral about twenty times, Elena raises her hand and says, "Think you're ready to try going a little faster?"

"Whoa." Julia pulls on the reins lightly, and Leia slows to a stop. She steers the horse and approaches Elena. "Elena, I don't know if I can—"

"Can't learn if you don't try." Elena swings open the gate to the corral.

Julia watches her walk over toward Samwise, quickly unloop the lead from the fencing, and mount the horse easily. Elena looks fantastic sitting atop Samwise with the sun hitting his coat just right. The image is so striking that Julia cannot find the words to tell Elena that she's not ready to try running yet. What if she gets bucked off? She doesn't think she can handle that embarrassment in front of Elena. "I'm not sure if I'm ready," Julia says with a shaky voice.

"If you aren't ready, it's fine. We'll trot there. But you're going to have to learn eventually."

Julia adjusts her baseball cap as she watches Elena slide on leather riding gloves. Elena looks so sexy with that smirk on her face. She takes a deep breath and gathers all of her courage. Fuck it. "Let's do it."

"Attagirl," Elena says with a smile. "Follow me." She turns Samwise toward the pasture, heading west.

❖

After an hour of riding, Julia can tell she's going to be sore tomorrow. Her thighs, her ass, and her arms. Probably every single muscle. Aside from that, though, it is the most fun she has ever had. Not only is riding a horse coming to her like she was born to do it, but it's so calming. Even though she was so nervous to take off, so nervous to spur Leia to a run, it all came to her like it was nothing, like she had been doing it her whole life. It made her so very happy.

And it was obviously making Elena happy, too; she had smiled at Julia more in one hour than she had the entire time Julia had known her.

Julia sees Elena slowing as they approach a clearing. She steers Leia to where Elena is stopped. "Is everything okay?" Julia asks.

"This is Miller's Gap." Elena is looking out over the clearing. She pushes her hat up and then off her head. It's hanging from the string now around her neck. "This land has been in my family for years and years. There's a story my dad would tell about the miller's wife." Julia notices that Elena's eyes seem to tear up as she tells the story of the miller's wife and how she ran away after finding him with his lover. "The wife was never heard from again; it's lore that when there's a shooting star, it's the miller's wife crying from heaven."

"That's so sad," Julia whispers.

"It is." Elena glances over at Julia, and their eyes lock. "It's beautiful, too, though. That kind of love."

"The kind that breaks your heart?"

"The kind that consumes you."

Julia's breath catches in her throat. Elena's facial expression, her eyes, her lips, everything is so goddamn gorgeous. She cannot take her eyes off Elena when she finally speaks again about the land and the weather patterns. Elena moves her hand nonchalantly from one side of the gap to the next, explaining how the valleys are important to a Colorado rancher. The valleys hold the sun's warmth, and the snow doesn't get as deep, so it's good for the cattle.

"And what's 'deep' here?" Julia asks as she reaches down and runs her hand along Leia's neck. "I mean, I've seen snow, obviously. Chicago gets slammed with snow."

"We've seen as much as twenty feet on the peaks. Fourteen or fifteen feet in the valleys."

"Holy cow. That's a lot."

BREAKING DOWN HER WALLS

"It's a different cold here, too." Elena squints as she looks across the gap. "It's a *dry* cold. Some days, in the winter, it's almost warm because of the sun—even though the temperature reading might say ten degrees." Elena glances over at Julia. "You should probably put some sunscreen on." Elena pulls out a tube of sunscreen lotion and hands it over. "Your fair skin is going to be very sunburned if you don't watch yourself."

Julia had noticed that she was starting to turn pink. "Yeah, is this part of that same phenomenon? Being closer to the sun and all that?"

Elena smiles. "Yes, and the air is thinner because of the altitude. It's all very true."

Julia quickly slathers some on her arms and then rubs it over her face, pushing her hat up so she can get her forehead. Afterward, she hands the lotion back to Elena and says, "Thank you." She gets a laugh from Elena in response. "What?"

"You did not get it rubbed in." Elena laughs. "You have it everywhere."

"Well, it's not like I brought a mirror with me!" Julia shouts. "Where's it at?"

"Come here," Elena says as she leans over, braces herself on her saddle horn, and rubs her hand over Julia's cheeks and nose. "There. Sunscreen and dirt. It's a great combination."

Julia can't feel her legs or her arms, and her heart is caught in her throat from the sensation of Elena's skin against hers. Whatever is happening to Julia is not stopping regardless of how hard she fights it. Her efforts are futile. Especially when Elena does something like that. Or looks at her. Or talks. Or *breathes.*

"Hello?" Elena snaps her fingers and laughs. "Earth to Julia!"

"Geez, zoned out there," Julia says, trying not to stammer. "How much farther?"

"It's just over this ridge."

The two women ride to the ridge, their horses' hoofbeats hitting in time with each other. When they reach the edge of the rocks, the only sound that comes out of Julia's mouth is a breathless "Whoa."

The mountains are in the distance, and the wide-open range stretches before them. The land is littered with so many cattle that Julia can barely begin to count. The very top of the peaks of the mountains

• 87 •

has minimal snow coverage. It's clear that the past week has helped the runoff because Elena commented about the depth of each stream they passed.

"I know," Elena says.

"This is," Julia says, her voice snagging in her throat. "This is *breathtaking*."

"It really is."

"Now I know why you love it so much. Thanks for letting me come with you today."

Elena clears her throat. "Let's get started. Have to count and make sure all are accounted for."

Julia is quickly learning that Elena Bennett hates these moments of kindness. She wonders if Elena knows that all her protesting does nothing but encourage Julia to be kinder and more sincere. And she's not going to stop. Ever.

Chapter Eight

The ride back to the ranch is mostly silent. Julia listened intently to what Elena had taught her about every step they needed to do each and every time they ride out to check on the cattle. It's all about counts and checking on the young calves and making sure everything is accounted for. It's actually a lot of fun, which surprises Julia that she is enjoying the learning process so much. Of course, she knows it has a lot to do with the teacher.

Elena also mentions that in a week, it'll be time to herd the cattle home for branding and vaccinations. The day is one of the most important days out of the entire season, and because it'd be too hard to do all on their own, people come in from the town to help out.

And there's a large feast afterward, which is music to Julia's ears. She's getting used to eating like a cowboy. The rest of the day sounds like it'll be hectic, and the idea of branding a young calf makes Julia's stomach twist, but Elena explains the significance of it and why it's absolutely necessary, especially during open range season when cattle can escape and get away from the herd.

As they're rounding the large patch of aspen trees that surrounds the log cabin, Julia spots Cole riding up to them on his horse.

"Mom!" He's coming at them fast and pulls his reins not nearly far enough away. Sweetie rears up, and Cole handles him expertly. "You gotta get back to the house. *Now.*"

"Goodness, dear, where's the fire?"

"She's back, Mom."

And that's all it takes for Elena to fly away on her horse, shouting, "Yah!" and losing her hat in the process.

"What the hell?" Julia asks, and Cole looks back at her.

"Penn."

Julia is taken aback, and even though she doesn't know the whole story, she feels like she knows enough to realize this isn't good.

"Come on," Cole says, taking off on Sweetie.

Julia urges Leia to a gallop and follows Cole to the barn. She dismounts easily and ties the lead against the horse post next to Sweetie. She jogs up behind Cole and grabs his arm. "What the hell happened with them, Cole? No one will tell me."

"Look, Julia, you really need to hear that from my mom—"

"Tell me," she says, cutting him off and folding her arms across her chest. She taps her boot as he tries to do anything but make eye contact.

"You can't tell her I told you," he says, pointing a finger at her.

"Deal."

They shake hands, and Cole gulps before saying, "They were running the ranch together, and well, it wasn't perfect, but it was what it was. And then Penn just left my mom with no warning or reason. Mom woke up one day, and Penn was gone. And, well, she was in love with her, or at least, I think she thought she was or whatever. In love with the idea of being happy again? First time since my other mom—" Cole adjusts his cowboy hat, wipes his brow, and pushes the hat back on his head from the top. "She hasn't been the same since all of that happened. She and I haven't been the same. Geez, Julia, it's not really my place to tell you this." His eyes meet Julia's, and he glances back over his shoulder at the house. "You'd better never tell her I told you," he says. And then adds, "And close your mouth, for shit's sake."

Julia slaps him lightly on the arm. "Don't cuss. Your mother will kill you."

"Tell me about it," he says softly as he turns to walk toward the house. "Are you coming?"

Julia doesn't know what she should do. Should she go inside with Cole? Should she stay outside with the horses? Even with barely knowing Elena, the protective feeling Julia has for her is a little disconcerting. She figures if she ends up meeting this Penn woman she'll end up wanting to fight her. So, in the end, she decides to stay and take care of Leia. It was a long day, after all. A lot of riding and a lot of new information to process, and she *is* responsible for Leia's care.

And the last thing she wants to do is go inside that house and meet this woman that she already can't stand.

❖

It takes her about an hour to unsaddle Leia and groom her after riding. She takes her time with the grooming, making sure her tail is free of debris and tangles, getting all of the dust she can out of Leia's coat, and checking her hooves and shoes. The horse is so easygoing, only snorting at her a couple times when Julia snags a knot in her tail. Of course, the horse happily goes back to munching on the grain she was given as a snack.

It's when she's finishing up that she hears voices. She stays in the stall because she knows one of the voices is Elena but the other voice? That's definitely not someone she knows, which can only mean one thing.

Penn.

She stands next to Leia, smoothing a hand over her withers and down her back when she sees the two approaching the stalls.

"Penn, you didn't even leave a note. You just left. What was I supposed to think?"

"Elena, please, you have to understand. I got spooked."

"Do *you* understand, though?"

Julia watches Elena, how her arms are crossed, how her jaw keeps clenching. And she can see Penn as well, and she looks like a real jerk. A beautiful jerk, though, and it instantly causes jealousy to flare up in the pit of her stomach. Her hair is light brown and is in a long braid down the middle of her back. She is tall, built, very tan, and she looks like a cowboy should look. Of course, she still has her cowboy hat on, which any idiot knows should be taken off when you're talking to a lady, begging for forgiveness. Julia wants to punch this stupid, beautiful jerk in the face.

"I do understand!" Penn shouts, standing in front of Elena now, her arms hanging at her sides. Pretty smug for someone who's apologizing.

Elena shakes her head at Penn. "I don't think you do. All I told you is that you needed to figure yourself out. If leaving is your way of figuring yourself out, then so be it."

"Why didn't you try to contact me, then?"

"*I* was supposed to contact *you*?"

"Yes," she says with a huff.

"Penn, you broke my heart," Elena says, her voice breaking.

"I won't do it again." She reaches for Elena and pulls her into a hug, still not removing her dumb black hat.

Elena doesn't reciprocate the hug. She pulls away and crosses her arms again. "Look. I need help with the herding. So, for now, you can stay. The room upstairs isn't being used."

"In the barn?"

"Yes, Penn, in the barn. That room will do, and you know it. You don't get to come back into my life and also stay in my house. That isn't how this works."

Penn rubs her hands together. "Fine."

"Don't get comfortable. You leave when I tell you to leave. You hear me?"

"Fine."

"And don't try to be your same persistent self with me."

"Fine," Penn says one more time, but this time she's way tenser. "Elena, I promise I'll be better."

"You were wonderful before."

Julia hears the words come out of Elena's mouth, and her stomach bottoms out. She glances at Leia as if the horse can respond, then looks back over the wall at the couple.

"I won't hurt you again."

Elena shakes her head. "We'll see about that," she says as she turns to leave the barn, Penn hot on her trail.

Julia watches as Penn catches up and slings her arm over Elena's shoulders. "Guess that's the end of that," Julia whispers to Leia when she looks back at the horse. And as if on command, the horse nudges Julia's face and breathes out.

❖

When Julia cracks open her beer on the porch of her cabin, she can feel her mouth watering in anticipation. To say it's been a long day would be an understatement. Her muscles hurt, her back is aching, and the shower she took may have very well been the most amazing shower she has ever taken. *Ever.* In her entire life. The water was brown from the caked-on dirt and dust. It was the first time she truly felt like she was worked like a dog, and all she did was ride a horse all day!

The craziness that happened after she and Elena returned from riding was enough to ruin her amazing day, though. She had a feeling Elena felt the same way, even though she didn't get a chance to talk to Elena because she wasn't at dinner. Cole had mumbled something about how his mom wasn't hungry, and when Julia's eyes found his, he shook his head. She knew it meant that things weren't great and to not ask questions, but it bothered her no end.

She isn't exactly sure why it is upsetting her so much that this Penn woman just showed back up in Elena's life after clearly breaking her heart with nothing more than a horrible apology and a piss-poor excuse. It's not like Julia has any claim to Elena whatsoever. Up until recently, she was fairly sure she'd never get on Elena's good side. But now? After all their interactions, she is feeling things for Elena, things that have lain dormant for quite some time. This attraction to Elena isn't hard to understand. She knows what is stirring in her heart, but Julia shouldn't be feeling this. Elena is her boss, and she is not on the market. Especially now.

There is absolutely no way that this woman, Elena *freaking* Bennett, with her gorgeous hair and perfect skin, was going to reciprocate.

No. *No. way.*

Julia leans back against the wood beam of the porch and takes a deep breath. She can see the lights on in the kitchen of the log home and the television light flickering from the family room. She often finds her mind wandering. Wondering what Elena is doing over there in that big house. Is she watching TV with Cole? Is she doing bills or keeping the books for the ranch? Is she wondering what Julia is doing?

She shakes her head, laughs to herself, and stands, making her way back inside, where she flops on the couch and props her feet up on the coffee table. The room is quite cozy now that she's finished cleaning, with two leather chairs, a sofa, and a coffee table that all sit in front of a fireplace. It's been too warm, of course, to try the fireplace, but Julia is excited for the first time she can give it a whirl.

If she's still around, of course.

There are a couple lamps on, but the light is so low that she has lit candles to help. It's actually becoming very comfortable there at the cabin, and even though sticking around is not normally something Julia would be all for, she's actually settling in well.

So much so that now when she hears a knock on the door, she shouts, "Come in!" without even getting up to check who it is.

After the screen door opens and slams closed, she hears a familiar throat clear and then, "You realize that even though this isn't the big city, you should probably still check to see who's at the door, Miss Finch."

Julia jumps up, immediately pulling at the T-shirt she has on as well as the running shorts. "Elena, hi. I'm sorry. I didn't realize—"

"How could you?" Elena asks, a small smile on her face. "May I come in?"

"Oh, gosh, yes, please." Julia motions toward the chairs in the living room. "Make yourself at home."

Elena notices Julia's beer and raises her eyebrows. "Have any more of those?"

"Yes! In the fridge. Help yourself," she says through her very nervous breathing. She watches Elena walk into the kitchen and immediately looks up at the heavens and silently curses herself for being such a basket case. Seeing Elena after everything that happened today is shocking. And also, seeing her with her hair down again and curly again and dressed in black yoga pants and a light pink tank top with flip-flops is startling. She never wanted to imagine Elena in anything other than jeans and boots because anything else would mean she's human. And soft and sexy and dammit, so, so beautiful. Not that Julia's imagining her in other clothes. *Or whatever. Ugh.*

Elena walks over to the couch, beer in hand, and sits a space and a half away from Julia. "Is this okay?"

Julia nods because honestly, she couldn't talk if she wanted to. The whole series of events has sent her into a tailspin.

"I had to get out of the house." Elena sighs. "It was too closed up."

Julia nods again.

"And I don't want to be in there alone, *thinking*."

This statement is followed by silence until Julia finally says, "I understand that completely."

Elena takes a long drink from the Coors Light she picked. "I know you know what happened with Penn."

Julia chokes on the sip of her beer. After a cough or two, she blinks rapidly at Elena.

"Cole confessed that he broke down and told you. He is such a sweet boy. He simply cannot keep things from me," Elena says as she slips her feet out of the flip-flops and pulls her legs up so she can sit with them crossed. "It's both a blessing and a curse."

"I'm really sorry. I made him tell me. I just, everyone is always walking on eggshells because of this chick, and I didn't get it and then she shows up, and like, I should probably know."

"Julia." Elena places her hand on Julia's bare leg, right above her knee, and Julia stops immediately. "I'm not mad that you know."

The breath that Julia was holding releases from her lungs. "Whew," she says with a laugh.

"You were bound to find out sooner or later, right?" Elena asks. "I guess I shouldn't be surprised."

"Oddly enough, Elena, no one was talking about what happened. If it makes you feel any better."

"Maybe a little," she says. "It wasn't a shining moment in my life."

Julia is very aware that Elena's hand is still on her leg, and it takes everything in her to focus on Elena's words and *not* the feel of her very warm, surprisingly soft skin. "I'm sure it wasn't," Julia replies, her voice barely above a whisper.

"It's just, as the boss, the owner, I really do strive to be professional and keep things separate. But Elijah is part of my family now, and Caroline will always be as well, so when Penn started, it was hard at first. I welcomed her and, well…" Elena glances at Julia and raises her beer to her lips. Before she drinks she says, "She was very persistent."

"I can only imagine." Julia breathes in, holds it, then breathes out slowly. She cannot handle the way Elena is looking at her.

After Elena drinks, she licks her lips, and then presses them together. "After Gloria, I kind of just stopped trying. I didn't want anyone. I didn't even want Penn. But again, she was…" Elena's voice trails off.

"Persistent. I got it."

Elena chuckles. "Yeah, well, I let her in, and she broke me. Being left with no explanation is never easy. And when you didn't want to open yourself up to begin with and some stranger comes into your life and makes you? And you're left saying, 'I fucking knew it'?" Elena pauses and drinks. "Let's just say, I was very broken. Probably even more than after losing Gloria. Because when someone just leaves you, you feel as if it's all you. But someone being taken from you? That's at least…hard to argue with?"

"I think they both sound like they suck." Julia doesn't want to take her eyes off Elena. Looking at her has become Julia's favorite thing to do, and it's scaring the hell out of her because Elena is turning out to be just as broken as Julia is.

"You're right. They do both suck." Elena drinks again, and Julia wishes she was that beer bottle. "For some reason, Julia Finch, I trust you. I don't really know why." Elena's line of sight is focused somewhere across the room. Julia wishes Elena would look at her, but she knows the second Elena does, she is a goner. "It might be because the horses trust you, which is sometimes the best sign you can ask for. But either way, I do. I trust you." Elena pauses, looks at Julia in the dim lighting, and squeezes Julia's leg very gently.

Julia blinks twice and opens her mouth to say something but can't figure out exactly what to say. She really is a goner. She can barely remember how to breathe, let alone speak. She clears her throat and says, "I trust you, too."

Elena finally pulls her hand away from Julia's leg and rests both hands in her lap where she instantly starts to fidget. "It's oddly weird that she's in the barn right now," Elena says softly. Julia lets out a nervous laugh, and Elena rolls her eyes. "What?"

"I'm sorry." Julia takes a drink of her beer and then meets Elena's eyes. "You know, we all do things that, at the time, aren't exactly the smartest decisions. And when we make them, it's always with the best intentions. So, I get what you're doing."

"I sense a 'but' coming."

"*But* she left you with no explanation. And broke your heart." Julia shrugs and twists her mouth a bit. "She's stupid for leaving you in the first place."

Elena arches an eyebrow and tilts her head. "Oh, really?"

"Yeah, really." Julia feels a little like an idiot for speaking so freely, but she continues her thought. "I would never leave you for anyone." She shakes her head, realizing what she said and how it came out. "I mean, wait, that's not…I just mean that, like, I wouldn't leave *you*, but that—" She looks at Elena's wide eyes and goofy grin. She is obviously enjoying how Julia is fumbling her words like a fool. "Shit," she says at the end of her rambling. "You know what? Let's act like I didn't say that."

"No," Elena replies, her lips displaying a rather large smile. "I understand what you're saying. Even if you aren't sure."

Julia pushes her hands through her hair and laughs. "I sure do have a way of sticking my foot in my mouth."

"I can see that."

"Part of the reason I have so few friends, I'm sure."

"It's actually quite endearing. Don't sell yourself so short."

"Yeah, well." Julia downs the rest of her beer and stands to get another one. "I wouldn't ever call anything I do *endearing*." She makes her way into the kitchen, opens the fridge, grabs two beers, twists the cap off one, and tosses it onto the counter. She's so nervous now. Listening to Elena, seeing her in such a casual setting, it's getting under Julia's skin. And now Elena just said Julia is endearing? What the hell? She turns around, and Elena is leaning against the doorframe; her hair looks so soft, and Julia instantly sees herself running her fingers through it, and she has to snap herself back to reality. But it's this moment, with Elena standing there so casually, her hair without any product, her skin without any makeup, her tank top tight enough that it's accentuating all of her curves, that Julia begins to admit to herself that all these feelings for Elena Bennett are going to become a real problem. "I got you another one." Julia hands over the opened bottle. She watches as Elena reaches for it, and her hand lightly lands on Julia's. There's a very long pause where the two women just look at each other before Elena takes the beer and raises it to her lips. She drinks one, two, three big gulps, and the sound of the carbonated liquid in Elena's mouth is almost deafening in the small kitchen.

They stand in silence for a few more moments, Julia now leaning against the countertop next to the sink. Elena smiles as she motions toward Julia with her beer bottle. "What are you thinking, Julia Finch?" she asks, taking a step closer to Julia, the floor creaking slightly under her weight.

"I'm thinking I'm really glad my car broke down," Julia says, turning on the smallest bit of charm.

The smile that lights up Elena's face almost takes Julia's breath away. "Oh, really?" Julia nods and watches as Elena closes the distance between them and places her beer on the counter, her eyes never leaving Julia's face. "You're making things really confusing for me."

Julia keeps eye contact with Elena even though, in this circumstance, Julia's height difference is making it difficult. Elena is so close, and her scent is so amazing, and her breath is warm as it brushes past Julia's skin. She pulls her gaze from Elena's eyes and glances down to the floor. After a deep breath and mental pep talk, she makes herself look back into Elena's dark eyes. "Confusing how?"

Elena pulls her bottom lip into her mouth and bites down. "I think about you a lot," she says, her voice so soft it's almost a whisper.

The night breeze that is blowing softly in the kitchen window causes goose bumps to form on Julia's arms. But the chill that washes over her has more to do with Elena's confession than anything else. "What about me?" Julia manages to ask even though her brain seems to be short-circuiting at the moment.

Elena reaches forward and lightly runs her fingers down Julia's bicep and forearm to her hand that is clenched into a fist. Julia relaxes her hand slightly when she feels Elena's touch before she says, "I think about your hands and what it would feel like for you to touch me."

"Elena…"

"I think about your green eyes," Elena says, "And your mouth. And how you say my name."

Julia can barely feel her legs. If she didn't know for sure, she'd be positive that she's standing in the middle of a dream.

"I didn't want this to happen again," Elena says. "I shut this part of me down."

"I know."

"I didn't ask for this. For you. In your stupid Converse shoes and skinny jeans." Elena squeezes Julia's hand a little tighter. "But you got into my head, and I can't get you out of there."

"Did you think putting me in Wranglers and boots would make it easier?"

"Yes, but it backfired. It actually made it worse."

"It makes me really happy that one of your plans backfired," Julia says, lifting her head and smirking.

Elena takes a step backward, pulling on Julia's hand as she says, "I should go."

Immediately, Julia wants to beg her to not go. *Please don't leave now.* Not when this all feels so damn good. Elena motions to the door. "We have to go to town tomorrow morning to run errands."

"Who does?"

"Well, me, Cole, you, if you'd like to join us."

They get to the door, and Elena turns to look at Julia, who instantly hates the idea of letting Elena leave. "You could stay," Julia says, her voice cracking from her nerves.

"I wish I could."

"Another night?"

Elena's smile is enough of an answer to make Julia's heart explode.

"I'll go with tomorrow," she says as Elena leaves the cabin, the sound of her flip-flops walking into the night the last sound Julia hears before she shuts the door.

Chapter Nine

Julia hates admitting it, but not only is she so sore from riding that she feels like she was trampled by wild animals, she's also insanely nervous as she walks out of the cabin at eight in the morning. She's so nervous, in fact, that she forgets that there are steps that she needs to walk down and stumbles, has to catch herself, and lets out an exasperated groan because none of that felt good on her muscles. She can't quite seem to wake up, either, because of course she could barely sleep the night before. She tossed and turned and tossed and turned. Woke up at three to take ibuprofen for her aches and pains and then found herself launched back into thoughts of what had happened only hours earlier.

How was she supposed to sleep after all of that?

Julia shakes her head as she walks up the path toward the log home, her sunglasses on, her hair pulled back into a very messy ponytail, and her black tank top already attracting the sun's rays. She opted for skinny jeans today, but she still pulled the boots on her feet. Even though everything in her body screamed for a nice, relaxing day in her Chucks.

She glances at the sky. Not a cloud in sight; the blue color amazing in the early morning hours. It still strikes her how gorgeous this place is. How everything is so crisp and clear. How even in the sweltering heat, the shade offers much-needed relief from the blazing sun. Her eyes move over to the back of the house, and just like that, the calm brought from the outdoors is washed away. The thought of Elena marching out that back door makes her heart lodge in her throat. Julia is so nervous to see her this morning after everything that happened last night. It's too fast and too soon, especially considering the fact that Julia hasn't shared a single meaningful thing about herself with Elena. And now this? How in the world is she supposed to handle *this*?

This whole thing has turned into a giant cluster of nerves and feelings and emotions that Julia did not sign up for. Or maybe she did sign up for it? How is she supposed to know? Is she supposed to actually open up and talk? To Elena?

"I can't do that," Julia whispers as she approaches the garage where she assumes Elena and Cole are waiting.

"Can't do what?"

Julia jerks her head up and sees Cole standing there, his normal cowboy attire on, except this time he's wearing a very worn T-shirt that has the Phish emblem plastered across the front. "Nothing," Julia says. "Nice shirt."

Cole smiles. "I love them. Favorite band ever."

"I am actually surprised you've even heard of them."

"Oh, Jules, I listen to everything," Cole says as they both take a seat on the bumper of the red Jeep Wrangler that is parked in the garage. "So, Mom said she told you that I told her."

Julia looks at Cole and shakes her head. "About what?"

His chuckle is deep, and he moves his hands in the air and then rubs his face. "Penn. Everything that happened."

"Yeah, she told me not to tell you that I knew you cracked." Julia laughs, and then it hits her. "Wait. She's talking about me to you now?" She rubs her palms on her jean-clad knees.

Cole huffs. "Um, yeah, *duh*. I told you she likes you the other night. If she didn't, she would have fired you already."

"I guess you're right," Julia says with a smile. "Have you thought any more about applying to schools in Chicago?"

"Like, all the time. I just don't want Mom to get mad at me. She's going to be so upset..."

"I get that." Julia nudges Cole on the shoulder. "The pizza is worth it, though."

Cole laughs, sweeping his hair away from his forehead. "I need to get out of Colorado."

"Your mom wouldn't like you getting out of Colorado without

her," comes a smooth, deep voice from right outside the overhead garage door.

Julia whips her head toward the voice that obviously belongs to Penn and stands immediately, pushing her hands into her back pockets. She looks at Penn for a brief moment. She cannot get over how pretty this woman is. It's unsettling. It's not that she thought Penn was going to be ugly, but damn, all the stories about her made her seem like she was going to be sort of, well, *handsome*. Julia turns her head, stares off into the distance, and tries to avoid eye contact at all costs.

"You must be Julia," Penn says, taking a couple steps inside the garage toward where Julia is standing.

"What's it to you?" Julia's voice is laced with contempt. She knows she just came off very rude, but she honestly doesn't care right now.

"I'm Penn," she says. She wipes her hand on her jeans and holds it out for Julia to shake. "It's a pleasure to meet you."

Julia eyes the hand, looks at Penn, and then back at the outstretched hand before she decides to shake it. She wants to tell Penn that she wishes she could say the same, but she doesn't. She takes her hand back and folds her arms across her chest. She looks down at Cole who looks just as uncomfortable as she feels.

"So, you're here from Chicago?"

Cole goes to respond, but Julia cuts him off, answering the question with a simple, "Yep." She glances at Cole and shakes her head as nonchalantly as possible.

"I've never been," Penn says with a faraway stare. "You like it there?"

Julia shrugs. "Yeah, I mean, sure."

"What are you doing here, then?"

"I could ask you the same question," Julia quickly says, hoping she looks far more badass than she feels right now.

"I have more right to be here than you do."

"Um," Cole says, his hand rising into the air. "You kinda left, Penn."

Penn looks at Cole, then back at Julia. "So, you think you can just come in here and replace the work I did?"

Julia can't help it when a laugh escapes from her throat. "I'm sorry. What is that supposed to mean?"

"It means I can very easily find a reason to stay."

"I don't think my mom would be okay with that," Cole says. "And neither would I."

Penn shakes her head and looks around the garage before finally setting her gaze back on Julia. She moves into Julia's space with a look on her face that means business. "You'd better watch yourself." Penn's voice cracks at the end of the threat, and it makes Julia smile.

"Thanks for the advice." Julia glares at her and doesn't give up her footing. She watches as Penn turns around and leaves the garage in a huff. She can feel Cole standing up next to her now, and he nudges her side with his elbow.

"That was badass," he says, holding up his hand so Julia can high-five it.

She turns toward him with her hand raised and notices that Elena is standing in the garage now, her arms crossed, shaking her head. *Busted.* "Hey," Julia shouts. Obviously, she doesn't know how to play it cool. Ever.

Elena walks toward Julia and Cole. "You know that wasn't necessary, right?"

"I know." Julia sighs.

"Yeah, it was, Mom. Penn was being all crazy ex, asking Julia questions and stuff. Like, she needs to lighten up."

"Cole Daniel Bennett," Elena says lightly, raising her hand to place on Cole's cheek. "I can fight my own battles, my love." She smiles and glances at Julia. "The same goes for you, too."

Julia shrugs. "Hey, I don't do well when I'm cornered. What can I say?"

Elena walks over toward the driver's side of the Jeep and opens the door. She looks way more casual than normal; her hair isn't pulled up, and she has just a simple white T-shirt paired with her jeans and boots. "Come on, you two. Let's go."

❖

Julia discovers the ride into town is much more fun when in good company. While Elena drives, Cole talks about fifty-five different topics from the passenger seat, which he protested, but Julia told him she likes riding in the back seat. Truthfully, she wanted to be able to see Elena's eyes in the rearview mirror. So far, she hasn't been disappointed with her decision.

When they get to the general store, Elena pulls into a parking spot and puts the Jeep into park. She looks over at Cole. "Do you want to go to the video store?"

"Yeah!" he shouts.

Elena hands him a twenty-dollar bill after they climb out of the vehicle. "Try to get something other than comic book movies!" she shouts after he starts running toward the video store. She shakes her head. "We'll be watching Marvel movies for the next four nights. I just know it."

"At least they're not horror movies."

"True, although when I was a teenager, I watched *Halloween* for the first time, and still to this day, I love it." Elena pushes through the doors of the general store and grabs a cart.

"I do love me a little Jamie Lee Curtis," Julia says, watching Elena's every move, making a mental note of how amazing she looks from the back in those jeans. They turn the cart down an aisle, and Julia gets plowed into by none other than Toni.

"Hey, girl! What's up?" Toni yells, frantically collecting the items she was holding from the floor. She stands and looks at Julia, then glances at Elena. Her eyes widen, and she grins like an idiot. "Um, hi, Miss Bennett."

"Miss Carson. How are you, dear?"

"Good, good. Business is good. Just putting back stray and discarded items. Are you two here *together*?"

"Yes, Miss Carson, we're getting the shopping done. Cole is getting movies at the Family Video."

"Oh, little man, how's he doing? Caroline done homeschooling for the year?"

"Yes, herding starts tomorrow. Will you be around to help?"

Toni smiles. "Of course! You know how I *love* to get *dirty*!" Her answer is so sarcastic that it doesn't need the eye roll, but Toni does it just for good measure. Julia starts laughing, partly because of Toni, but also because her nerves are shot at the moment. For some reason, Toni calling them out about being together has made Julia's stomach fill with butterflies.

Elena, on the other hand, does not laugh. She motions over her shoulder toward the deli counter. "You know your grandmother is the one that volunteers you?"

"Oh, I know." Toni groans, then glances at Julia. "How's it going on the ol' ranch? I heard Miss Bennett got you a new mare, Jules."

"I'll never get over how news travels in this town, I swear to God."

"Oh, it's no big thing. I occasionally sleep with one of the guys that works at Dusty Hearts."

Julia lets out a laugh. "My God, Toni. You're crazy."

"I believe Miss Carson asked you a question, Julia," Elena says with a smile and nudge.

"Oh, yes, the ranch. It's really great, actually."

"*Actually*? Wait a second…" Elena tilts her head, but her voice has a joking tone.

"You know what I mean, Elena," Julia says, her eyes locking on to Elena's.

"Mm-hmm." Elena steers the cart down the aisle. "I'm going to continue the shopping."

Toni watches as Elena turns out of the aisle, then throws her hands up. "Whoa, whoa! First-name basis? Forgive me, but what the hell? That has *never* happened before."

Julia can feel her cheeks turning pink. She knows she's not doing a very good job of acting cool, calm, and collected, but she can't control herself. "I know, right?" Julia whispers, leaning in. "I don't even know what happened."

"Well, well, well, it's about time someone softened that hard-ass exterior," Toni says, real low, with a chuckle.

"I can still hear you, Miss Carson," comes Elena's voice from the next aisle over.

Toni and Julia both hide their laughter, and Julia slaps Toni's arm. "Nice going, Toni."

"Someone needs to call you out," Toni says as the two women walk down the aisle together. "You just be careful. I heard that asshole Penn is back in town."

Julia sighs. "She is. She's back. Staying in a room in the barn."

"No way!"

"Yes, way." Julia eyes the bag of Doritos behind Toni on the end cap of the aisle and grabs them. "It's weird, right?"

"Yeah, man, just be careful. And make sure Bennett keeps her guard up around her." Toni leans in toward Julia's ear. "Believe me, Penn is a smooth character."

"That sounds an awful lot like you're speaking from experience."

"Sort of." Toni sighs. "It's a long story."

"Maybe you need to keep *your* guard up? Geez."

"Nah, I can handle it. And her. But Bennett? I don't know."

"I just…I don't want to push her. You know what I mean?"

Toni starts restocking the items she was holding before she says, "You realize you can only be as charming as she will let you?"

Julia tilts her head, her face screwed up. "What does that mean?"

"It means…" Toni takes a deep breath and turns toward Julia, readjusting the box of Frosted Flakes she's holding and the cans of Hormel Chili, Bumble Bee Tuna, and Spam. "Look, I know her fairly well. I have helped out on that ranch since I was sixteen. She's *complicated.* In a good way. And I know what happened with Penn. And I get it. And it sucks. But look, Julia, she's not going to let herself get hurt again. So, like, if you want to be charming and fun and find a way to get over those walls she's built, she's probably going to let you."

"I hardly know her." Julia's voice is soft, almost a whisper.

"She's ready, though."

"How can you tell?"

Toni places her free hand on Julia's shoulder and turns her around gently so she can look at Elena standing by the deli counter. "Look at her," Toni whispers. "Look at the way she's standing. Look at the way she's dressed. Look at her hair. *Look.*"

"But how—"

"Because I know her," Toni says. "And that is not the way she normally is. She's normally wound tight and mean and unhappy. Ugh. I would dread when she would step foot in this store because heaven forbid we didn't have the freshest apples in stock. Like, really, lady? We're in Colorado. Not Washington. Trust me. You can tell now just by, like, looking at her that she's relaxed. A white T-shirt? Come on. I don't think I've ever seen her in a white T-shirt. Seriously. *Believe* me."

"She is really hot, isn't she?"

Toni laughs. "Um, yes! Hello! She's gorgeous! Now go before I get in trouble for 'talking too much to the customers.' I'll see you tomorrow."

Julia takes off toward Elena, watches as she talks to Agnes, watches as she laughs, watches as she runs a hand through her hair. She really is stunning. And that white T-shirt she apparently never wears? Julia would be absolutely fine if she wore it every day for the rest of their lives. *Damn.* Julia knows that it's outrageous and uncharted territory to have these feelings for Elena after hardly knowing her, but for some reason, it feels more natural than anything she has ever felt in her entire life.

It's scary, yes.

It's probably something she shouldn't be doing, yes.

It's probably going to get messy, yes.

But…

Elena glances over at Julia when she strides up next to her at the counter. "Smoked turkey, right? Isn't that what I saw in your fridge?"

A warmth washes over Julia's entire body when she smiles and nods. "Yeah," she says, her response breathy from her racing thoughts.

"You okay?" Elena tilts her head slightly. Julia nods and throws out a soft *mm-hmm* as her response.

"I see you decided to stick around," comes Agnes's voice from over the deli counter. "I wondered if you were going to run screaming from this town."

Julia glances at Agnes, shrugs, and says, "My car broke down. Didn't have much of a choice."

"Maybe it was a blessing in disguise, eh?" Agnes asks, and she adjusts her glasses.

Julia glances at Elena, then back to Agnes. "Seems like a good place to put down some roots."

Roots.

Now, there's a concept for a girl who never even planted a seed before.

CHAPTER TEN

Y ou're going to end up kicking a rock into someone's truck." Elena is leaning against the side of the Jeep, one leg crossed over the other.

Julia scoffs, but after kicking another rock that careens awfully close to a vehicle, she ends up listening. The last thing Julia needs is to cause trouble and draw even more attention to herself. "So, how long does it typically take to pick out movies?"

Elena looks up at the sun for a few seconds before moving her view out across the parking lot toward the west. "About an hour. Give or take thirty minutes."

"Good Lord. There can't possibly be that many movies out." Julia leans on the Jeep next to Elena but with enough distance to not make either of them uncomfortable. "Are movie nights a normal occurrence?"

Elena takes a deep breath, glances over at Julia, then looks back across the parking lot. "Gloria started them. I continued the tradition after…"

Julia watches how Elena's face hardens, her lips as they press together, and her brow when it furrows. "It sounds nice, you know. *Family movie night.*"

After Elena clears her throat, she pushes away from the Jeep, takes two steps away from Julia, and turns on the heels on her boots. "You realize that I'm not letting Penn stay forever."

"Uh," Julia says, her mouth hanging open slightly. "What brought this up?"

"Well, I just know how people in this town love to gossip.

Especially Caroline and Toni. If I could have hid it from this whole town, I would have!" Elena folds her arms across her chest and looks at the ground. "How do you tell someone you're only using them for the labor?"

"Elena, look—"

"No, Julia, *you* look," Elena says, almost too forceful, but clearly, it's something she needs to get off her chest. "I know I seem like a real bitch on the outside, but I honestly hate hurting people. And Penn? I just…I don't know what to do."

Julia reaches up and pulls her sunglasses from her face, folds them, and slides one arm in the neck of her tank top. She squints a little at Elena, but then as her eyes adjust, she looks at her fully. "I need you to understand something here." Julia's voice is shaking the tiniest of bits. "I have absolutely no say here in how you handle *anything*. So, whatever you want to do with Penn is entirely up to you. It really is. If you're not done with her, that's your business. Not mine. Or anyone else's in this town." She watches as Elena looks away from her, focuses on the ground, and hugs herself a little tighter. "But just know, I will never treat Penn with any kindness. *Ever*."

"I don't expect you to be *nice* to her," Elena says softly, loosening her arms before letting them hang at her sides. "There's just so much history there."

"Elena, you don't have to explain it to me. I may shy away from talking about feelings, but I totally understand having them." Julia forces herself to smile. "Just promise me one thing?"

"What?" Elena asks as she looks at Julia and tilts her head.

"Please, do not ask me to let her stay in my cabin with me. I fear I would murder her in her sleep."

"Oh, Julia, after seeing how you handled her today, I am fairly confident that the feeling is mutual, dear." Elena lets out a laugh in unison with Julia just as Cole comes running up to the Jeep. He's holding a plastic bag full of Blu-rays in one hand and a king-sized bag of Peanut M&M's in the other. "Well, well, well, it's about time."

"Sorry, Mom, there were like, at least fifteen movies I wanted to get," Cole says before he throws a couple more M&M's in his mouth. "And I got five movies because some aren't due for a week. But yeah, and also, there isn't any change." The last part of his sentence is mumbled around the remnants of candy.

Julia starts to laugh when Elena lets out a gasp. "You spent that entire twenty dollars on movies and candy?"

Cole shrugs, looks at Julia, then back at Elena before saying, "You didn't say I couldn't."

"He does have a very valid point."

"Would you like to walk back, Miss Finch?"

"Miss Finch? Oh, no! The *last name*! You're back on her shit list!"

"Cole!" Elena shouts as they all climb into the Jeep. "How many times do I need to tell you not to curse?"

Julia lets out a snort as she says from the back seat, "*Now* who's on her shit list, hmm?"

And Cole descends into giggles. And really, so does Elena.

❖

Julia spends the rest of the day mucking stalls and trying to find a balance between obsessing about how Elena's lips look and how they might feel and figuring out how to handle these feelings without constantly wondering what Elena is thinking. A part of her is already annoyed at this whole thing because if this is how it's going to be having feelings for someone else, with the obsessing and the freaking out over every little thing, then fucking *never mind*!

"Julia?"

She swings herself around, the sound of her name frightening her, and grips her heart while gasping. She sees Caroline standing there holding a large water bottle. Her short black hair is swept over her forehead to the side. "Jesus, you scared the shit out of me."

"I'm sorry," Caroline says. "I just wanted to bring you this." She offers the water bottle, the ice inside rattling against the sides of the plastic. "And I wanted to ask you a question."

"Ugh, why?" Julia asks after propping up the pitchfork. She's had a number of conversations with Caroline, but they're typically while everyone else is present. So, this seems weird right away. Julia takes the bottle from Caroline and takes a very long drink from it. She stops, water spills down her chin, and she slides her forearm across her lips. "I am so sick of questions."

Caroline laughs and crosses her arms. "You realize this question might not be about you, right?"

"Touché."

"Is Elena okay?"

Julia's eyes go wide. She leans against the wood frame of the stall and clears her throat. "Why would I know if she's okay or not? You talk to her a hell of a lot more than I do."

"Not lately," Caroline says. Her voice is laced with *something*. Is it irritation? Is it jealousy? Is it nothing at all, and the heat is just getting to Julia's senses? She can't be sure.

"Well, why don't you *ask* her?"

"Why can't you just *tell* me?" The huff that follows Caroline's question sounds like the start of a temper tantrum. Julia fights the laughter that is bubbling within her. Seeing Caroline like this is so comical.

"Because," Julia says. "I know how people love to gossip. And I'm not one for it. So, I think you should ask her."

Caroline lets out a deep breath. "I know," she says quietly. "I just…I don't know how to tell her that I don't want Penn here. And neither should she."

"This is about Penn?"

"Yes!" Caroline says. "She really hurt Elena, and I do not trust that woman. And she just breezes in here with her long hair and her beautiful eyes and that really nice personality that wins people over. She just rubs me the wrong way. I feel like she's up to something. I have a sixth sense about things like this. Normally, I'm right."

"Well, I don't like her, either, my friend."

"As much as I love hearing that you don't like Penn, because the more the merrier, can I ask why? Because you barely know Elena. How do you even know what happened? If you're so against gossip and don't want to talk about anything *ever.* How do you even *know*?"

It's obvious to Julia now that Caroline's words aren't just laced with *something*. They're *dripping* with irritation! "Look, Caroline, I don't really like to talk about myself—"

"Ever."

"Yeah, ever."

"Well, *why*?"

Julia pushes off from the side of the stall and starts to walk away. "I just don't." She sighs, hearing Caroline's footsteps quick behind her.

"Is there a reason?"

"I thought you came in here to talk to me about Penn?" Julia asks as they continue to walk.

"I did," Caroline says. "But I hate talking about that woman. She just makes me angry."

"Me too," Julia mumbles, smiling at Caroline. "One thing we definitely agree on."

"I bet we agree that Elena isn't thinking clearly right now."

Julia pauses when they approach the fence to the pasture. She steps onto the bottom rung, places her arms through the open area of the fence, and leans into it. "Yeah." She's watching three of the horses grazing and Sully and Scout chasing after each other. Leia is watching Julia and Caroline, though, her eyes never leaving Julia.

"What do we do?"

"You've known Elena far longer than I have." Julia looks over at Caroline and smiles. "What do *you* think we should do?"

"Kill Penn."

The answer comes out of Caroline's mouth so fast and without any emotion that for a split second, Julia thinks she's completely serious. It's only when the corners of Caroline's mouth start turning upward that Julia realizes it was a joke. "Jesus." Julia shakes her head and stares forward again.

"I don't know what to do." Caroline mimics Julia's position against the fence and props her chin against her bicep. "Are you coming to the movie night tonight?"

"Nope."

"Why not?"

"Wasn't invited," Julia replies.

"Elena said she was going to ask you."

"She didn't mention it to me."

Caroline sighs and looks back at the horses. "Your horse is really taking to the others. She's so calm."

Julia feels herself start to smile, barely able to hold it back. "Yeah, she's pretty awesome."

"You know she doesn't just give anyone a horse." Caroline takes a deep breath and lets it out slowly before saying, "Penn never got a horse. She rode Sully for all of her ranch hand duties."

Julia stays silent, not really knowing how to take that information. She continues to watch the horses, paying special attention to Leia, who is slowly making her way over. What is Caroline saying without actually saying it? It's clear she's pussyfooting around something…but what is it?

"Of course, Elena seems to really like you."

"Okay, Caroline. What the hell are you getting at?"

Caroline smiles, shrugs, then turns to leave. "See you later, Julia."

"Not fair!" she shouts after Caroline as she walks away. Julia shakes her head before she glances back at the pasture. Leia has grazed her way to the fence and is now nuzzling Julia's hand. Julia climbs over the fence and lands on the other side, a couple of feet from Leia, who doesn't get spooked like the other horses do sometimes. Leia moves closer, nudges Julia with her nose, and breathes out when Julia finally starts petting her head. "Did you hear all of that, Leia?" Julia asks softly, next to the horse's head. "Caroline thinks Elena has a thing for me because she gave you to me. What do you think about that?"

The horse lets out a ragged breath and then perks her ears and stomps her front foot a few times while looking toward the house. The back door of the house opens abruptly, slams, and Penn comes barreling down the steps. Julia observes with curiosity as Penn approaches the old Ford truck. Elijah is underneath it, changing the oil, when Penn lets out a very loud and very gruff, "She's letting me help as long as possible, but I have to stay in the barn!" Julia can't hear Elijah's response, but Penn takes her cowboy hat off and throws it into the dirt. "Well, she's being ridiculous," she shouts. "I apologized. What more can I do?" Elijah's response must be something she's not happy about because Penn kicks her hat, and it goes flying. "I'm not leaving. I'm going to fix this." And she takes off toward the barn, cursing the entire way.

"Great," Julia mumbles. Just what she needs. "Competition."

❖

Julia swings Leia's stall door closed. All of the horses are happily munching away on dinner in their clean stalls. Julia felt like she was never going to get done with her chores, and now she's beat. She cannot wait to take a shower, pull on her sweatpants, and prop her feet up. Hell, just thinking about it is making her anxious for the relaxation.

When Julia exits the barn, Elena is standing on the walkway to the cabin with a smile on her face. The mid-afternoon light is amazing, but the clouds are rolling in, and it smells like rain is on the way. "Hey there," Julia says with a soft voice when she approaches Elena. "What brings you 'round these parts?"

Elena folds her arms across her chest and looks at the ground. "Just passing through." Her tone is playful, and Julia feels it in her stomach.

"Oh, yeah?"

"Yeah," Elena says right before her eyes meet Julia's.

Julia watches as Elena reaches up and tucks some stray hairs that have pulled from Julia's ponytail behind her ear. The gesture is so tender and familiar and all Julia can do is swallow.

Elena brushes her fingertips across Julia's sunburnt cheeks. "Are you coming for movie night?"

Julia can't fight the rush of emotion that fills her heart. She nods. She feels light-headed looking at Elena. "Elena?"

"Hmm?"

"There's something I want to ask you."

"Ask me. Ask me anything."

Julia smiles. "Did you really not get Penn a horse?"

The laughter that spills from Elena's mouth is intoxicating, and Julia cannot help but drink it up. She chuckles along with Elena, the two of them sharing a moment that a while ago, Julia never thought would happen. "Miss Finch, you are too much."

"Aw, man. Too much? That makes me sad." Julia lets out a defeated sigh. She's joking, of course, but she's laying it on thick.

Elena licks her lips, then purses them together before saying, "Actually, you're just right. And I don't know how to handle it anymore."

The admission takes Julia by surprise, especially considering her and Elena's conversation earlier about Penn and history and Elena's obvious internal struggle. She isn't sure what to say in response. She knows what she wants to *do*, of course, and that's slide her hands through Elena's hair and pull her into a deep kiss.

"So, go clean up." Elena's voice interrupts Julia's thoughts. "Movie night starts at seven." Elena brushes Julia's arm as she passes and walks toward the house. Julia, still breathless, looks behind her and watches her walk away.

❖

Cole seems practically giddy when he answers the door and sees Julia standing there. "You came!" he shouts as he grabs Julia's hand and pulls her inside. "Mom said she invited you, but I wasn't sure if you'd come!"

Julia gets tugged through the grand entryway into the kitchen, the smell of freshly popped popcorn surrounding her. Elena is standing near the stove on the other side of a large island complete with a white farmhouse sink. She's pouring popcorn into a giant bowl, and the sight makes Julia's knees weak. "Well, hello there," Elena says, glancing up at Julia, then back down at the bowl.

"Do you need help with anything?" Julia asks as she walks around the island toward the stove.

"I'm glad you came."

"So am I," Julia says, noticing the twinkle in Elena's eyes when their eyes meet.

"How was your shower?"

The question doesn't sound intimate. But dammit, Elena's voice is soft like velvet, and she's looking at Julia with this intense stare that sure as hell makes it *feel* intimate. "It was amazing," Julia says. Does she sound as breathless as she feels?

Elena reaches around Julia and grabs a stick of butter from the cement countertop on the other side of the stove. "You smell nice," Elena says quietly. "Is that lavender?"

Julia nods. She needs to pull herself together, or she's going to melt into a giant puddle on the slate-tiled floor.

Elena looks at Julia. "Promise me you'll start putting sunscreen on your face." She reaches and runs her fingertips across Julia's cheeks again. And it causes the same feeling in the pit of Julia's stomach.

"I promise," Julia whispers.

"Are you okay?"

"I'm more than okay."

"You sure?"

"Elena," Julia says. "You're making me feel so many things…"

"Isn't that good?"

"It's incredible."

"Then I won't stop," Elena says.

"Please don't," Julia says. "I don't want you to stop."

Elena starts to lean forward, her face within inches of Julia's.

"Mom!" Cole shouts from the living room, and the pair jerk away from each other. "What's taking so long?"

Elena shakes her head while clutching her chest. "It's almost ready, Cole. My goodness."

Julia chuckles softly after she dislodges her heart from her throat. "Okay," she says through her laughter. "What do you want me to do to help?" She can feel Elena's gaze as it rakes over her body from her head to her toes, and it is too much. Too, too, too much.

"You can melt this butter."

Julia is immediately filled with regret. She honestly hoped for something that had nothing to do with cooking. Like, wash the pan or get everyone a drink or maybe get herself a shot or two of vodka. Anything but cooking when she can't focus.

Elena must sense her trepidation, though, because she slides a glass measuring cup toward Julia and smiles. "Don't worry. Just microwave it for ten seconds. Stir. Then do it again."

A nervous laugh bubbles out of Julia, and she shakes her head. "You'd think I could handle melting butter."

"You can." Elena's words are soothing, which is pretty comical considering they're only talking about butter. It's when Elena finishes with, "I think you can handle more than you realize," that Julia's hands start to ache.

She looks over at Elena, at her hair, her profile. She doesn't glance up, doesn't flinch, really doesn't even look like she said a word except for the tiny pull on the corner of her mouth.

"What are you two doing in here?" comes Elijah's voice from behind them. Of course, it sounds like he knows *exactly* what they were doing.

"Butter," Julia shouts and points at the microwave.

"Oh, really? Just butter?" Elijah laughs, shakes his head, then leans against the counter. "City Girl, I meant to tell you earlier. Your car is done."

Julia hears Elijah, but she can't move. She's instantly filled with fear. For the first time since being on the ranch, she legitimately doesn't want to leave. And now she may have to. How does she find the courage to ask if she can stay? Oh man, she did not want to have to think about this right now. She plasters on a fake smile like she's had to do for most of her life as she looks over her shoulder at Elijah. "Oh, okay, that's good."

"Don't worry." Elijah's heavy hand lands on Julia's back with a thud. "You haven't paid me off yet, so you're not going anywhere."

"Oh, thank God," Julia says with an air of sarcasm. She looks back at Elijah. "Here I thought I could finally escape manure and dirt."

"Yeah, once you get that in your veins, you never get rid of it, so don't even try." Elijah turns back to the family room. "Can you please hurry up so we can start this movie?"

Caroline's annoyingly sweet, "Yeah, come on you two!" shout from the other room makes Elena roll her eyes.

"You realize perfect popcorn takes time?" Elena yells back. She walks over to Julia with the giant bowl of popcorn. "Now, this is the hard part. You have to make sure you get just the clarified butter. Not the separated part at the bottom. You see that?"

Julia watches Elena hold the glass measuring cup toward the light. She says, "Mm-hmm," even though she's not even looking at the butter. She can't take her eyes off Elena. There's something about the way she looks tonight that is making it difficult for Julia to function. Her hair and the way her skin looks, and does she have mascara on?

"Do you see what I mean?" Elena looks at Julia. "You haven't heard a single word I've said, have you?"

Julia feels her cheeks get hot and her entire body flush upon being busted. "Um, no. Sure didn't."

Elena shakes her head. "What were you thinking about?" Elena's eyes lock on to Julia's.

"Your lips."

"Jesus." Elena raises an eyebrow to her hairline.

"Did you want me to lie to you?"

"Never," Elena replies. It sounds like she really means it, which is not normal for the people that have come and gone from Julia's life. They all lie to her and expect the same in return. But not Elena. Not this wonderful woman who Julia thought she was going to hate. "Shake the bowl. I'll drizzle the butter over it."

Julia does as she's told, tries not to look at Elena's eyes because she'll lose focus again, and is pleasantly surprised when she doesn't screw up. "Look at that. I *can* handle it."

"Told you," Elena says, her voice soft. "Grab those individual bowls and follow me."

Julia takes the smaller bowls that actually say "popcorn" on them and follows Elena into the family room. The room is dark, illuminated only by the light from the large, flat screen TV. Cole is seated on the recliner, Elijah and Caroline are on the love seat—*how appropriate*—and the couch is left for Julia and Elena. She sits on the left-hand side of the couch, as far away from the right side as possible, and hands over the bowls. Elena fills each one with popcorn, and Julia passes them out. It's almost like they've done this before with how smooth the process is going. Cole, of course, is the first person to notice.

"First time I passed out popcorn, I spilled it all, Julia." Cole smiles while shoving his mouth full of the buttery goodness.

"Well, I'm more mature. I'm sure that's why I can handle it," Julia replies, smiling and laughing when she sees that he is rolling his eyes dramatically.

"*Sure.*" Elijah chuckles from the opposite side of the room.

Julia whizzes a piece of popcorn at Elijah and gets a gentle smack on the arm from Elena. "Sorry," she whispers, a smile gracing her lips.

"Okay, Mr. Impatient, you can start the movie." Elena sighs, nodding at Elijah, pulling her legs up onto the couch.

Julia leans over. "What movie?" Her eyes land on Elena's profile, study the way her eyes are fixed on the screen.

"*Jurassic Park*," she whispers, shielding her mouth from Cole.

"Has he not seen it yet?"

"Yes, I've seen it," Cole says. "Are you one of those people that talk through movies?"

Julia hides her laughter when Elena smiles and looks over at her. "Damn, tough crowd," she says softly as she goes back to eating her popcorn.

❖

Obviously, Julia has seen *Jurassic Park* before. She's probably seen it a few too many times since, for a while, it was the only movie she owned. But what she hasn't done is watch the movie while sitting next to someone she honestly cannot stop thinking about. And it's most definitely making it very hard to pay attention to the plot.

Thank goodness she knows what happens.

And knows most of the words.

And hums along as often as possible to the music.

And makes sure to jump when the velociraptor attacks Dr. Sattler after she turns the power back on.

And even sheds a tear when the sign falls from the ceiling in front of the Tyrannosaurus Rex.

She's acting as if she's watching every second, when in actuality, she hasn't stopped checking her peripheral to see Elena's reactions. She wants to smile when Elena laughs at Dr. Malcolm's attempts to woo Dr. Sattler. She wants to hold Elena's hand when Timmy doesn't wake up after being electrocuted. She wants to be the arm for Elena to grip when the raptors are chasing Timmy and Lex. And she absolutely cannot get over how Elena eats one piece of popcorn at a time and has almost a full bowl the entire movie.

But as the movie wears on, it becomes clearer and clearer that Julia isn't the only one not really paying attention.

When the credits roll, Julia glances over at Elijah and Caroline. They're sound asleep. She looks at Cole. He's passed out as well. "Guess it's just you and me," Julia whispers as she locks eyes with Elena, who is somehow way closer than when the movie started.

Elena smiles and moves her partially full bowl of popcorn to the coffee table in front of the couch. She leans back into the cushions and looks over at Julia. "You seemed to know most of that movie. Almost like you've seen it a few times."

Julia feels herself blush. "Yeah, I kind of love that movie." Their faces are insanely close considering present company. It makes Julia's heart ache, looking at Elena, wanting so much from her but knowing it's not the right time.

"I have to tell you something," Elena whispers.

Julia's voice is gone upon hearing that. She nods, tries to say *okay,* but realizes nothing is coming out.

"Penn is going to stay as long as we need her." Elena looks like she's gathering her courage as she says, "We talked, and I think it'd be good to have her here to help out."

Julia looks away from Elena, at the TV, where the very end of the credits is still rolling. "That's probably a good idea," she says, trying to not let her voice crack.

"You think so?" Elena asks. "Because I don't think you sound like you believe it's a good idea."

Julia glances back at Elena, then pulls her eyes from her again. "It's the best for the ranch." She takes a deep breath. "I'm sure Penn is really good at this job."

"Yes." Elena sighs. "But she's not…" She pauses, presses her lips together, then bites her bottom lip lightly. "She's not you," she finishes, and when Julia finally finds the courage to look at her, she smiles. "So, remember that, okay?"

Hearing that from Elena's mouth makes Julia's chest tighten in a way she's only experienced one other time in her life. "I don't want to lose you." Julia hears the whispered words come out of her mouth and realizes she's said the thought out loud. "Oh my *God*, I'm so sorry," she says, sitting upright, rubbing her palms on her knees.

"Don't be," Elena says gently, mimicking Julia's position. Julia watches Elena's eyes and how her gaze shifts down to her feet. "I feel the same way."

"Maybe we can talk about this one day? Not here, of course, while everyone is sleeping literally steps from us." Julia motions between the sleeping people and gets a smile and a nod in response.

"I'd like that," Elena says, and then in one smooth, fluid move, she gets up from the couch. After grabbing the bowls from around the family room, she turns the TV off, then moves over to pull the blanket on Cole around his shoulders. She places a hand on his forehead and whispers some words in Spanish to him. Julia doesn't catch them all, but she does hear *te quiero* and *mijo*, which, for some reason, makes her heartbeat speed up. Is it sad to say she's even more enamored with Elena after hearing her speak in another language?

"You know Spanish?" Julia asks when they're safely in the kitchen.

"Gloria used to call him *mijo*. She was Cuban." Elena glances down, then back up at Julia. "I try to keep the memory of her alive for him."

"That's really special."

"It's really sad, is what you mean." Elena crosses her arms and leans against the doorframe by the front door.

"No." Julia shakes her head. "It's special. I never had that."

Elena chuckles. "An overprotective mother?"

"A mother." She makes her way past Elena and opens the front door. "I'd better get going. Big day tomorrow."

Elena stops Julia by placing her hand on Julia's arm. "What? Julia, are you serious?"

Julia nods. "I'm okay, though."

After taking a step closer, Elena takes Julia's wrist in her hand and wraps her thin fingers around it. "You're lying to me."

"I promise I'm okay."

"You're a horrible actress."

Julia's mind flashes back to how she thought she was a great actress, and she wants to smile and laugh.

"You can talk to me," Elena says quietly.

"Herding starts tomorrow." Julia's voice is strained; clearly, her racing heartbeat isn't the only thing affected by Elena's touch.

Elena takes another step closer to Julia, the space between them getting smaller and smaller. "You'll be great," Elena says. "As always." She tightens her grip around Julia's wrist, then pulls gently on her. "Don't."

"*Don't* what?"

"Don't pull away. Don't *run*—"

"I won't," Julia says. "You *don't* either."

Elena tilts her head and lets out a laugh. "And leave all this?" She looks around the house and motions outside through her low laughter, letting go of Julia's wrist and running her fingers along Julia's forearm.

She nods, then waits a half second before turning to walk through the front door. She says her good-bye, feels the warmth still radiating from her wrist, and wishes she had the courage to kiss Elena Bennett.

CHAPTER ELEVEN

Julia smooths her hand down Leia's side after she tightens the riggings on the horse's saddle. "Good job," she says, making sure to pat the horse's neck affectionately. She hears Elijah talking to his horse as he walks her to the saddle station. "Good morning," she says.

He smiles, bright-eyed and bushy-tailed. "Well, good morning to you. How are you on this fine day?"

"Why are you in such a good mood?"

He looks at Julia with his eyebrows raised and tilts his head. "No reason," he says, his grin almost too much to handle.

"Oh my God!" Julia's scrunches her face when she realizes what he's talking about, holds her hand up, and shakes her head. "Please stop! Spare me the details!"

Elijah lets out a hearty laugh as he lays the saddle blanket on Jazz's back, then hoists the saddle on next. "Well, you asked."

"I will never ask again," Julia almost shouts.

"Speaking of good evenings...How was yours? Did you enjoy the movie?"

Julia continues to pet Leia's head as she thinks about how she left things with Elena. She has some regrets in her life, but not kissing Elena last night may be her biggest one right now. "It was really great, actually. I can't believe you guys fell asleep."

"Oh, we weren't *sound* asleep," Elijah says and smiles.

"What is that supposed to mean?"

Elijah moves around Jazz, tightening the riggings and the straps.

He pulls on the saddle to check it and looks at Julia over his shoulder. "I think it's fairly obvious."

"I have literally no idea what you're talking about, Elijah," Julia says. "Honestly. What the hell?"

"Let's just say, it's obvious to us what's going on. And you know we're totally okay with it. I mean, aside from you not really telling us much about yourself…"

Julia feels the cooler morning air get instantly heavy and hot. "Wait a second. What do you mean?"

"You," Elijah says, "and Elena."

"What about us?"

Elijah readjusts the bridle on Jazz, then turns toward Julia. "City Girl, I know you're supposed to be pretty quick on the uptake, but damn, I feel like I'm really needing to spell this out for you."

"Well, yeah, because I'm lost, man. Seriously." Julia wants to capture this moment so she can show Elena later and say, *And you think I'm a horrible actress, eh?*

Elijah pulls on Jazz's lead, and they start to walk past Julia and Leia. "Let's go. Daylight's burnin'," he says with a grin as they make their way out of the stables.

Julia rolls her eyes when she looks at Leia. "What a weirdo," she says to the horse and receives a snort in return.

As they follow Elijah and Jazz outside, a steady stream of cars arrives at the ranch. Julia watches as a conversion van side door slides open, and one man after another after another stumbles out. Eight men in total, all shouting at each other: one of them yawns, another laughs, and another punches one in the back, which starts a small scuffle. It looks like a band of fools, but Elijah leans over and says they're a group of rodeo clowns that always help out.

"Like legit rodeo clowns? Seriously?" Julia asks, her voice low.

"As a heart attack." Elijah motions toward the one with a very full gray beard. "Don't mess with that one. He's a real live wire."

The bartender from Julia's first day in town pulls up in an Oldsmobile that looks as big as a boat. Next is Toni and Agnes climbing out of an old station wagon with wood paneling along the sides. Agnes pulls an old crossbow out of the way back of the wagon and slings it over her shoulder while shouting something about Toni's short shorts making her look like a hooker.

"Elijah," Julia says calmly. He turns back and looks at her and nods. "Why does Agnes have a crossbow?"

"She's the protection."

"From *what*?"

"Mountain lion. Bear." Elijah chuckles when he sees Julia's shocked expression. "She's a sure shot. Just wait."

"What about a gun? Or like, someone who *isn't* eighty-five years old?"

"She could hit a target from a hundred yards out, City Girl," he says, pointing at her. "Don't you let her hear you calling her an old woman, either. She'll shoot you next."

"Christ," Julia mumbles under her breath. She sees Toni jogging up to her and motions to her clothes. "I like your ranch hand attire."

Toni laughs and takes a very elegant bow. "Why, thank you, miss. Of course, I am just here to look pretty and help with the food. Besides, you and your guns look like they can handle it," she says while slugging Julia on the arm.

"Look at this, the city girl is really settling in," Agnes shouts while walking up to Elijah, who's been joined by Cole and Caroline. "You look like you were made to strut around in those boots and Wranglers there, missy. Maybe you should consider staying here for good."

Julia smiles and looks down at the ground after shoving her hands in the back pockets of her jeans. "Yeah, well, I'm sure I'll wear out my welcome eventually."

They all chuckle until, from behind them, Penn's voice breaks the laughter with a snide "I'm sure your welcome is already wearing thin, my friend."

Julia shakes her head before she shouts after her, "You should know better than anyone when a welcome is worn out." She mumbles, "Bitch," under her breath and starts to walk away. She feels Toni grab on to her bicep.

"Don't let Penn get to you," she says quietly.

"I won't. But I am hoping a bear attacks her. Is that wrong?"

Agnes lets out a low chuckle and leans in closer to Julia. "I won't shoot if I see that happening. Deal?"

"Deal." She's happy to know she isn't the only one that is having issues with this woman being here.

"Ed!" Elijah shouts as a slender older man with a bald head comes walking toward them. He pushes his dark-framed glasses up the ridge of his nose and waves before shaking Elijah's outstretched hand.

"We haven't seen you in forever. How was vacation?" Caroline asks.

"It was wonderful," the man replies. A golden retriever comes running up behind him. Everyone starts petting the dog, whose name, she learns, is Bentley. Ed turns and looks at Julia. "You must be Julia, the new ranch hand. I'm Ed. I help Elena with the business side. Not great with the physical side," he says with a laugh. "But I try."

Julia smiles. "It's really great to meet you."

"Likewise. Boy, am I glad to be back in beautiful Colorado." He pauses when he sees Penn over by the barn. "What the heck is she doing back? How long have I been gone?"

Elijah snorts and shakes his head. "About a week. She's staying through the herding, then she's gone. According to Elena."

"Oh, Lord." Ed sighs. "What does *Penn* have to say about that?"

"She's going to try to win Elena over, *apparently*," Julia says, clearly irritated.

Ed glances from Julia to Elijah to Caroline and back to Julia. "Interesting that you barely know Penn, and you feel all the same feelings we do," he says. "I am going to get along just fine with you, Julia."

"We actually call her City Girl," Elijah says as he drapes an arm over Julia's shoulders.

"It really is a perfect nickname." Toni smiles and crosses her arms. "I'd like to think I helped come up with it, but sadly, it was all Elijah."

"You all suck!" Julia says just as she sees Elena coming out of the barn leading Samwise.

Penn is following with Sully, and Ed gasps. "She's not!"

"Oh, I think she is," Elijah says softly.

"What the hell?" Julia rolls her eyes. "That's bullshit."

"No, *that's* Penn. She gets what she wants."

"We will see about that," Julia replies calmly. "We will definitely see."

❖

The ride to the ridge is just as much of an awesome experience as it was the first time. Julia and Leia are walking near the back of the group, taking in the view, trying to soak up as much knowledge as possible. Cole and Sweetie are beside her. Sweetie and Leia seem to get along really well, which makes Julia very happy. They are next to Agnes in the red Ford while three of the rodeo clowns sit in the back with the alfalfa and hay that will be spread out for the cattle as they make their way home. Agnes laughs at Julia when she asks how she got so good at shooting.

"When I was a little girl, my pappy used to take me up in the mountains with my brothers and teach them all how to shoot," Agnes says, eyeing Julia over her rickety glasses. "One day, there was a bear that came close to attacking us all. My pappy started teaching me that night how to shoot to help protect our family." Agnes raises her voice a bit over the engine of the truck. "If you ever come visit, you'll see that bear's skin hanging above my mantel."

Julia's eyes are wide. "Holy shit," she says. "That's crazy."

"I've seen it, Julia. That bear was huge. Bigger than the one we saw that one day," Cole says, his hands and arms shooting outward, depicting the size of the pelt. "It had to have been as big as this truck."

"It wasn't *that* big," Agnes says, a twinkle to her eye.

The bartender, whose name is Benjamin, is riding Scout and has made his way alongside Julia now. He's been slowly creeping closer and closer, and even though Julia is not interested, he seems like a nice enough guy; he may actually be friend material. He latches on, asking her tons of questions that she dodges expertly. He's definitely full of stories, and after about the tenth one, Julia realizes that he isn't shutting up. It's starting to annoy her because as he rambles on and on about his years as a traveling rodeo star, all she can see is Penn trying to weasel her way in with Elena at the front of the line. And Julia's jealousy is driving her absolutely insane.

After the group has slowed the pace to give the horses a break, Benjamin asks, "What's going on there, love? You jealous, or you just dislike that woman as much as the rest of us?"

"Is it that obvious?"

"That you dislike her or that you're jealous?" Benjamin smiles. "Because I definitely think you're jealous."

"Oh, for shit's sake, I am not jealous. I am annoyed. Clearly. You don't even know me. How would you know if I'm jealous or not?"

Benjamin pulls the reins on Scout and clicks his tongue. "You realize I know what it looks like to pine after someone you'll never get?"

"Of course. Because bartenders always fall for their regulars, don't they?"

A guffaw comes out of Benjamin's mouth, and he winks. "The regulars fall for me, love. You should know that."

Julia rolls her eyes. "Yeah, well, I'm not a regular."

"Yet."

"Ever," Julia adds and points at him. "I'm sure this dashing scoundrel routine works with other girls, but it's not really doing much for me."

"It's not, is it." His sentence isn't a question as much as it is a statement. "Partly why I know you've got a thing for Elena. Which is fine, and definitely hot, but love, you're letting *that* scoundrel woo her, and believe me, Elena is seconds away from forgiving her."

Julia looks toward the front of the riding party. Elena is listening to something Penn is saying, and she's smiling, and dammit, Benjamin may have a point. The feeling that is absolutely not jealousy flares in her chest. "Not today," Julia says softly as she spurs Leia to a gallop and steers toward the front of the group. When she gets close to Elena and Penn, Elena's attention immediately turns to Julia.

"Hi," Elena says as Julia rides up. Her entire face lights up, and it's enough to throw some water on Julia's smoldering jealousy. "How's it going back there?"

"Good," Julia replies. "Wanted to come say hi. See how the front of the line looks."

"Better now," Elena says quietly. "I mean, don't get me wrong; I'm glad you're learning from Elijah, but it's nice to see you."

A smile spreads across Julia's face, and she instantly feels stupid for being so worried. "I'm glad I came up here, then."

"Yeah, well, Mr. Rodeo was talking your ear off. I'm sure it's nice to get away."

"It's definitely a very fitting nickname."

"Oh, yeah." Elena echoes Julia's laughter. "I see he told you his life story."

"Yes, he did." Julia looks over at Elena, at her hat pushed up a bit on her forehead, the sun shining on her cheeks and nose. Julia can't help but be taken back by how absolutely gorgeous she looks in that moment. It's amazing to her that after all of these days, Elena's beauty still has the ability to take her breath away. "You're in your element out here, aren't you?"

Elena closes her eyes and turns her face toward the sun. "It's moments like these that make me happy I'm still here. Still alive," she replies. When she opens her eyes, she adjusts the reins in her hands and smooths a hand down Samwise's neck.

"I'm really happy my car broke down here," Julia says. And the best part is that she's actually telling the truth. "Like, really *happy*."

Elena looks at Julia and moves her hand to push her hat back on her head. "Yeah, well, that makes two of us."

Julia hears Penn scoff from her horse on the other side of Elena, and she leans back to look at her. "Everything okay over there?"

"Oh, sure, just watching the show," Penn mumbles, rolling her eyes.

Elena turns to look at Penn. "What show?"

"Nothing," Penn says, shaking her head. She shouts, "Yah!" at Sully, and the horse takes off toward the ridge.

Julia lets out a breath and tries not to pump her fists in the air in victory.

Julia, 1
Penn, 0

❖

Julia quickly observes that herding cattle is not so much a *job* as it is an *art*. Elena, Elijah, and yes, even Penn, move together like they've been doing this for years. It's amazing how they know exactly where to go and how to move the giant animals without even touching them. Julia learns a lot about horse placement and why certain people will ride on each side of the cattle on the way back to the house. She learns about flight zones and how each flight zone has a point of balance. This is where you can move the cattle without really trying by being in their peripheral vision; being behind the point of balance moves the cattle forward; being in front will stop them. She stays alongside Elijah and listens intently when he tells her how it's the biggest and one of the most important jobs to bring up the rear of the herd and make sure there are no stragglers. He tells her that he wants her to be that person today because the best way to learn is to *sink or swim*.

She hates that saying. She's never been a fan of swimming, and to say she's nervous is an understatement. But she's getting the hang of this herding thing, and she's impressing herself.

Julia knows how important this all is. She remembers the speech Elena gave her after the bear incident all too well. In fact, it's the first thing Julia thinks about every time she starts her day. This is a real job. This isn't just something to do to occupy her time. Or until she decides to take off again.

Although the longer she stays, the more those roots she talked about putting down look tempting. It's weird how easy it has been settling into everything. Even riding horses seems to come naturally to her, which obviously scared her at first. Julia doesn't do familiar. She doesn't do safe and easy. It means she's getting attached.

Julia watches Elijah as he turns Jazz to look toward the back of the herd. He's in front about a hundred yards. He told her to keep her eyes on him because he'd be leading the herd. Everything would start and stop with him. She sees him raise his cowboy hat in the air and wave it back and forth as if to ask if everything is good. She mimics his signal and waves her baseball cap in the air. Julia totally gets now why cowboy hats are definitely more helpful.

❖

Arriving back at the ranch at the end of the line is pretty hectic. There are people everywhere as the cattle are moved into the corral a few at a time from the pasture.

Julia rides toward the corral and dismounts from Leia. Caroline hurries up to Julia with grain for the horse and tells her that she'll take care of Leia, and everything is under control. "You need to get in there. Elijah's ready for you."

"Thanks, Caroline!" Julia moves away quickly toward Elijah. "Okay, where do you want me?" She claps and rubs her hands together eagerly.

Elijah smiles and pulls Julia by the arm into the corral. "You get to handle the vaccinations," he says, a crazed look in his eye. "It's not hard, but you gotta be tough, so are you ready?"

"It's now or never, right?" She follows Elijah over to a long chute hooked to one side of the corral.

"Okay, the calves come in this way." Elijah signals toward the end of the chute that's inside the corral. "The gate closes, keeping them semi-restrained—"

"Does it hurt them?" Julia asks, her eyes wide.

Elijah shakes his head. "Not at all," he says. "Once the gate is closed, you give the vaccination with this injection gun, right behind the shoulder. Come with me and watch."

Julia does as she's told, following Elijah to a space on the side of the chute where there's room to stand. Ed is on the other side of the chute, and he shoos a young calf inside. Elijah administers the shot with ease, then unlocks the gate so the animal can leave, running into the pasture where the chute's exit is located. It's over and done with fairly quickly, and Julia just looks at Elijah and says, "That's it?"

"That's it. Think you can handle it?"

"Absolutely," she says and takes the vaccination gun from Elijah. "Okay, Ed, let's do this!" The determination on Julia's face is equal to the nervousness in her body, especially when she sees Ed start leading calf after calf into the chute. Julia struggles at first, fighting with the vaccination gun, then missing the side of the animal and shooting the liquid everywhere but where it needs to go. She's starting to get more and more frustrated when all of a sudden, it all starts clicking. After about the twelfth head of cattle, Julia finally gets the hang of what she's doing. She's feeling pretty good about herself, too. Maybe she really is cut out for this ranch hand business. Even though everyone thinks she's just some dumb City Girl. She's proving all of those haters wrong. *Yeah!*

Just as Julia is finishing her internal pep talk, one of the females gets into the chute, and a loud noise goes off, startling the animal. She springs free from the chute like a horse out of the racing gate, and unfortunately, the ruckus and thrashing on the chute ends up pushing Julia down in the process. Julia is thrown airborne for a second, hits the dirt square on her back with a thud, and knocks the wind clean out of her.

Ed climbs the wall of the corral and is next to Julia in the blink of an eye. "Julia!" he shouts. "Are you okay?"

Julia tries to sit up and starts coughing. "Holy," she breathes deep, a string of coughing again, "Shit!" she finishes, another string of coughs following. "That hurt like a son of a bitch!"

Ed laughs as he helps Julia up. "Yeah, that happened to me the first time I helped, too. It's not fun—that's for sure!"

She dusts her face off and adjusts her baseball cap. "Let's try again," Julia says, watching the escapee as it eyes them from inside the corral. She does a quick scan for Elena and can't find her anywhere at the moment. Julia thanks God that Elena didn't see her totally fall on her ass.

After multiple attempts, two more head of crazy cattle, three refills on the injection gun, and a good hundred or so curse words, Ed and Julia are finally successful and get all of the calves vaccinated.

Ed makes his way over the fence again and walks over to Julia. He hands her his handkerchief and smiles. "You are a mess, my friend."

Julia wipes her face off, then hands the cloth back to Ed. "That was *crazy*."

"You handled yourself well." Ed stuffs the cloth into his back pocket.

"Yeah, sure, if you call being beat up by a baby cow *well*." Julia rolls her eyes.

"Oh, I'm sure Elena approved," Ed says.

"She wasn't even over here. She's been over with Penn branding the calves." Her words come out a lot more accusatory than she was intending, so she backtracks with, "I mean, I think that's where she's been, right?"

A smile spreads across Ed's face, and he adjusts his dark-framed glasses. "She was watching you from across the way, Julia," he says softly. "And that hasn't happened in a very long time."

Julia feels her pulse quicken. "Nah, she is always watching her staff."

"Not like that she isn't." Ed puts his hand on Julia's shoulder and squeezes. "Not in a very, very, *very* long time. Not since…" His voice trails off, and he looks over at Elena.

"Yeah, yeah," Julia says. "Not since Penn. I know." She is letting

Penn piss her off left and right, and honestly, it's starting to grate on her last fucking nerve.

"Oh, Julia. I don't mean Penn," he says. "I mean *Gloria*."

Julia's pulse that has been going nuts since the start of this conversation seems to almost stop when she hears Ed say that name. "What?" she says, dumbfounded.

"So, you've heard about her?"

Julia continues to stare at Ed, at his kind eyes.

"Let's just say," he says, glancing over at Elena as she works to brand the calves, "I knew her before. I knew her when she was in Miami with Gloria. I've been in her life for a very long time. And even throughout everything that went on with Penn, Elena's heart has always only beat for two things." Ed looks back at Julia. "Her son and Gloria. So, I don't know what your story is, Julia Finch, or what your plan is, but this woman? Ever since losing Gloria and then her parents? Her plan has always been to merely survive. And now?"

Julia feels a lump start to grow in her throat.

"Now, it looks like, for the first time in a long time, she's not *just* surviving. She's living." Ed takes a couple steps away from Julia and looks over his shoulder, "Come on, City Girl. Let's go help the rest of the crew."

Julia huffs at the usage of the nickname. "What the hell? I was actually starting to like you," she says as she takes a few fast steps to catch up with Ed.

❖

The day ends up going very smoothly. The branding, vaccinations, and de-wormer injections go off without a hitch. Julia feels very successful considering that it was her first time helping. She knows her body is going to feel it in the morning, but as they all sit around the fire enjoying s'mores and beer while Elijah plays guitar and sings campfire songs, she feels absolutely no pain whatsoever.

Toni is sitting next to her on a big blanket, leaning against a log made into a makeshift bench. Ed and Scooter and his friends are all lined up next to Caroline. They're singing "Rocky Mountain High" like they've been in a band together forever, and it's definitely one of the best nights Julia can remember.

"City Girl!" Benjamin shouts from across the fire. He is leaning against another makeshift wooden bench. Agnes is sitting next to him, and he's inebriated. *Highly.*

Julia lets out a sigh and nudges Toni, rolling her eyes when Toni looks at her. "What?" Julia shouts back. She braces herself for whatever his drunk ass is going to say next.

"You got your cherry broke today," he slurs. "How'd you like it, love?"

All Julia can hear is a loud *whack* and then Benjamin saying, "Ow!" before she can answer.

"Julia, forgive this buffoon," Agnes says, her voice low. "That was uncalled for, you scoundrel."

"Damn," Benjamin says while rubbing his arm. "I was just teasing her."

"Cole is right there," Agnes says, pointing at Cole, who just came outside. "Don't be so vulgar in front of him."

Cole sits next to Julia. "What happened?" he asks, his voice low.

"Don't worry about it," she says, leaning into his shoulder. She looks over and can tell something is wrong. "What's going on? You okay?"

He shakes his head, keeping his eyes on the fire. "Nothing," he mumbles. "Just done with her being here."

Julia has a feeling that when she asks, "Who?" he is going to answer with, "*Penn,*" but she still holds her breath and hopes.

Cole looks at her, his mouth held in a way that looks so much like Elena it's startling. "Who do you think?"

Toni leans in then and says, "Julia isn't *that* bad, Cole, *geesh.*"

Julia's mouth falls open, and Cole starts to laugh. "Thanks, Toni," Cole says softly. "I needed that laugh."

"Anytime, little man," Toni replies, reaching around Julia to mess up Cole's dark hair.

"I'm sorry," Julia whispers. She nudges Cole with her shoulder. She watches as he nods, takes a deep breath, and then looks at her.

"I don't want her to take Penn back."

Those words make Julia's stomach plummet. Her mouth goes dry, and she blinks three times before saying, "What?"

"They're in the house now. Penn's talking to Mom. Begging her for forgiveness." Cole looks back at the fire, a sigh escaping from his lungs. "I don't understand my mom at all."

"Women are hard to understand," Julia whispers. "But people do crazy things when…" She wants to say when "they're in love," but the idea of Elena still being in love with Penn is too much of a gut check to even mention. "When they're not thinking straight," Julia says as she lifts her arm and drapes it over his shoulders, pulling him into her side. It feels fitting that Elijah would pick right now to start singing Van Morrison's "Brown Eyed Girl."

"Here," Toni says as she stands and starts toasting a marshmallow. "This will make you feel better, Cole. S'mores always make me feel better."

Julia lets out a snort. "It does help," she says, watching Toni make the s'more like an expert. She hands the completed masterpiece over to Cole, and he laughs.

"I'm sure this will do the trick," he says before he takes a huge bite.

It's then that Julia turns her head and sees Elena and Penn walking to the campfire together. They're walking too close to each other for Julia's liking, and the suspicion inside her is so strong that she can taste it on her tongue. She can't stop watching, wondering, hoping to God that Elena isn't giving in. But if she is, what the hell is Julia going to do about it? She can't make Elena's mind up for her. Oh, how she wishes she could, though.

"How many is that?" Elena asks Cole as she struts over and sits next to him on the blanket.

Cole's mouth is stuffed with the last part of the s'more. "It's only his first one," Julia answers. Elena looks at her, raises an eyebrow, and Julia responds with, "I promise."

Elena sighs before she takes a drink of the beer she's holding. She leans her head back on the oak tree. "Today was *rough*."

"I thought it went really well," Julia says. She looks over at Elena, whose mouth is hanging open. "What?"

"You have literally never done this before. How would you know if it went well or not?"

"I have a good feeling." Julia raises her beer to her lips and drinks two long swallows. "Things went well on *my* side. Maybe you should have worked with me where things were going right." She really shouldn't be saying that to Elena right now, especially in front of Cole, but she can't help it. She really regrets it, though, when Cole pipes up and says, "Yeah, instead of working with that jerk the whole time," motioning to Penn, who is now sitting next to one of Scooter's friends.

"Cole," Elena's says. But her voice is soft with not an ounce of discipline.

"I gotta say, I agree with Cole." Julia locks eyes with Elena over the top of Cole's head.

"Yeah, well," Elena says, "I think you both need to remember that I'm a grown woman, and I know what I'm doing."

Julia waits a beat before asking, "Do you?"

Cole's quick to echo with, "Yeah, do you?"

Elena doesn't hesitate when she says, "Since when did you two decide that it's a good idea to band together against me?"

"Not against you, Mom," Cole replies. "*For* you."

Elena places a hand on Cole's face and smooths her thumb over his cheek. "You don't need to worry."

"You promise?" Cole asks, his voice cracking from emotion or the last lingering effects of puberty, Julia isn't quite sure.

"I promise." Her voice trails off, and she looks at the fire, takes a deep breath, and closes her eyes. After she licks her lips, she looks down at Cole. "Cole, dear, would you please go get me a beer?"

Cole narrows his eyes. "You already have a beer." He tilts his head. "What's going on?" he asks.

"Beer. Now, please." Elena points at the coolers, and he reluctantly stands and takes off toward them. She looks back at Julia. "Is he really that worried?"

Julia doesn't know how to answer that except to be blunt, and she doesn't think now is an appropriate time to remind Elena that she's spending way too much time with a woman that left her with no real explanation except for a piss-poor excuse. "Cole loves you, Elena," Julia says softly, deciding that's probably the best answer she can give. "You're his mom, his whole world. And that dumbass over there really fucked you up, which fucked up his world. I think he's just worried." Julia looks at Elena and smiles, shrugging. "For good reason."

"Penn isn't going to get what she wants." Elena sighs deeply, her eyes never leaving Julia's. "Even if she wants to keep trying."

"Does she know that?" Julia asks, her heart full of fear as she awaits the answer.

"She's getting the idea," Elena replies. "Okay?"

Julia feels her heart skip a beat at the way Elena is looking at her and the sound of her voice. "Okay."

"Here you go, Mom," Cole says, sliding in between them again.

Julia watches as Elena leans over and kisses him on top of the head.

Penn's getting the idea?

That's not good enough. What is going to happen if Julia falls for this woman and… Ugh, Julia can't bring herself to finish that thought. It's too much. Her guard is already so far down she may as well just throw in the towel, but something inside her shouts to tread carefully. Elena's not finished with Penn. And Julia has no idea how much fight she has in her anymore.

CHAPTER TWELVE

When Julia finally strolls to the dimly lit cabin, it's way past her bedtime. The whole gang should have turned in hours ago, but the music, the fire, the stories—it was all too great to miss. And knowing that tomorrow is actually a day off makes it way too hard to say no to booze and music.

She stumbles in through the screen door and realizes that maybe she had a bit too much to drink because dammit, she miscalculates the distance from the door to the bench and just barely misses falling onto the floor. She starts laughing, leaning her head against the wall, and listening to the music still coming from the fire. She left Benjamin and Elijah out there, both insanely inebriated, but they promised they'd be able to find their way inside. Elijah had assured her, though, that even if they didn't make it inside, they'd be fine outside by the fire all night. She wasn't sure how either of them was still coherent—especially Benjamin, who had put away the better part of a mason jar of homemade moonshine.

After she finally toes off her shoes, she thanks God that she had enough sense to actually clean up before going out to sit by the fire because if she had to shower now, she'd never make it. Her body is starting to feel the aftermath of herding. And her backside is starting to feel the aftermath of being thrown onto the ground.

Julia finally pulls herself up, stretches, and decides to head straight to bed when she hears a soft knock at the door. Dread fills her mind because if it's Benjamin trying to win her over, she's literally going to punch him in the face.

Opening the door, though, and seeing Elena standing there in shorts and a T-shirt was honestly the farthest thing from her mind. She smiles, pushes open the screen door, and notices the way the air seems to get lighter when Elena enters the cabin. They exchange no words, just the looks of two people who aren't sure what the other is thinking.

When Julia shuts the wooden door, the noise from it latching is so loud that it sounds like it was slammed shut. Julia stands behind Elena and looks at her backside and her loosely done ponytail. Julia is wondering if she should say something. She takes a breath, and before she can even let it out, Elena is speaking.

"Can I stay with you tonight?"

The question is so wonderfully out of character that Julia can hardly even find the words to answer. It's not like Elena to seem vulnerable. She smiles, though, and says, "Of course," before taking a few steps around Elena. "You can sleep on the couch if you want. I can pull it out into a bed?" Julia motions to the couch, shrugs, and keeps her eyes off Elena. "It won't take long."

"Can I just sleep," Elena says and pauses. Julia looks back at her. "With you?"

Julia practically forgets how to speak as she stands there and looks at Elena standing in front of her. She opens her mouth, and nothing comes out.

"Is that too forward?" Elena asks, sounding very self-conscious.

And Julia lets out a laugh that has no reason being in this conversation, but she can't help it. She reaches out and takes Elena's wrist, smiles, squeezes softly, then asks, "Aren't you *always* too forward?"

A smile spreads across Elena's face as her cheeks turn pink. She takes a step closer to Julia, making the distance between them almost nonexistent. "I can go if you want." Elena's voice is so soft and has so much emotion that it literally makes the hair on the back of Julia's neck stand on end.

"Elena," Julia whispers, finally finding the courage to look directly into Elena's eyes. "I want you to stay." She watches as Elena physically relaxes: her shoulders, her neck, her spine. "Come on," she says, linking her fingers with Elena's and pulling her toward the bedroom. She leaves the lamp in the living room on but doesn't switch any other lights on as they walk through the dark hallway. Julia's heart is thudding away, keeping her from saying too much for fear that her voice will shake with anticipation? Excitement? Desire? *Need?*

Julia excuses herself and quickly does what she needs to in the bathroom. There's no way in hell she's going to sleep next to Elena and not make sure she at least brushes her teeth. And takes some ibuprofen. She's going to be a hot mess tomorrow if she doesn't.

Hell, she's a hot mess right now. She's so excited, yet apprehensive. Elena is becoming everything Julia never realized she needed. She actually never really wanted anyone before. Wanting someone means trusting the person. And trusting someone means heartache. At least, it always has before. So, wanting and needing Elena Bennett means two things: one, Julia's going to have to start trusting her; and two, Julia's definitely going to have to work on controlling her blood pressure around her.

"Sorry," Julia whispers. "I had to take medicine. Or I'll never be able to move tomorrow. You'll have to pick me up to get me out of this bed."

Elena turns onto her side. Julia can feel Elena's eyes on her even in the dark bedroom. "Sore?"

"Uh, yeah, I feel like someone beat me up."

"The cattle beat you up," Elena says. "I saw when that one threw you backward."

"Great," mumbles Julia, rolling her eyes as she lies on her back, all too aware of Elena's eyes on her.

Elena reaches out and places her hand on Julia's arm. "You were so good today," she says. "I couldn't stop watching you."

The feel of Elena's skin on hers as they lie next to each other in bed is something Julia is sure she will never forget. "Well, you were pretty good, too." Julia finally finds her voice and replies, glancing to her right. She can see Elena's silhouette illuminated by the moonlight spilling in the window. "Not that I was watching that much."

Elena licks her lips. "Oh, yeah? Not that much?"

"I mean," Julia looks away and smiles at the ceiling, "maybe I saw you a few times across the way."

"A few times, hmm?"

"Yeah, just a few."

"I feel like it was more than just a few," Elena whispers, tightening her hold on Julia's arm.

"It probably was." Julia's voice quavers when she responds, and she wonders if it's hot in the room or if it's just her.

"Julia?" Elena asks, her voice low.

There's a calmness to the air that Julia knows won't last. It must be the way the room is aglow with the light from the moon, the breeze that is gently blowing in through the window, and the smell of the fire still stuck on them. It takes Julia a second to respond because she is a ball of emotions right now—and hearing Elena say her name like that, all deep and seductive, makes Julia want to light herself on fire. "Yeah?"

"You realize I don't do this with just anyone…right?"

A smile tugs at Julia's lips as she looks over at Elena. "I think I'm starting to figure that out," she says softly.

"Good," Elena whispers, keeping her hand on Julia's arm as she closes her eyes and takes a deep breath. "Good night, City Girl."

Julia lets out a low chuckle. "Night, Elena," she replies and closes her eyes to go to sleep.

❖

Waking up at nine with Elena draped across her body is the last thing Julia expected. So, when she opens her eyes and finds an arm across her abdomen and a leg flung across her with the sun already high in the sky, it's definitely a shock. A *welcome* shock, but a shock nonetheless.

Very gently, she tries to pull herself out from under Elena. It's difficult at first, but eventually, she is able to slip out of the bed. Elena is sprawled out on the sheets now, her tan skin a stark contrast against the white sheets. Her T-shirt is hiked up, and her shorts are riding low, exposing her skin and the waistband of her black panties. Julia isn't going to pretend that sight doesn't do things to her body. It's *such* a turn-on. Especially the way the shirt is pulled up on Elena's side, exposing far more side-boob than should be legal at this time in the morning. It feels good that a woman who earlier had confided in her that she rarely sleeps is snoozing away without a care in the world.

Julia pads into the kitchen, flips on the power to the coffeepot, and waits patiently as it starts the brew process. She opens the refrigerator, looks around for eggs, some veggies, and a loaf of bread and then gets going on making breakfast. It won't be spectacular, but it'll be something.

Julia is the first person to admit that she doesn't like to cook. Cooking stresses her out, makes her anxiety spring into action. But she hates the idea of being a bad hostess. And isn't it customary to feed the person you slept next to all night?

After chopping the veggies, she throws them in a pan with melted butter, sautéing them until they're perfect. The sound of the veggies sizzling in the pan reminds her of her childhood in foster homes and running away. There's always something that happens to make her remember why at seven years old she knew how to cook a full meal for herself. Cooking typically makes her remember. And she has spent years running in order to forget.

Just as she's pouring the beaten eggs into the veggies, she hears a throat clearing behind her. She turns her head and looks at Elena. "Well, good morning, sleepyhead." Julia grins. "You were sound asleep. I didn't want to wake you." As if Elena could be more perfect, she actually looks even more beautiful after just waking up.

Elena smiles, pushes a hand over her face, and moves the loose strands of hair that have pulled from her ponytail behind her ears. "I slept like a rock," she says as Julia moves toward her and hands her a steaming hot cup of coffee. "Oh, why, thank you." Julia beams and gets back to cooking the eggs. "I thought you didn't like to cook?"

Julia lets out a laugh and looks over her shoulder at Elena leaning against the counter. "I don't." Julia looks back at the skillet. "But breakfast is different." She plates the eggs and reaches over just as the toast pops from the toaster. She hands the plate to Elena. "I set the table out there."

Elena pads barefoot toward the dining room table where Julia has laid out silverware and two small glasses of orange juice. "How long have you been up?" Elena asks, sitting down at one of the spaces.

Julia rushes into the room and sits at the empty spot. "Not long," Julia says, immediately starting to dig in. "You just looked really peaceful…"

"Well done, Miss Finch," Elena mumbles around her first bite of omelet. "Not that a person can screw up eggs."

"You'd be surprised," Julia says. She takes a drink of her coffee and looks at Elena. "Where does everyone think you are?"

Elena shrugs, her mouth full of food again.

"You're not worried?"

Another shrug and a smile this time.

"All right then."

"I think everyone kind of has an idea."

Julia looks across the table. "And you're okay with that?"

Elena screws up her face, then takes a sip of orange juice. "I'm not thrilled, but—"

"Because I'm an employee?"

"No!" Elena almost shouts, her voice an octave higher. "No, I mean, I just…Just after everything that went on with Penn."

"Does she know?"

Elena shakes her head and eyes her toast. "It's not really her business."

Julia doesn't like that answer. It's not at all what she thought Elena would say. And now she's instantly worried.

"So, now that you started telling me about yourself, think you feel like telling me something else?" Elena asks, not making eye contact as she eats her toast.

No. "What do you want to know?"

"Well, I want to know everything." Elena's eyes are locked onto hers, and Julia's not sure if she's ever been looked at with so much intensity and so much emotion. "But I don't think you'll tell me everything."

"Probably not."

"Tell me about Chicago?"

Julia instantly feels her stomach start to roll. A common occurrence with someone who cannot stand talking about herself. "Well, it was cold." Julia laughs when Elena rolls her eyes. "It was actually really awesome. I loved the city. Culture and constant change and the ability to just blend in…I loved that part. No one knew me there. It was wonderful." She can hear the apprehension in her voice. "I mean, I had some people, but no one was like, my *person* or whatever."

"I understand that," Elena says, her eyes full of hope. She props her hand under her chin and leans on the table.

Julia pulls a deep breath into her lungs, leans back in her chair, and looks around the dining area. "Okay, one more question." Julia sighs.

"Oh, wow, one more?" The twinkle in Elena's eyes is hard to resist, so Julia nods. "Did you like school?"

"Truthfully? No. But…" Julia stiffens and decides to say one more thing. "Since I'm an orphan and my foster parents were typically assholes, I had to pick up a lot of slack all the time. And I was made fun of a lot. So, the first chance I got, I dropped out. I barely have my GED." She stands, grabs her plate, and rushes past Elena into the kitchen. She tosses the rest of her omelet into the trash.

"Hey," Elena says quietly.

"Look, I'm not good at this—"

"I know you don't want to talk about yourself, Julia, but, honey, I love getting to know you, whatever that entails."

Julia feels Elena's hands land on her hips, then turn her around so she's facing her. She looks into Elena's eyes. "I don't know how to do this," she whispers.

"Do what exactly?"

Julia freezes because she doesn't even know how to answer the question. She wants to say she doesn't know how to trust anyone, but it's not just trusting Elena that is scaring her. It's letting anyone else see how messed up her past is, and how even in her attempts to escape it, it always sticks with her.

"Why don't you just breathe?" Elena says with a voice so sexy Julia can barely do as instructed.

"Because it's hard to breathe when I'm around you."

"Oh, yeah?"

"You know what you do to me."

"Do I?"

Julia huffs. "Um, yeah. Don't act so coy."

"Me? Coy?"

"Yes, Elena. You."

"Maybe we could do something that might help you breathe?"

"Like what? Do you have an inhaler or something?" Julia laughs. "I mean, that might help."

"Not exactly." Elena starts to lean into the space Julia is occupying. "I was thinking, maybe we could distract you." Her fingers have found their way to the skin above Julia's running shorts, and they're starting to roam.

"Distract me how?"

Elena takes a step closer so that her leg is touching Julia's now. "Do you think you'd be okay if I kissed you?"

Julia swallows and nods.

"Are you sure? You think you could handle it?"

Another nod.

"So, if I place my lips on yours right now, you're not going to pass out on me, are you?"

"Maybe you could just do it and see what happens?"

Elena smiles and moves closer, her lips within an inch of Julia's. "I guess we could just do it," she whispers against Julia's lips.

Julia closes her eyes when she feels Elena's breath brush past her skin. And then all she can feel is Elena's lips and mouth and teeth and tongue, and it feels like coming home and being free, and Julia isn't sure how to handle all of these feelings. She has never felt like this before. Her mind is racing, her skin is on fire, and all she can focus on is the fact that Elena Bennett is kissing her.

"Elena?" Julia asks between kisses.

"Hmm?" she says as she places gentle kisses along Julia's jawline and down her neck.

"I'm going to end up falling in love with you," Julia whispers.

Elena raises her head and looks at Julia. "I'll catch you when you fall."

"I hope so," Julia whispers. She leans forward and kisses Elena again, wraps her arms around Elena, and holds on for dear life.

❖

"Julia!"

Elena's eyes are wide as she looks over at Julia. They're cleaning the kitchen from breakfast, Elena doing most of the cleaning, and Julia sitting with her legs crossed on the counter next to the refrigerator. "Is that Cole?" Elena turns the faucet off. Julia catches Elena's eyes as they roam over her body, her T-shirt and no bra, and then smiles when their eyes lock. "He's going to know," Elena says with her left eyebrow arched to her hairline.

"He brings me the paper every morning," Julia whispers, cupping her mug of coffee.

"I wondered why my damn paper was missing all the time."

Julia scrunches her face. "Sorry," she says softly with just the right amount of sass.

"Julia!" comes Cole's voice again, this time followed by knocking on the door.

Elena sighs and grabs a towel from the counter to dry her hands. She takes off toward the door and is swinging it open before Julia even realizes what's going on. "Good morning, dear," Elena says with a smile, looking at Cole's very shocked expression.

"*Mom?*" he asks, standing on the porch with the latest copy of the newspaper.

"*Yes*, sweetie, now get in here, please?"

Cole does as he's told, walking inside around Elena, who is holding the screen door open. She closes the wooden door and walks back into the kitchen, draping the towel over her shoulder as she continues to wash the dishes.

"Hi, Cole." Julia smiles, hiding her nervousness by casually sipping on coffee.

"What's...going...on?" Cole asks as he stands in the middle of the doorway to the kitchen. He removes his cowboy hat and holds on to it like a lifeline. "Are you two..." He motions to both of them, and his eyes go wide with the realization. "Whoa."

Julia's eyes land on Elena's, and it's quite clear that when faced with the stark reality of actually *being* questioned, Elena is nowhere near close to coming to terms with this—whatever *this* is. "Cole, no, that's not it," Julia says. "We just had a sleepover because I was drunk last night and needed help."

"But Mom went to bed first," he says quietly.

Screw being an architect. This kid should join the FBI. "She just came to check on us around the fire, so we didn't burn down the property." When did she get so good at lying? "She saw how tipsy I was." Another lie. "And decided to walk me back to the cabin." All lies! "That's all." Her eyes dart to Elena, who is looking at Julia with nothing but admiration and a silent *thanks*.

Cole takes a couple steps into the kitchen, hands over the newspaper to Julia, then leans against the counter. "*Okay*," he finally responds. He doesn't look convinced, but he also looks like he is nowhere near needing to know the truth. At least not right now, anyway. "Penn has been looking for you all morning, Mom." Cole rolls his eyes and sighs. "I told her you were still sleeping."

Julia notices immediately how Elena's spine straightens at the mention of Penn's name.

"Thank you, sweetie." She turns the water off after she finishes the last dish and faces Cole. "Are you packed for the ride back tomorrow?"

Cole nods, and then, like he's been to Julia's a thousand times, he moves over to the cabinet that holds the glasses and grabs one. He slides across the kitchen to the refrigerator and fills the glass with milk, then grabs the chocolate syrup in the door. After he gets a spoon from the drawer, he adds the syrup, then stirs it feverishly. Elena watches him, her mouth slightly hanging open. "You realize you're a guest here, Cole?"

"He helped me move in." Julia smiles. "And he's not technically a guest since this is his property, too."

Elena shakes her head. "What am I going to do with you two?"

Julia swings her legs around and slides off the countertop. "So, we take the cattle back to the range tomorrow?"

"Yeah," Cole answers while wearing a chocolate milk mustache. "We camp up there, though, so you want to make sure you bring that sleeping bag I gave you."

"You gave Julia a sleeping bag?"

"Well, duh, Mom. She didn't have one."

"Duh, 'Mom,'" Julia echoes and gets a slap on the arm from Elena.

"Okay, Cole." Elena takes her son's empty glass and places it in the sink. "Let's go so I can get cleaned up."

They walk to the front door together, Julia trailing behind Cole and Elena. She watches as Cole runs out the door first, skipping down the front steps before taking off toward the house.

Elena turns, faces Julia, and looks into her eyes. "Thanks for letting me sleep with you," she whispers as she leans forward and places her lips on Julia's. When she pulls away, she very quietly adds, "I'm sorry I was such a bed hog."

Julia lets out a small snort as she reaches forward and holds on to

Elena's hand. "You can hog my bed whenever you want," she says and squeezes. "I kinda liked waking up with you all over me."

A blush fills Elena's cheeks as she pulls away from Julia and starts walking down the porch steps. "Just wait," she says while she's walking away. "You might think differently one day."

"I doubt it," Julia shouts as she watches Elena walk away. Julia is so far in over her head she can't even handle it.

CHAPTER THIRTEEN

There aren't many days on the ranch where it's encouraged to actually *not work*. So, after Julia finishes laundry and cleans herself up, she looks out her screen door and sees Elijah, Benjamin, and Ed all sitting around the fire already—at two in the afternoon—she knows right away that she needs to take advantage of this.

She grabs a six-pack of PBR out of her refrigerator, slips on her ratty Chucks, and heads out the door, hearing the screen slam shut behind her. The boys all look as she's walking over, and of course, Benjamin is the first to react.

"Would you look at that?" he says, his words already slurring together. "The City Girl herself has decided to join us. And she's wearing shorts. And *gym shoes*? What is going on here?"

Elijah lets out a laugh as he pats the seat next to him on the blanket. He's leaning against the log, his legs crossed, his jeans rolled up to his knees, and he's wearing flip-flops. It's a strange sight, seeing him so casual, but it's much deserved. Julia plops down and immediately pops open a beer. "Well, hello, boys," she says while holding her beer up. "Bottoms up."

"My bottom has already been up," Benjamin mumbles, raising a half-empty bottle of red wine to the sky.

Thankfully, the firepit is situated where the afternoon sun is shielded by the large trees that surround the yard; otherwise, it wouldn't be relaxing. The breeze is blowing just enough to make it comfortable, and the weather isn't nearly as warm as it has been.

"Julia, how's your backside this morning?" Ed asks while he pets Bentley the golden retriever, who's sprawled out next to him.

Elijah looks over at Julia. "What is that supposed to mean?"

"Oh my God, I fell yesterday. Calm down," she says. "It's actually not nearly as bad as I thought it was going to be. I did take medicine, and I have the start of a very beautiful bruise. Otherwise, it's okay."

"The cattle give you some trouble, City Girl?"

Julia rolls her eyes and looks over at Benjamin. "Yes, as a matter of fact." She watches as he takes another long swig of wine. "I'd rather cattle give me trouble than women," she says, raising her eyebrows. Benjamin just hiccups in response, then leans his head back, promptly passing out.

"Good one." Elijah laughs, nudging Julia on the shoulder. "How was last night?" His voice is low, and only Julia hears him, but she feels as if he's shouted it from the mountaintops.

"What do you mean?"

He tilts his head, gives her a knowing look, then smiles. "Really?"

"Ugh," Julia groans. "How?"

"I saw her walk over there last night. Don't worry," he says softly. "He didn't see." Elijah motions toward Benjamin, then glances over at Ed. "And he's totally cool with whatever is going on."

"Well, that's just *great* because I'll be honest. I have no fucking idea what's going on," Julia says, her voice showing how out of her element she is.

Ed raises his beer bottle at Julia and smiles. "Welcome to the world of women." He laughs.

"Women? Where?" Benjamin's head pops up, and when they all three look over at him, he leans over onto the ground and passes out again.

"Jesus." Julia takes a breath. "What a guy, eh?"

Elijah chuckles and so does Ed. "You realize Elena is probably just as nervous as you are, right?" Elijah asks.

Ed raises his hand and says, "May I be frank?"

Julia nods, drinks her beer, and waits for him to speak.

"Elena Bennett is a *very* complicated woman. For years, she mourned the loss of Gloria. *Years*, Julia. I mean, there were some women here and there, but nothing was ever serious. And then in walks Penn, who was new and different and wasn't Elijah or me or someone she already knew."

Elijah laughs and adds, "So true."

"And then Penn breaks her heart. And while I don't believe she was really the right person for Elena, it still hurt, and she was still wrecked—"

"So true, *again*," Elijah says.

"And now? Penn waltzes back into her life. It would be confusing for Elena even if you weren't here—doing whatever you're doing to her heart and mind." Ed looks around, then checks over his shoulder. "You've done something to her that I haven't seen in a really long time." He looks at Elijah as if expecting a response or confirmation.

"Yeah, man, me either," Elijah replies. He looks over at Julia. "Seriously. I've known her for a while, but this is all brand new. She's never had a worker call her by her first name. Julia, that's big. Even Penn was calling her Miss Bennett."

Ed takes a deep breath and keeps his eyes on the fire. "Like I said. She's a complicated woman."

"Then why? Why me? Why even do this?"

"Can't help who you have feelings for, right?" Elijah smiles when he puts his arm around Julia's shoulders and pulls her into him.

"Penn's easy," Ed says. "And you make Elena feel things that she's not used to."

"How do you even know this?" Julia rolls her eyes. "You act like you're her therapist or something."

Elijah starts to laugh as he squeezes Julia's shoulders. "Well, he's been in her life the longest. Even longer than Caroline." Elijah looks over at Ed. "Didn't Elena's dad hire you?"

"Wait, *what*?"

Ed smiles. "Yeah, Danny hired me when I was eighteen. Elena was only twelve at the time. But damn, could she ride a horse better than me."

"Wow." Julia's mind is stuck on twelve-year-old Elena and how adorable she probably was.

"We hung out a lot. She's like a little sister to me." Ed is petting Bentley, and the dog looks like he's in heaven. "I was very sad when she left to go Miami, but I understood. I did try to talk her out of it, though. But it's hard to argue with Elena when she's in love."

"So, you've been here through it all?" Julia clears her throat. "Through the death of her parents, Gloria, and even her relationship with Penn?"

Ed nods.

"That's incredible."

Ed smiles. "We still talk, you know. Not as much lately, but only because she made me take a vacation. Either way, I know her. And I know when she's feeling things and doesn't know how to handle them. Believe me."

"Great." Julia sighs. "She's gonna be so mad at you if she ever finds out that you're telling me this."

All of a sudden, Elena's voice interrupts them. "You think so?" she says loudly, a few yards away still.

Julia gasps, Elijah starts to laugh, and Ed just raises his beer at Elena. "Hello, Miss Bennett," he says calmly, as Elena approaches. "Just trying to talk some sense into your City Girl here."

Elena climbs over the log and slides down next to Julia. "Worrying yourself to death will get you nowhere. You know that, don't you?"

"Hey." Julia finally finds her voice. "I don't *worry*. I *obsess*. Two completely different things."

A laugh spills from Elena as she nudges Julia's side. "You're an idiot."

"Yeah, well, can you blame me?" Julia replies, her heart still feeling like it's lodged in her throat. She offers a beer, and Elena takes it, her fingers brushing Julia's. It's moments like these that make Julia mad at herself for needing to know so badly what Elena is thinking. Why not just go with the flow? Take these little acts of kindness—or attraction—and be okay with them.

"What time tomorrow, Boss?" Elijah asks, finishing his beer and letting out an insanely loud belch. He covers his mouth, and his eyes are wide when he says from behind his hand, "I am so sorry, Miss Bennett."

Elena shakes her head. "I wanna be on the way by eight. And, Elijah?" He looks at her. "I'm not your boss right now. Deal?"

Elijah glances at Ed before looking back at Elena. "Deal."

Ed jerks his thumb toward Benjamin. "This guy. What's his deal? He didn't used to drink that much."

Elena lets out a very audible sigh while looking at Benjamin passed out on the blanket he was sitting on. "Toni really broke his heart."

"Toni?" Julia gasps. "Get out of town."

Elijah nods. "Yeah, they were in love. Getting married. And then—"

"She ditched me for a mechanic," Benjamin mumbles, pushing himself up and rubbing his eyes with the heels of his palms. "Not a fun time for me."

"Please tell me it wasn't Ray." Julia pauses before she drinks and says, "Of course, I wouldn't be surprised."

Everyone laughs and answers with a resounding, "No!"

"She's not with that guy anymore, you know that?" Elijah says.

"Yeah, well, pal, I'm not into getting my heart broken twice by the same person."

"Great advice." Julia glances nonchalantly at Elena, who's looking down at her hands.

"I see you looking at me," Elena says, never making eye contact. "For the record, I'm not going back to Penn."

Ed clears his throat and says, "I told you I knew her."

"Yeah, well, Ed, you haven't really been around here the last couple of weeks." Elijah raises his beer at Ed. "No offense, of course. Everyone's allowed to take a vacation."

"None taken."

"Do you all think I'm going to just take her back?" Elena asks, her tone exasperated, while leaning forward to look at Elijah. "After *everything*? You think I'm going to allow Penn to just waltz back into my bedroom?"

Elijah flashes a lopsided smile, one that looks as if he's had the better part of a case of beer because, well, he has. "You said you aren't my boss right now, right?" Elena nods, so he looks around, then says, "Between you and me, you haven't really been acting like a woman scorned, if you know what I mean."

Julia looks at Elena's face. It's a mixture between pissed off and shocked, and it's making her want to rethink a lot of things in life, namely where she's sitting at the present moment. She cannot believe this conversation is happening. Obviously, Elena Bennett does not talk about her life with just anyone. She knows Elena has known Elijah for a really long time, and now she knows the same thing about Ed but Benjamin? And she's just word-vomiting her feelings? And Elijah is talking back like a *friend*? How is this happening? Oh God, Julia hopes she isn't confronted at all about what's going on right now. She wouldn't be able to handle it. She'd clam up and probably die.

"I know it isn't necessarily the nicest thing to do to a person, but I am using Penn for the herding season," Elena says. "Is that so *wrong*? I'm not going to pay her, and she's leaving as soon as we get back from herding the cattle back to the range. We needed the help. She came back. I wanted to shoot her with my pistol, but I refrained. The end."

"Okay," Elijah mumbles. "But you should know that Penn's thinking otherwise."

Julia looks at Elijah. "What is that supposed to mean?" she asks. All she knows is the part she heard—about *I'm going to fix this* and *I'm not leaving*, which was enough for Julia to want to shoot Penn with a pistol herself.

Elijah sighs before he looks around his surroundings. "She told me Elena's gonna take her back if it's the last thing she does."

"It's gonna be the last thing that asshole even *tries* if I have anything to say about it." Jealousy is dripping from Julia's words.

Elena lays a hand on Julia's leg, a bold move, considering present company. "Calm down," she says. "It's not for you to worry about."

"Yeah, well, I *will* worry about it. Obviously."

"So will I," Elijah says with a hint of sadness. He was here when Elena went through it, after all.

"I won't." Ed smiles. "I have your back, Elena."

Elena smiles back at Ed. "Thank you, my dear friend." She bows her head at him, then motions with her hand. "The rest of you need to take lessons from this man here."

"Any chance Toni would take me back?" Benjamin asks, completely changing the subject. They all laugh, and he smiles. "What? It's just a question."

"No harm in trying," Elena replies and nudges his boot with her foot. "Maybe she'll go to the hoedown with you?"

"Hoedown?" Julia asks.

"After herding, we do a huge hoedown in the barn. The entire town is invited. It's to celebrate the end of another successful year. It's a great time. Food, dancing, live music," Elena says. She leans into Julia's shoulder. "We get all cleaned up—"

"I wear a new hat." Elijah grins. "*Real* special."

"I'll not wear leather for once," Benjamin says. "And maybe Toni will wear that one dress she wore a couple years ago…" His voice trails off as he stares into the distance.

"Man, you've got it bad." Julia's secretly relieved that he's not out to make her his wife, though—that's for sure.

"By the way, you guys," Elena says, moving her hair over her shoulder and running her fingers through it. "Campfire snacks are your job today."

Elijah's eyes go wide just as Ed takes a drink of his beer. And Benjamin—honest to God—*giggles.*

"Hot dogs," Julia says.

"Go get them, then, because I refuse to cook on the only day I have off." And they all four start to stand. Until Julia is pulled back down. "Not you," Elena murmurs. "You stay with me."

And Julia's heart swells as she sits back down, watching the three boys stumble their way to the house.

❖

The boys are gone for a good ten minutes before Elena finally looks at Julia and with a voice that is so low and seductive, says, "You have got to stop worrying so much, dear."

Julia sighs. It's the only response she can come up with.

"Julia," Elena whispers, "I want this. I want *you.* I'm just…" Elena moves her hand and lets it drop into her lap, fidgeting with the clasp on her watch. "I'm scared. *Nervous.* I swore off love."

Julia moves so she can see Elena's face. "Love?" And when Elena's eyes say more than words ever could, Julia shrugs, and says, "So we don't rush it. We figure it out."

"Take things slow?"

"A snail's pace if we need to," Julia says. "For once, I'm not itching to go anywhere."

Elena's eyes lighten. "You're going to stay, then?"

"Until you're ready for me to leave."

"I won't be ready for that. Ever," Elena says before looking at the fire.

Elena's deep breathing makes Julia think that maybe she's

positive, even though her voice sounds unsure. "Elena, look at me." When Elena turns her head and their eyes lock, Julia tilts her head. "I won't hurt you."

Elena's face softens, the tiny lines around her eyes deepening when she smiles. "I know you won't," she whispers.

"Let go, then."

"I will if you will."

Julia shakes her head and looks back at the fire. "That's not fair."

"I have *never* played fair."

Elena's voice is so full of desire that it takes Julia by surprise. She clenches her fists together, then releases the pressure, looks at Elena, and raises an eyebrow. "I'm not sure whether to be scared or turned on by that confession."

A sultry laugh spills from Elena, her perfect deep pink lips curved into a smile. "If you want to take it slow, you shouldn't admit when I turn you on."

"Elena," Julia says softly. "That would be all the time. Everything you do…everything you say…everything."

"Jesus." Elena bites her bottom lip, then releases the pink flesh. "Taking it slow is going to suck."

"Snail's pace, remember?"

"Can we make it a racing snail?"

Julia leans her head back and laughs a hearty laugh.

"I'll never survive," Elena whispers. "Especially when I see you laughing like that."

Those words make Julia's hands ache. "I'm ready to throw in the towel now, so I probably won't survive, either."

Elena flashes her smile, her perfect teeth, and tosses her hair over her shoulder. "You won't."

"You're so sure?"

"I'm positive."

Julia watches Elena clench her jaw, the outline in her cheek, the way her muscles flex in her neck. Julia's mouth has gone dry, and she's pretty sure she lost the feeling in her hips all the way down to her toes. When Elena's eyes finally land on Julia's, it takes all the self-restraint ever created for Julia to not ravish every last inch of Elena's lips, neck, and breasts. Julia tries to swallow and looks back at the fire when she hears one of the guys clear his throat. *Busted.* How is she going to do this? Talk about torture!

❖

Needless to say, a snail's pace is extremely infuriating.

Trying to not touch Elena proves to be insanely difficult. Especially when dinner is complete, and the drinks start flowing, and the soft music plays from Elijah's battery-powered radio. Julia is trying her hardest to stay in line, to not flirt, to not softly run her fingertips over Elena's arm or leg or side…But it's so hard. She can't stop herself from reaching over to brush a stray crumb from Elena's lips. She can't restrain herself from pressing her leg into Elena's as they sink lower into their seats on the blanket. She can't fight the goose bumps that form when Elena looks over at her and whispers, "Your skin is so warm."

Julia turns her head and looks at Elena. The light from the fire is dancing on her skin. She looks like summer feels, free, invigorating, and remarkable. "Come here," Julia says. She watches Elena lean closer. When her ear is next to Julia's mouth, she whispers, "I want to kiss you." Elena's intake of breath makes Julia smile.

"Is that all you want to do?" Elena asks as she leans back a couple inches. She runs a finger down Julia's hand to the tip of her middle finger, and Julia feels as if she might combust.

"No. I can think of about a thousand things I want to do."

"You think we'll last this whole 'taking it slow' thing?"

All Julia can do is laugh. And when she finally breaks eye contact, she realizes that all three guys are staring at them. "What?" she asks, and they all smile.

"Oh, nothing," Ed says.

"Get a room," Benjamin says right before he lets out a loud belch.

Julia shakes her head and smiles. "You are such a dick." She feels Elena's fingertips continue to lightly stroke her fingers. The feeling is so erotic. And it's just a light touch on the hand! She cannot believe how deeply she has fallen for Elena.

❖

Julia opens the door to the cabin and immediately feels hands on her hips turning her around. She has her lips on Elena's before she even has a moment to think about closing the door or turning on a light.

The door slams behind them, and Julia pulls away. Elena smiles and reenacts a kicking motion with her foot. "I kicked it closed. No worries," she whispers before Julia pulls her back into a searing kiss, searches her mouth, revels in the way her teeth feel as she nips at Julia's lips. It's so satisfying to kiss Elena that Julia isn't aware of the sounds she's making until Elena says between kisses, "You sound so fucking sexy."

Julia moans, fights away the embarrassment of being so vocal, and says, "You do this to me." She slides her hands up Elena's shirt to the soft skin of her stomach, to the warm small of her back, then to Elena's breasts. In one fluid motion, she slips her hand under the silken fabric of Elena's bra, feels the hardness of her nipples, the fullness of her breasts, and the soft, soft skin that she honestly never thought she'd get the chance to feel. The sound that pours from Elena's mouth when Julia gently rolls each nipple between her forefinger and thumb is enough to send Julia straight over the edge. "Dammit, Elena."

Elena laughs as she slides one hand under the waistband of Julia's running shorts to Julia's warm center. She cups it, lets her fingers roam over Julia's panties, tracing the edge with her middle finger. "I want to fuck you so bad," Elena says into Julia's ear before she grabs her earlobe and bites down.

"This is so the opposite of snail's pace." All Julia wants is to feel Elena's fingers inside her, but this is so fast, so furious, and so not what they just discussed. "Elena, God, I don't know what to do."

"I know." Elena moans, and the sound reverberates into Julia's ear, and she almost comes right on the spot.

"Fucking hell," Julia says through clenched teeth. "We have to stop."

"I know," Elena says. "I don't want to stop. I want to taste you and feel you come in my mouth."

Julia cannot even describe how wet she is. Her panties are soaked. She wants to just let go and do it. Say *fuck it* and tell Elena to do it, have her way with Julia, with anything she wants. Julia leans her head back, feels Elena's lips on the hollow of where her neck meets her collarbones, and she knows this isn't the time. "We should wait,"

Julia whispers when she bends her head back, and her eyes lock on to Elena's. "I want you to love me when you do this."

The look that washes over Elena's face is so wonderful. If Julia didn't know any better, she would have thought it *was* love. Elena places her lips on Julia's. "That won't be hard to do," she says against Julia's lips. "I'm already most of the way there."

Julia has run so far away to find something, to find this, to find love and kindness and a home. And all it takes is those words for Julia to know that this relationship could be the very thing she needs to fix her, to make her whole, to protect everything that her self-built walls were supposed to do.

CHAPTER FOURTEEN

The ride to take the cattle back to the range is far slower than herding the cattle down. It seems like they've been riding forever. They've been going for the better part of six hours now. Thankfully, Leia handles like a breeze and hasn't given Julia an ounce of trouble. She's riding next to Benjamin now, and even though it has been confirmed that he's not really interested, it's hard to take his compliments and eyebrow game without wanting to punch him right off his horse.

"I thought you have a thing for Toni?" Julia finally asks after his tenth try to act like a dashing asshole.

"Pal!" Benjamin almost shouts as they're riding, waving his hand as he looks back quickly over each shoulder as if making sure no one heard Julia. "What are you getting on about? You need to keep your freaking voice down!"

Julia chuckles, glances over at Elena, who is riding next to Elijah and, of course, Penn. "You realize no one is listening, right?"

"I don't give a damn," Benjamin says. "Do you know what it's like to get dumped by someone you love? It's not a carnival. And I'm not proud that I still love that woman."

"I do know what it's like." Julia looks at Benjamin and pulls her baseball cap down to shield her eyes from the harsh sun. "I know exactly what it's like. But I also know what regret is."

Benjamin wipes his brow with the back of his gloved hand and looks at Julia square on. "You mean you think I should try again?"

"Why not? What do you have to lose?"

"My dignity?"

"You've already lost that, my friend," Julia says. He rolls his eyes, and she puts her hand in the air. "No, no, all joking aside. Has she told you to leave her alone?"

"Quite the contrary," Benjamin mumbles, to which Julia raises her eyebrows. "She's been frequenting my bar more and more. Staying until last call. Playing darts and accidentally dropping the dart so she has to bend down…" His voice trails off, dreamy-like.

Julia has to almost stop her horse so she can stare at him. "Jesus, *pal*, you need to get your act together," she says with an air of sarcasm and friendliness she didn't think she'd ever have with this man.

He laughs, tilts the brim of his cowboy hat, then motions toward the red Ford where Agnes and Toni are riding. "I'll give it a whirl on one condition."

"Oh, yeah? And what's that?"

"That you quit lollygagging and fuck Elena already."

Julia's mouth drops open, her words completely lost.

Benjamin throws his head back, a hearty laugh escaping. "You're not the only one with great advice, love," he finally says, winking.

"Yeah, well, you're a bit crass, you *asshole*!" Julia tries to wipe the shit-eating grin from her face. Another laugh echoes from Benjamin's mouth, and goddammit, Julia can't help but laugh with him.

❖

They arrive at the camp sometime after five o'clock. It's an awesome area that Julia hasn't seen yet. They're about five clicks farther north to account for southerly grazing, according to Elijah. The view is spectacular, of course, and the sun is still high in the sky, making it almost too hot to think. It's a welcome reprieve when Caroline grabs her by the arm and drags her to the small river about a hundred yards from where they're setting up. Both women strip off their boots, roll their pants up, and plunge their feet into the water, sounds of relief uttered in unison.

"Julia, I'm so happy that I've gotten to know you a little bit better." Caroline smiles with her hands in the water, cupping handfuls to pour over her arms. They're both sitting on the large rocks that line the river bank. "I just…It gets a little lonely around here."

Julia glances at Caroline, wonders how she can say they've gotten to know each other when Julia has barely said ten things about herself, but she plays along. "I agree." She props her elbows on her knees. It's been a really long time since she's had anyone go out of their way to be her friend, and now she has Toni and Caroline, who both seem really *normal.*

"I'm happy you're here. That you stayed. I wasn't sure you were going to."

"I wasn't sure, either."

"I figured." Caroline laughs. "I mean, don't get me wrong."

"No, don't worry, I know what you mean." Julia looks up and then down the river. It's so peaceful, so beautiful. "I can't get over how beautiful everything is."

"It's definitely a sight, isn't it?" Caroline sighs and closes her eyes. "Sometimes, I just sit here and listen. Listen to the way the wind catches the trees, how the birds sound, their chirps, their wings spreading. It's just so—"

"Peaceful," Julia says, closing her eyes. "I've almost forgotten how traffic jams sound."

Caroline laughs. "You'll never want to go back to Chicago."

Julia opens her eyes when she hears someone approaching them from behind. She glances over her shoulder. "Oh, great."

Caroline's eyes shoot open, and she checks behind her. "What the hell does she want?"

"To get under my skin, I'm sure." Julia groans.

"You want me to stay?"

"No, but thank you for offering." She watches Caroline pick up her socks and boots and make her way toward dry land, limping with every step from the rocks on the side of the river. Julia chuckles at the sight.

"So, you found the promised land?" Penn asks when she approaches the area where Caroline was sitting.

"Do you mean the river?" Julia asks, an eyebrow raised.

"No, actually, I meant Elena," Penn replies, her voice low, dirty, full of something that Julia can't quite pinpoint. It sounds an awful lot like hatred, but it's probably jealousy.

"Don't talk about her like that," Julia says. "Ever."

"Oh, great, she has you to stick up for her now, too."

"Penn, I swear to God—"

"What? What will you do, Julia Finch?" She turns her body fully toward Julia. "Shank me?"

Julia's heart rate starts to pick up the pace. "Excuse me?"

"Well, I decided to do a little research."

"Surprised you can read." Julia delivers the barb with as much accuracy as a sharpshooter.

Penn lets out a low chuckle, one that is laced with far more than jealousy. "Oh, I read. I read a lot about you."

"And?" Julia knows full well that Penn didn't get as much dirt about her as she'd have liked.

"Jail at seventeen? Sound familiar?" Penn's face looks as if she just unearthed a secret from hundreds of years ago that would prove aliens exist or that George Washington was really a woman.

"Yeah? *So?* Everyone has a past. I'm sure you do, too. If I cared enough to even find out."

Penn's face falls, as do her shoulders. Julia is pleased, but her heart is still in her throat. Jail at seventeen is not a shining moment, and honestly, she hadn't planned on telling anyone, especially Elena. But now she's going to have to.

"Seriously, Penn, I don't mean to sound like a bitch, but you have got to stop trying to make me look bad. All it does is make you look bad. And you already look pretty bad."

"Don't attempt to give me advice," Penn mutters, hanging her head.

"I'm just trying here."

"Yeah, trying to ruin my chances."

"Um." Julia lets out another laugh. "You ruined your own chances when you decided to fuck Elena over and leave with no warning. You did that."

"You think I don't know that? I'm trying to fix it!" Penn shouts. Her blue eyes are piercing, and she's holding her black cowboy hat in both hands. It's actually taking a lot for Julia to not feel bad for the woman.

"Did you love Elena?"

Penn takes a breath as if she's going to respond but stops. She runs her hand over her face. "Y'know, your car is done. It's been waiting down at the auto body shop for the past month. Ray told me Elijah paid for it."

Julia stands and gathers her boots. She knows exactly what Penn means, and it makes her stomach twist. "Look," she says, her voice calm, even though she feels like there's electricity coursing through her veins. "I'm not going anywhere."

"I know your type. You'll run. Your type always does. All I have to do is figure out how to make that happen."

"Well, good luck."

Penn places her hat back on her head, swipes two fingers over the brim, and looks out over the river. "You're the one that's gonna need the luck, sweetheart."

❖

"Do you need help with that tent?" Elena asks Julia, motioning toward the pile of polyester and poles.

"I know I might not be a cowgirl, but I certainly know how to camp." Julia tilts her head, grabs the tent pole, and gets to work. In no time at all, the two women have the tent erected and the stakes hammered into the ground. Julia holds her hand in the air. "Awesome job!" she says, waiting for Elena to high-five her. Elena is still looking at the tent when she nods, and Julia shakes her head. "C'mon, Elena, don't leave me hangin'!"

"You want me to high-five you? For putting up a tent?"

"Yes!"

Elena high-fives Julia. "You are a child," she says.

Julia pulls the brim of her baseball cap down. "Yeah, but at least I'm cute." Julia beams, her hands in the back pockets of her Wranglers. She watches Elena's cheeks fill with pink, and it makes her heart swell. "So, now what?"

"Well, there's the campfire." Elena motions toward the roaring fire where the rest of the group has congregated. Cole is laughing along with Ed; Benjamin is regaling some tale to Agnes and Toni, who both seem to be enjoying whatever is being said; Elijah has his arm around Caroline, and it's sickeningly sweet; and Scooter and the rodeo clowns are singing their own rendition of Dolly Parton's "Jolene" (it's actually quite good, and Julia is impressed). "Which is what we've been doing the last three nights. Or you could come with me."

"Where you gonna take me, Miss Bennett?" Julia asks quietly, a smile creeping to her lips.

"It's a surprise."

"You know," Julia glances back at the fire and then at Elena, "I typically hate surprises."

"I feel like you might like this one," Elena whispers as she leans into Julia's personal space.

❖

"So, you want me to follow you into the dark with only a flashlight to protect us?"

"Oh, come on, don't you trust me?" Elena has slipped a black fleece over her shirt and has a folded blanket over her arm.

Julia shakes her head. "I don't trust anyone."

"Come on." Elena nods. "I know this area like the back of my hand."

"You sure?"

"Julia, you realize that 'trust me' means that you actually need to do just that?"

"Fine, fine." Julia sighs, following as Elena takes off east, blazing her own trail. She slips her hands into the front pocket of her hooded sweatshirt. They're walking for a good ten minutes before Julia realizes she has absolutely no idea where the edge of the mountain is. "You're not gonna march me off a cliff, are you?"

"I probably would have when you first started." Elena chuckles, glancing over her shoulder. "But I've actually grown to like you since then." She reaches back to wrap her fingers around Julia's forearm. "I won't let you get hurt. I promise." She squeezes gently. "Besides, this is where I'm taking you."

They take a few more steps, and they're on rock instead of dirt. Julia looks out and notices that they're almost to the edge of the mountain. The light from the small sliver of moon is enough to make it clear that Elena was not marching her off the side of a mountain but damn near close. Julia takes a deep breath and looks over at Elena.

She can make out Elena's facial features: the curve of her lips, her gorgeous jawline, her perfect cheekbones; the sight takes her breath away.

"Here," Elena says as she snaps the blanket into the air, and Julia helps spread it out onto the rock surface. She sits promptly, reaches to grab on to Julia's hand, and pulls her down beside her. "Now, look up."

There are so many more stars in the night sky than Julia has ever seen, and she's been looking at the stars her entire life. Wishing on them, wondering about them, trying her hardest to understand them, and now...Now she's sitting next to Elena Bennett on a blanket in Colorado with no earthly idea how to handle what's happening between them, and she's more at peace than she ever has been. "Elena," she says, one hand on her chest, the other pushing her hair back from her face. "I can't...I can't find the words."

"That group of stars right there?" Elena points. "That's my favorite constellation."

"What is it called?" Julia whispers, still barely able to form a sentence.

"Pegasus," Elena says. "Gloria used to say she was *my* Pegasus. And I was her muse."

Julia can feel her chest tighten. "That's pretty powerful," she whispers, keeping her eyes on the sky.

"Have you ever..." Elena's voice trails off, and the silence that follows is deafening.

"Have I ever what?"

"Loved someone like that?" Elena asks. "Like they were your everything?"

Julia finally pulls her eyes from the sky, focuses on her hands that are now folded in her lap. "No," she replies, softly.

"Oh."

"Don't get me wrong. I sure thought I was in love a number of times." Julia looks back at the sky, at Pegasus, and fights back tears—which is making her so uncomfortable. Why does she want to cry right now? "Never had someone be my everything, though." Julia kind of hopes that Elena will say something, but when Julia looks out of the corner of her eye, it's clear that Elena isn't going to talk right now. "I'd like to think that I could," Julia breathes. "But how do you keep a handle on who you are if you've let someone else be your everything?"

"You find who you are when you love someone like that," Elena whispers, her voice cracking.

Another silence falls between them. It's not awkward. It's comfortable and reassuring, especially when Julia feels Elena lean into her and hears Elena's deep breaths and can smell her fabric softener and her deodorant, and everything about it is intoxicating.

Elena raises her finger toward the eastern sky. "That's a satellite," she says. Julia follows the direction Elena is pointing and sees the light moving across the sky like a slow-moving shooting star. She pulls away a little and looks at Julia. "You ever going to tell me more about yourself?"

"I hadn't planned on it," Julia mumbles. "It's not a good story."

"I'd still like to know you. The good and the bad."

"Well, the me you want to know and the me I really am are two different things."

"Are they?" Elena asks. "Because I can't believe that."

"Elena." Julia sighs. "I really don't want to talk about it."

"You can't tell me at least one thing?"

"Why, Elena? Why? You said you wouldn't push me, yet you always seem to. I don't get why you want to know so badly. So you along with everyone else that has come and gone from my life can finally know that I'm a fucking screw up? That I'm a huge mess? That I've done some really stupid fucking shit? Because I don't think I want you to know that."

"We've all done stupid shit, dear."

"I was in prison six years ago." Julia looks at Elena and sees her eyes go wide. "Yeah, that face right there?" She motions to Elena's expression. "That's exactly why I didn't want to tell you."

"Look, I'm sorry," Elena says. "It just took me by surprise."

"Why? Because I don't *look* like a convict?"

"No, Julia, come on. Don't be like that, please. It just surprised me. That's all."

Julia can't fight the tension coursing through her veins.

Elena takes a deep breath and shrugs. "You can't let the horrible define you."

"Oh, yeah because it's super easy to just forget about the time I spent there. The sleepless nights, the solitude. You have no idea what the hell I went through there and in the rest of my life. And here?" Julia pauses and looks back at the sky. "Here no one knows. No one needs to know my background for me to be able to scoop horse shit into a wheelbarrow. So, why is it so important to you?"

Elena doesn't answer right away. And even though Julia does not want to talk, the silence is killing her. All it's going to take is a little more pushing, and Julia's floodgates are going to fly open, and all of her past is going to come spilling out. And Elena will be the one running this time, straight for the hills and not looking back.

"Julia," Elena says as she leans forward, crosses her legs on the blanket, and bends her head down. "Is it that out of the realm of possibility that I might actually be interested in learning more about you because I really like you? Do you honestly think I'm going to use anything you tell me against you? Because I can assure you, I will not. I don't want to hurt you." Elena looks back at Julia. "I want to help you."

The insinuation that Julia needs help pisses her off. Why the hell would she need help? "Help me do what?" Her voice is laced with the irritation she's feeling, and she hopes Elena is getting the message.

"Help you see that you're worth it." Elena shrugs. "Worth getting to know. Worth fighting for. Worth *falling* for."

And just like that, the pissed-off feeling, the irritation, it all falls away and leaves Julia speechless. Her mouth has gone dry, her hands are aching, and she wonders if she is really in this moment or if it's a dream.

"So, take that chip off your shoulder and try to remember that. Okay?"

Julia takes a deep breath, waits one beat, two beats, three, before she finally finds a little bit of courage to trust Elena and says, "I met my real parents right before I ran this last time."

"Julia," Elena says, barely above a whisper.

"And they didn't like me." Julia fights back the tears threatening to escape. "And this is why I don't want to talk. Because who wants to talk about their parents not liking them?" The laugh that follows is not because it's funny; it's because Julia cannot handle this emotion. She has never been able to do this, to open up, to trust, to be human.

"Julia, honey, how do you know that? How could they not like you?"

"Because, Elena!" Julia shouts, and the echo it creates is eerie. She sucks in a breath and twists her hands. She knows she shouldn't yell at Elena. But dammit, she can't help it. "My real father said it. I heard it with my own ears. He said they didn't want anything to do with me. And my *mother* sat there and didn't say a thing. She didn't protest it. She didn't fight for me. I don't know why I thought she would fight. She didn't want me to begin with, why would she want me now?" Julia stops and looks down at her hands. She's shaking. She's only opened up one other time, and it turned out awful, and now that there's a crack in her façade, she can't stop talking. The words just keep coming. "They knew I had been in jail. That's ultimately how they found me, and they asked what happened"—she shakes her head—"so, I told them everything. I started at the beginning, from my first foster family until the last, and laid it all out. I told them everything, Elena. How I only did what I did to survive. They're supposed to love me unconditionally, right? Isn't that what parents are supposed to do? Love their child no matter what?"

There's no noise coming out of Elena. It hardly even sounds like she's breathing. And there's a part of Julia that feels as if maybe she should just shut the hell up. Stop talking, stop sharing, and start running again because now another family is going to disown her. But when she feels Elena's warm hand cover hers, something that feels an awful lot like strength springs to life inside her chest, and she tells the story of Johnny and Sophia, the only foster parents she ever loved. She remembers the time when Johnny brought her a new set of markers and pens to draw with, and Sophia had taught her how to draw, and it was so much like a family that it for once felt *normal*. And then Johnny was killed at work at the steel mill. Sophia couldn't take care of Julia anymore, so she had to go to a different family.

"His name was George. And her name was Franny. And he beat her all the time. She was a lovely woman with beautiful eyes, and she would always play the piano. But he was horrible. I will never feel bad about hitting him with that car."

Elena gasps.

"Jesus, Elena. I didn't kill him."

"Well, what the hell *happened* then?"

"I tried to run away a lot, but Franny would always find me and ask me to come back. She said I helped. I don't know if that's really the case. It felt nice to be needed. So, I stayed. One day it got really bad, and I had enough. He had my car on lockdown, though. I ripped apart his garage to find the keys, and I came up empty, so I said, 'fuck it' and stole his car to run away. He came out of the house and saw me in it, so I tried to peel out. He kind of jumped in front of me, and I swerved, but I was so shaken up that I slammed into him." When Elena seems to stifle a chuckle, Julia can't fight the urge to laugh right along with her. "Yeah, looking back on it now, it was kind of funny. I mean, I really slammed into him. He flew up onto the hood, broke the windshield; I think it broke some of his bones."

"Julia, my God, you weren't kidding," Elena still cannot contain her shocked laughter. "What did Franny do?"

"Well, she didn't want to press charges, but George, of course, did, so...I was right on the cusp of being a kid and an adult, so George pushed and pushed until they tried me as an adult." Julia leans back and looks up at the stars. "The judge was a total dick and believed George's lies. So, to prison I went. Franny came to visit me in jail, though. A couple times. She was such a nice lady."

"Julia," Elena says softly. "Wow."

"Yeah..."

"Let me get this straight."

Julia glances at Elena and smiles. "Are you too shocked to comprehend it? It is a little convoluted."

"No, I promise," Elena says. "So, you were in jail for four years, got out, found a way to live a life on your own, and *then* your parents found you? What took them so long?"

Julia shrugs. "I mean, I guess I was hard to find since I was in and out of the foster system. And as soon as I got out of jail, I pretty much flew under the radar. Stayed out of trouble, of course."

"Wow."

Julia laughs at Elena's response. "That's all you have for me, eh?"

"Well, you were right. It's a lot to put on a person." Elena nudges Julia's side. "But I can handle it."

"You sure?"

Elena nods. "So, your parents?"

"What about them?"

"They didn't even give you a chance, did they?"

Julia rubs her hands over her face. There is still a fine layer of dust covering her skin, so all it does is make her feel even uglier and more like an outcast. "They didn't want to even try," Julia whispers. "So, instead of dealing with my own feelings of rejection, I packed up my car, and I ran from everything again."

"Now I know why you don't want to talk about it." Elena takes a breath, runs her hand down Julia's back, and then back up it. Her voice is so caring and wonderful that it makes Julia's heart hurt.

"I'm so messed up. I run. I never want to stay because I'm a fucking wreck."

"You're not old enough to be a fucking wreck," Elena says. She runs her hand up and down Julia's arm, then reaches up to her face, cupping her cheek and slowly urging Julia to look at her. She lightly brushes her thumb across Julia's bottom lip. "You can stop running now," she whispers.

And Julia's only response is to lean forward and capture Elena's lips, kissing her as if she is her lifeline, tethering her to this place that has started to feel an awful lot like home.

❖

When they get back to the camp, the fire is still roaring, as are the men plus Toni and Penn, who are settled next to Benjamin, and Penn is saying something to Toni that is making her laugh. Benjamin is annoyed, clearly, but what the hell is Penn doing? Doesn't she know that Toni is off-limits? Julia nudges Elena. "What the hell is going on there?" she whispers as they approach the fire.

"That's Penn being Penn. Trying to make me jealous."

"Is it working?" Julia asks.

Elena looks at Julia, her perfect eyebrows raised. "You're joking, right?"

"I'm just asking."

"Stop, please," Elena says. "You have nothing to worry about."

"Where have you two been?" Elijah asks, his eyes shifting from Elena to Julia and then back to Elena. "Did you take her to the looking point?"

"I did," Elena says. The two of them find a seat around the fire next to Cole. "Did you eat enough?" she asks, mussing his hair when he nods. He leans his head against her shoulder and lets out a giant yawn. "If you're tired, dear, you can go to sleep. I'll be in the tent shortly."

"Where will you sleep, Julia?" Cole asks, looking at her from his mother's side. "You should stay in our tent. It's big enough."

Julia looks at Elena. "Well, I set my tent up."

"I think your tent is called for." Cole motions to Toni and Penn. "They said neither of them brought a tent. Well, actually Toni said she isn't sleeping with her goddamn grandmother." Cole holds his hands in the air in mock surrender when he makes eye contact with his mom. "Direct quote, Mom! I promise!" He's quick to snuggle back into Elena's side, smiling when he makes eye contact with Julia. "So, Penn volunteered your tent. You stay with us, then."

"I guess that settles it," Elena says quietly.

Julia glances at Elena, notices how insanely attractive she looks in that moment. She has to wonder if it's from the fire or from everything that has happened. Either way, Elena has never looked better.

❖

Julia turns onto her side, pulling her sleeping bag back up to her shoulders. She looks at Elena, who is also on her side; her eyes are closed, her hair is down, falling across her chin. She looks so peaceful, so beautiful.

"Go to sleep, Julia," Elena whispers.

"How'd you know?"

"I can hear you breathing."

"Sorry."

Elena's eyes slide open. "Close your eyes. Try to get some rest."

"I don't want to miss anything," Julia whispers.

"What do you think you'll miss?"

"This." Julia places her hand over Elena's heart. She knows this is the first time in her life that she has felt this way about another person. And this feeling of love and desire is not going anywhere. It's settling itself inside her, right inside her chest, right where she knows she'll never stop feeling it. "This right here."

"Oh, honey," Elena says, her voice so low that Julia can barely hear it. "I'm not going anywhere."

"You look so beautiful tonight, Elena."

"You can barely see me," Elena says.

"I can see enough."

Julia feels Elena run a finger across her cheek and down her jawline before she says, "Sleep."

"Okay," Julia says, still smiling as she closes her eyes.

When she sleeps, she dreams of staying still, riding her horse, finding life when she thought she'd never be able to. She sees Elena and Cole and wonders if this is where her life has been taking her. She sees smiles and happiness and real love. She sees fear…and confusion. She sees it all being taken away within the blink of an eye.

And then she sees herself standing alone again.

Alone.

Alone.

Chapter Fifteen

After two weeks of being back at the ranch, the planning and preparation for the annual Bennett Ranch Hoedown has been wrapped up. Julia has barely seen Elena because of all the meetings with party planners. And when they do talk, it's nothing groundbreaking but enough to make Julia's heartbeat speed up. She misses Elena, though, which scares her. She's never really been in an actual relationship, at least not one with a woman she really likes. Of course, she had many flings and one-night stands, but now…Now there's Elena. Julia can't stop thinking about her in the downtimes, in the middle of the night, in the morning, in the shower. Elena's hands, her long fingers, her lips, and beautiful smile. Julia wants to feel Elena…Taste her…Make her scream…The thought alone is enough to make Julia wish for the sweet release of her own hands. She has touched herself and gotten herself off more in the past few weeks than she has in her entire life. So, needless to say, she's nervous about the party, about seeing Elena, about being in such close proximity to her. How is she going to handle the urge to kiss her, rip her clothes off, and ravish her as soon as she sees her?

The frustration is enough to cause a coronary.

So, the party will commence at 6:00 p.m. sharp, and thankfully, Toni and Caroline took Julia shopping in Boulder the day before for a suitable outfit. Apparently, the hoedown is *the* social event of the year. She is shocked to find that out, and her facial expression as Caroline explains it over a cup of coffee on Friday morning must not have been hidden, considering the smack on the shoulder she receives from Elena.

"Ow," Julia says through a soft laugh. "I didn't realize! I'm sorry!"

Elena points a finger at Julia and tilts her head. "Miss Finch, I can uninvite you as quickly as I invited you. Keep that in mind."

Julia smiles when she sees Caroline roll her eyes. "Believe me," Caroline whispers when Elena leaves the kitchen to go outside, the screen door slamming behind her. "There's no way you aren't coming. It really is a great time."

"I know we talked about this a little while we were all shopping, but why is this such a big deal?" Julia asks before biting into a bear claw that Caroline bought at the bakery in town.

"Well, Elena's parents started it forever ago. It was a way for them to say thank you to everyone for helping out during the herding season. And Elena has carried on the tradition. Which, honestly, is really nice because for a while there, we thought she was going to stop. Elijah and everyone else works so hard for Elena, and this ends up being a really nice way of saying thanks. And this year, for whatever reason, is supposed to be even bigger than last year. I think it's the twenty-ninth anniversary or something."

"Thirtieth," comes Elijah's voice as he rounds the doorway and glides toward the coffeepot. "Last year was the twenty-ninth, and that's when the shit hit the fan."

"Oh. *Yeah.*" Caroline sighs.

"God, what the hell happened last year?"

"That's when Penn up and left," Elijah says. He leans against the counter and drinks his freshly poured cup of coffee. "And so began the dark ages—"

"You know," Julia says. "I think I get it." She looks down at her hands, then back up at the two in front of her. "I'm glad we had time for me to buy a nice outfit because I certainly don't want to stick out like a sore thumb."

"Wait a second here. You mean you *aren't* going looking like a hoodlum?"

"A *hoodlum*? Do you think I normally look like a hoodlum, Elijah?"

He raises his eyebrows, a smile coming to his lips. "Oh, no, never. Except of course when you stroll in with your Ramones T-shirt on."

"Well, son of a bitch." Julia huffs, shaking her head, a laugh spilling from her mouth. "I look damn good in that T-shirt."

"Sure." Elijah laughs. "Sure."

Caroline turns and pats him on the stomach, standing on her tiptoes to kiss him on the cheek. "You stop teasing Julia," she says against his skin, nuzzling him with her nose.

"You two are disgusting." Julia rolls her eyes. "I'm going to go get busy on the stalls. I'll leave you two lovebirds alone."

They both laugh as Julia gets up and downs the rest of her lukewarm coffee and takes another bear claw to go. She heads outside, bracing herself for the heat today. It's supposed to be a record high with nothing but sun. No riding today, but the stalls still need to be cleaned, and regardless of how used to it she gets, the heat does nothing for the smell.

❖

It's Saturday afternoon about an hour before people are supposed to start to arrive for the party when Julia hears her screen door bang and then Cole's exasperated, "Julia!"

"What's goin' on?" Julia rushes out of her bedroom, curlers in her hair, shorts and a tank top on—thankfully—and barefoot. "Is everything all right?"

"I'm really sorry," he says, sweat beading along his hairline. He's near tears. "I couldn't get my tie tied. And Mom was all frantic about getting things ready for the party, and she'll be mad if I show up without it tied and have to have her do it, and clearly, Jules, I'm freaking out."

"Cole, dude, chill out," Julia says with a soothing voice. She puts her hands on his arms and pulls him farther into the cabin. "You're gonna sweat yourself into a frenzy. You gotta just take some deep breaths and relax. And take your suit jacket off. You have a vest on *and* a jacket. You're overheating."

He shrugs off his jacket and tosses it onto the overstuffed armchair in the living room. "I just fucking hate that I can't ever fucking tie stupid *fucking* ties. It's not fucking fair."

"*Whoa* there, cowboy," Julia says as she stifles a chuckle. She wants to laugh so bad because hearing him cuss like that really is funny, but he's on the verge of a literal meltdown. He needs a solid shoulder to lean on right now, not an asshole to make fun of him. "I know I'm your friend, but maybe calm down on the fucks."

"Sorry." Cole's shoulders slump. "I just…This girl Allison will be there."

"Oh, *really*?"

"Yeah, and she's older—"

"A cougar, eh?"

"Julia!" He giggles, his face blushing ten shades of red. "No, that's not it. She's just…she's really…I just like her a lot."

Julia lays a hand on his shoulder, "Let's get you looking like a million bucks, then. Lucky for you, I know how to tie a tie. And also, we gotta get you in front of a fan. You're sweating like a whore in church." Cole starts chuckling, his boyish laughter making Julia's heart swell. "So, tell me about this Allison girl."

Cole lets Julia lead him into the living room and over to a window fan. He takes a deep breath. "Well, she's seventeen. I think she just broke up with this guy from the next town over. I don't even know his name. But I guess he's a real jerk. We've talked a lot. She normally comes to herding, but she texted me and told me she had to work."

"Oh, so you text?"

Cole pulls out his iPhone and taps into the Messages app. He scrolls through his conversation with Allison. "That was just from last night."

"Wait. How do you get a signal up here?"

"We have Wi-Fi. Duh. It's not like we live in a vacuum or something. Focus." Cole rolls his eyes and continues scrolling through the messages. "So, Allison is gonna be there tonight, and she told me she's excited to see me and now, well, I'm freaking out."

Julia quickly ties Cole's dark purple tie in a double Windsor knot, then straightens it out.

"How do you know how to do that?"

Julia shrugs. "I, um," she says and takes a breath. "I used to have a foster dad that liked to wear ties to church. He taught me. I guess I just never forgot." Cole's looking right at her, into her eyes, and it's making Julia uncomfortable. "Okay," she says. She takes his arm and unbuttons his sleeve, rolls it up to his elbow, then does the same to the other sleeve. "May I make a suggestion?"

"Yeah, of course. You know I trust you," Cole says. He's watching her, though, his eyes taking in her handiwork.

"Lose the jacket. You look too hot, and it's like ninety-five degrees.

Also," Julia smooths the tie, then buttons up the dark gray vest, "this vest is sharp. You look good." She brushes his hair to the side. It's messy, but he looks good, like he's meaning to be trendy. "Now freeze. Don't mess your hair up. It looks perfect."

Cole looks at Julia, right into her eyes. "Thank you, Julia."

"No problem."

"No." He stops her by placing his hand on hers. "Like, for whatever is happening between you and Mom…for being here…for not leaving…for like, *everything*."

Julia's eyes start welling with tears, and she knows if this conversation continues, Cole won't be the only hot mess in this cabin. She places a hand against his cheek and offers the most genuine smile she can muster. "Honestly, I should be thanking you guys. Kind of saved my life."

Cole surges forward and wraps his long arms around Julia's shoulders; her breath leaves her body with a whoosh. A cough later and she's hugging the kid back, all of a sudden realizing this could be the family she's always wanted. And so desperately needs.

❖

Julia walks out her door and onto the wooden porch. She's insanely nervous. The buildup to this event feels so much more important than she ever imagined. She looks at Caroline and Elijah, who are standing on the stairs waiting because, according to Caroline, "They simply cannot be late."

Caroline looks adorable, of course, in her lace overlay pink dress complete with jean jacket and brown boots. Who would have ever thought that outfit would look nice? Certainly not Julia. But it actually does look really good on her. Her pixie hair is messier than normal, which Elijah apparently loves because he can't stop looking at her and grinning like a lovesick fool. And of course, he looks absolutely strapping in his pink button-down, black jeans, black boots, and black cowboy hat. They obviously planned their outfits.

Julia had picked out a simple black sundress that settles right above her knees, which she didn't really love, but Toni and Caroline said it makes her look amazing. She knows they were overselling. *Come on!* Her legs have barely seen the light of day. And she isn't a huge fan of dresses. The only benefit is that she decided to break the rules and wear a new pair of red Chucks, so really? It's worth being uncomfortable in the dress.

"You look adorable," Caroline says with a huge smile on her face. "Your hair is amazing. I love the curls."

"Thank you. It took forever," Julia says and then fluffs the curls one more time.

"Oh, yes." Elijah smirks. "The shoes are perfect. What a statement."

Julia does a twirl. "I figured you'd like that."

"Are you ready?" Caroline asks. She reaches for Julia's hand, holds it, and squeezes it. "You'll be fine."

"How do you even know that I'm nervous?"

"Because it's written all over your face. You look like you've swallowed a frog."

"Is that even really a saying?"

Elijah shakes his head and adjusts his hat. "Not that I know of. But it should be because I reckon it'd be a nerve-wracking experience."

Caroline's girlish giggle is disgusting, and Julia can't help but share in the laughter. "I honestly don't know why I like you so much," she says as they take off toward the barn. The music has already started, and there are string Edison lights lining the walkway up to the barn door. When they walk inside, Julia can hardly believe the transformation. There are white twinkle lights draped from the rafters, encircling the posts, and a giant, ornate chandelier with more Edison lights. She can feel that her mouth is open slightly when she hears that the music playing isn't country but a live band with a female lead singing a cover of ABBA's "SOS." *How fitting…*

"Julia, honey," Caroline almost shouts over the music. She reaches out and wraps her fingers around Julia's forearm. "Wait."

Julia turns and looks back. "What?"

"Just," Caroline says as she turns to look at Elijah; his face is without emotion. "Don't be upset if she isn't…*normal.*"

"What is that supposed to mean?"

"This night is always hard on her. Being the hostess with the mostest," Elijah says. "And with Penn being here."

Julia huffs. "Seriously, you guys?"

"Well, we just don't want you to get hurt."

"I won't get hurt. I'm a big girl." Julia pulls her arm away from Caroline and fluffs her curly hair. "Now, come on, let's go *drink*."

❖

Julia's drink of choice at a party has always been beer. For whatever reason, she gravitates toward it. Probably because growing up, it was so cheap it was practically free.

But for some unknown reason, when Toni hands a drink over and says, "It's an old fashioned, and it tastes like a dream," she doesn't protest. She stares at it, then eyes Toni, then stares back at the drink.

"What?" Toni asks, drinking her identical drink. She smacks her lips and says, "Ah."

"I don't casually drink bourbon. I get *drunk* with bourbon. And I don't know if *drunk* is a good idea." Julia, still hesitant, takes a sip and closes her eyes. It tastes amazing, and oh, man, it's going down real, real smooth, and shit, it's going to be a long night if she continues with this.

"Just drink it and shut up." Toni puts her hand on Julia's bare shoulder and turns her body slightly. "Elena is over there," she whispers.

Julia's eyes follow the motion of Toni's wrist and fingers, and she sees Elena standing across the pavilion in a gray skirt; a pair of boots; and a sleeveless white button-up shirt that's tied in a knot at her navel, and Julia literally can't even think about it because it's making her palms sweat. Her hair is pulled into a bun, and her skin is so tan and beautiful. Julia's mouth is dry as she blinks twice, licks her lips, and breathes out a simple, "Wow."

"Yeah, well, keep it in your pants until later," Toni says. "I know you haven't talked to her yet, but I want you to know something."

Julia groans, her free arm falling to her side in an exasperated motion. "Why is everyone being like this? I am absolutely fine!"

"I just think you need to know a couple things, okay?" Toni motions to an older man with flowing shoulder-length white hair who Elena is speaking with. "Mayor Jackson. Super good guy. Don't cross him, though." She points to another group of people off toward the stage. "Stay away from those guys. The Swine brothers and Jeff Doggly. They're all assholes." Toni looks around. "The band is the Sirens, all sisters and Mayor Jackson's daughters. The lead singer is

Kelly. So, like, if you're going to criticize the music, don't do it loudly or near Mayor Jackson or his secretary Heath over there. Or Kelly's best friend, Jess."

Julia starts to laugh as she downs the rest of her first drink. She breathes in through clenched teeth. The alcohol is burning all the way down to her toes. "Toni, I love you so much, and I'm so happy you're giving me the rundown, but seriously…" Julia clinks the ice cubes together in her empty glass. "Go get me another drink, please." She watches Toni walk away and then turns to find Elena through the crowd talking to a group of men. She watches her, the way she's standing with the group, the way she's talking, smiling, laughing.

"Take a picture; it lasts longer." Toni shoves Julia's drink in front of her face.

"Stop." Julia takes a drink of the dark liquid. The burn is starting to subside, but it still warms her from her head to her toes. "Why does she look so nervous?"

Toni fishes the orange peel out of her drink and nibbles on it. "Well, because she is. I mean, the mayor of the town is at her party. Wouldn't that make you nervous?"

"I guess so."

"She's just being the gracious hostess, kissin' babies and all that jazz. Let it go."

Julia does as she's told, but she doesn't take her eyes off Elena. It's hard not to stare. Elena is so gorgeous with her smooth skin and arms and neck and really, with the shirt tied at the navel?

"Close your mouth," Toni says over the top of her drink. "Let's go dance."

Julia feels a blush fill her cheeks as she follows Toni onto the dance floor. "You are ridiculous, you know that, right? And anyway, aren't you going to dance with *Benjamin*?"

"He's being a weirdo. Didn't want to pressure me. I told him I actually want to be pressured this time! Pressure me! Pursue me! Stop being a fucking pussy and step up to the plate!" Toni twirls around when they get to the dance floor as the Sirens sing their rendition of "Take Me Home Tonight."

"Well, maybe he's nervous you're going to dump him again." Julia shouts over the music as she spins around expertly. She sways her hips and finds Elena through the crowd again, and this time, she's pleasantly surprised to find that she's being watched. Julia bites her lip and nods at Elena, who winks in return.

"I am not going to dump him again," Toni shouts. "Have you seen the options in this town? He's the best one out there aside from Elijah, who is so clearly taken it is sickening." Toni rolls her eyes, and Julia bursts out laughing.

"Excuse me, ladies?"

Julia spins around and sees Elena standing there, a smile on her face. "Well, hello there." Julia tosses her hair over her shoulder, already sticky with perspiration.

"Can I steal Miss Finch for a moment, Miss Carson?" Elena asks, her hand reaching out and latching on to Julia's free hand. Toni's gigantic smile is enough of an answer for Elena to start walking away, pulling Julia behind her. When they get about ten feet away, Elena turns and faces Julia, still holding on to her hand. "Hi," Elena says as she leans into Julia's personal space.

Julia is trying to catch her breath from dancing, from seeing Elena, from everything. "Hi," she says, breathless.

"You look really…" Elena pauses, her fingers still holding on to Julia's hand. "Beautiful."

"You mean you're okay with my Chucks?" Julia asks, suddenly very unsure of her rebellious side. She watches Elena's eyes as they travel over her and finally land on her shoes.

"I'm more okay with everything you do than I thought I would be," she says softly, her voice wavering slightly at the end.

"Think you're going to be okay sharing a dance with me later?" Julia's eyebrows rise, and she hopes on everything meaningful in her life that she doesn't get shot down.

Elena leans forward, places her lips directly on Julia's ear, and says, "I hope to be doing more with you than *dancing* later."

Julia feels her body go numb; the air around her instantly stops moving. She swallows the rather large lump in her throat and lets out a very shaky breath.

"I have to go hobnob." Elena straightens, looks at Julia, and runs her hand over Julia's bicep. "Would you like to meet some very important people?"

"You're horrible. You know that, right?"

"Whatever do you mean?" Elena asks. Her dark eyes are shining.

"Get me all hot and bothered, then ask me to meet important people!" Julia smooths her hands over her dress and then fans her face. "Am I flushed? I feel like I'm flushed."

"No more than usual, dear," Elena says, her hand now linked through Julia's arm. "Just do this with me." They take a few steps toward a group of older men, all wearing cowboy hats, boots, jeans, and large belt buckles.

To say Julia is nervous is an understatement, but after Elena's gracious introduction of her as "My newest and maybe best hire, aside from Elijah, of course," Julia feels so at ease. The men are kind with their giant, weather-worn hands and deep, booming voices. It makes Julia squirm a little when one of the older men asks her if she realizes how important the Bennett Ranch is to this town and how if she and Elena are—with a dance of his bushy eyebrows—doing *you know what*, Julia better not mess it up. Elena explains later that the man is one of her family's oldest friends.

"A little warning would have been nice," Julia says when they finally leave the gaggle of men.

"And miss seeing you squirm? Never." Elena slips her hand into Julia's. "I'm pretty important in this town. You're kind of seeing a celebrity."

Julia tilts her head. "A celebrity? Well, then, Miss Bennett, just so you know, you're pretty important to me, too."

❖

Julia is about four drinks in when she silently thanks God that she's not wearing heels. Toni has already stripped hers off and is swirling around the dance floor—finally with Benjamin—and the bottoms of her feet look like a hillbilly's from the backwoods. She smiles, though, when Benjamin spins her and dips her expertly while Kelly sings "Hound Dog" as if she was born to be a performer.

Scanning the barn, the lights twinkling, the air a perfect temperature, Julia can see Elena laughing with Agnes off toward the side near the bar, and Cole, well…He's been wrapped up in Allison's attention the entire night, which makes Julia happy. And nervous. Like a *mom* or something. *Ugh*, she's never had *this* feeling before.

"Well, hello there, little lady," Elijah says as he strolls up to Julia, a bottle of Coors Light in his hand. He clinks the bottle against her glass of bourbon. "I saw you making the rounds with Elena."

Julia blinks, starting to feel her drunkenness but only slightly. "Yeah, she's um…*yeah.*"

"She's very comfortable tonight," he says, leaning against the wooden beam next to them. He crosses his right leg over his left. "I think that's partly your fault."

"I don't know about that."

"Well, I know Elena like the back of my hand. And this is the first time she's ever dressed like that. And this is also the first time she has ever introduced anyone to the town council." Elijah looks over at Julia, his cowboy hat pulled low on his head. He smiles and shrugs.

Julia doesn't really know what to say. This isn't really any sort of conversation she wants to have, so she's kind of speechless.

Elijah downs the rest of his beer and is promptly served another by the service staff. "So, Elena's parents were never okay with her being a lesbian. And this town was not okay with it at first, either."

Julia is silent, but now she is more nervous than speechless. What is Elijah trying to say?

"This has been a very long row for her to hoe, and it hasn't been easy. At all." Elijah takes a drink of his beer, starts to peel the label off, and doesn't look up when he says, "And it still isn't."

"What are you trying to say, Elijah?" Julia asks while staring out into the crowd of people dancing to Brandi Carlile's "The Things I Regret." "I feel like you're less okay with this than you originally let on."

Elijah sighs, removes his hat, and wipes his brow. "I'm fine with it, Julia, but…"

"But what, Elijah?" All of sudden, Julia is becoming more and more irritated.

"We know nothing about you," he says calmly. He's obviously better at handling himself while inebriated. "You share nothing. You tell us *nothing.*"

"Elena knows enough about me." Julia's tone is harsh, but she doesn't care.

"Does she?"

"What the hell are you trying to get at, Elijah? Huh? Are you trying to imply that I've been lying to you guys?"

"No, Julia, that's not it at all." Elijah moves the hat up on his head, smooths two fingers over the brim, and looks straight at Julia. "I just want to know if I can trust you with my family. Elena, Cole, Caroline, they're my *family*. And honestly? If you hurt them, I'll have no issues taking you out to the middle of nowhere and leaving you for dead."

His words are smooth, like the blade of knife. "Elijah," Julia says, repositioning herself so she can look him square in the eye. "Listen to me, okay? This? This person standing in front of you? This is the most authentic version of myself I have *ever* been. And just because I don't confide in every person I meet and tell my deepest, darkest secrets"—she pauses, fidgets with the straw of her drink, looks away from Elijah—"goddammit, it doesn't mean…I'm just…" Julia takes a very deep breath and lets it out, her breath probably smelling like a distillery, "I don't want to hurt her, Elijah. Or Cole. Or you *or Caroline*." Another pause, another deep breath, another chance to spill it all to yet another person. "Can you please, please, just try to trust me?"

"What are you running from?"

"Elijah—"

"No, Julia, tell me that. You want me to trust you? You need to trust me then. Trust is a two-way street, isn't it?"

Julia clenches her fists. Alcohol typically makes her feel bigger than she really is, so her usual behavior would be to punch this dick in the face and run. But this time, she knows she can't do that. She takes a deep breath, then looks away from him. "Please, don't make me do this."

"Julia."

"Okay. Listen." Julia downs the rest of her drink and looks at Elijah. "I hit one of my abusive foster parents with a car, then stole the car and ran away with it. I went to jail for four years for it. I worked odd jobs and found a way to survive for the next five years. And when I say, 'odd jobs,' I mean I did some *crazy* shit. And then, as if my life wasn't fucked up enough, I met my actual real parents, and they hated me because I'm a convict, and I didn't turn out how they wanted. So, Elijah, I'd really rather not talk about this. Ever again. Please fucking *stop* pushing me or—"

"Julia…"

"Elijah, just please stop."

"We love you. We can be your family, Julia," Elijah says, his voice deep, assertive.

Julia's breathing is becoming erratic as she tries to tamp down her emotions. "You *are* my family," she whispers.

"Okay, Jules. Okay."

Her smile is a silent *thanks* as she pulls away from him and walks away.

❖

Julia finds Elena at the bar, runs her fingertips down Elena's arm, and links their fingers together. "Would you dance with me?" Julia whispers, pressing her breasts against Elena's back.

Elena's sharp intake of breath makes Julia smile as she leads Elena onto the floor. Julia slides her arm around Elena's waist, pulling her closer than is probably necessary. She revels in the feel of Elena's arm around her shoulders and how wonderful it feels to have their hands linked together.

The Sirens are two notes into Aretha Franklin's version of "You Send Me" when Elena looks at Julia. "How did you know?"

"That this was your favorite song?"

Elena smiles. "Yes."

"A little birdie told me," Julia replies, softly, glancing at Caroline over Elena's shoulder.

"Well, tell Caroline I said thanks." Elena chuckles, stepping closer to Julia's body.

Julia's mind is running wild. Elijah pushing and pushing was almost enough to make her disappear into the night. And now? Elena dancing with her like this is enough to make her melt into a puddle onto the floor.

"Julia, dear, your heart is racing," Elena says softly, lifting her head to look at Julia. "Are you okay?"

"Yeah," Julia finally says after a very long pause. "I'm just…" She stops again, looks directly into Elena's eyes. "I'm ready to go back to the cabin…with you."

Elena stops moving, pulls away slightly, and their eyes lock. "Let me check in with the staff, then we can leave."

"Okay," Julia whispers. She watches as Elena moves through the thinning crowd over to the wait staff. And for maybe the millionth time, she wonders what the fuck she has gotten herself into.

And her only answer is, maybe it's love.

CHAPTER SIXTEEN

They're barely inside the cabin before Julia feels Elena's hands on her hips. Elena turns Julia around and pushes her against the wall as if Julia weighs nothing. When Julia feels the coolness of the wood paneling thud against her back, her eyes lock onto Elena's. There's a moment when she sees a flash of something there in those eyes that have captivated her since the beginning. Is it lust? Is it fear? Is it love? All Julia knows is that when Elena captures her mouth with hers, it's the most intense kiss she has ever had. And Julia has kissed before. But this is the first time a kiss has almost ruined her.

Elena's teeth are on Julia's tongue, her lips pressed into her as if she's searching for salvation. Elena moves, bites down on Julia's jawline, lays a path from Julia's chin to her pulse point. When Elena moves to Julia's earlobe and pulls it into her mouth, Julia's panties instantly become soaked. She can tell without even touching herself that she is drenched. Julia can't help but pull Elena closer, hoping she'll reach down and feel what she has caused.

"I need you," Julia says into Elena's kiss. Elena chuckles. At first Julia thinks it's because of her confession, but then she realizes that Elena has moved her hand up Julia's leg and is in between her legs and she knows…she knows how wet Julia is now.

"My God," Elena says, and it's followed by a low growl. "You are so fucking wet."

Julia is embarrassed that she let herself get to this point so quickly. Swollen, aching, ready to explode. And if Elena were to touch Julia just a little bit more, graze against her clit just a little rougher, Julia would come so fast it'd be laughable.

"What do you want?" Elena says against Julia's cheek before pulling back. Elena's eyes are so beautiful. Julia can't stand it. Her knees are so weak, and her calf muscles are quivering.

"I want you to," Julia says. She pauses because all of a sudden, she is so self-conscious.

"Want me to *what*?"

"God, Elena, don't make me say it."

"Say it," she says. The way she licks her lips and nudges Julia's nose with hers makes Julia's entire body shiver with anticipation.

"Fuck me," Julia says, and it comes out low and guttural, and she barely even recognizes her own voice.

"I'm sorry?" Elena's eyebrow arches, and her lips are a rose color Julia has never seen on her before. Her lips look bruised in a delicious way. "What was that?"

Julia groans and pushes her hips into Elena, who locks her eyes onto Julia's and smiles seductively. Julia shakes her head and whines. "You *heard* me."

"I didn't, though." Elena has her hands on Julia's hips; her dress is hiked up above those hands, and Elena's fingers are digging into her skin. Julia can feel Elena's thumbs pressing into the spot right under her hip bones, and *why the fuck does that feel so good?*

"I said, I want you to fuck me," Julia says, finally, giving in to her. Elena moves her left hand beneath Julia's lace panties. The second Elena's fingers touch Julia, Elena's eyes widen, and she bites her lip. She slides through Julia's folds easily, and when Elena pushes a finger inside, Julia can't help but moan. Julia realizes Elena likes the sound when she bites down even harder on her own lip. "Elena," she says softly as Elena pushes a second finger inside her. Elena is so gentle with her, and Julia can't stop watching her. Elena's eyes don't leave Julia's, either, even as she starts to thrust harder. Julia hikes her left leg onto Elena's hip, and it's Elena's turn to moan.

"You are so fucking beautiful," she says. Julia doesn't know what it is about the way Elena looks at her, but she is the only person that has ever made Julia feel beautiful.

"You're blind," Julia says quietly, and Elena thrusts into her hard. Julia cries out because it hurts so good.

"Take it back," she says.

Julia smiles. "No."

She thrusts into Julia, hard, and pulls out to do it again. "Take it back."

Julia bites her lip and shakes her head, and Elena thrusts into her again.

"Take it back, *please*," Elena says. Julia feels Elena slowly pull her fingers out. She immediately misses those fingers and feels so empty without Elena filling her up. Elena leans forward and kisses Julia, her tongue dipping into Julia's mouth in the most sensual way. Elena lets go of the kiss. "You know I can make you believe it."

"How?"

"By fucking you as hard as I can." It's so matter-of-fact that Julia can't help but smile at Elena. "Tell me you believe me," Elena says. "That you're beautiful."

"I'm beautiful." Julia's voice is soft, almost inaudible, but Elena heard her. The smile Elena gives Julia causes her already fleeting breath to leave her almost entirely. "I'm still going to fuck you hard."

Julia reaches down and pulls her dress up and over her shoulders. She's standing in front of Elena, black bra, panties, red Chucks, and in that moment, the look in Elena's eyes is unmistakable. It's love. This woman loves Julia. "What are you waiting for, then?"

Elena drops to her knees and grabs Julia's panties. She practically rips them off of Julia as she pulls them down her legs. She helps Julia step out them while sliding her shoes off at the same time. It's amazing, the push and pull; how one minute, Elena is ravenous, and the next, she's as gentle as can be. Julia wonders if Elena let herself go, didn't restrain herself, if she would wreck Julia completely. Julia watches when Elena leans forward and puts her mouth on Julia's center. She can see Elena's red lips as they land on her skin. She sees Elena's tongue dart out and lick Julia's swollen clit. Elena puts her hand on Julia's ass and pulls Julia's center into her. Elena's other hand is on Julia's leg as she guides it up and over her shoulder. The wood paneling is so smooth against Julia's back. She wonders if anyone else has ever been fucked so completely before in this space?

Elena pulls Julia's clit into her mouth, rolls it between her teeth, and it's then that Julia hears herself. She was so lost in the feel of Elena's mouth, her tongue, her lips, that she felt as if she left her body, left Earth and floated above, watching as the most amazing woman Julia has ever met has her way with her. She reaches down and runs her hand through Elena's hair and then pushes Elena's mouth harder into her wetness. "Don't stop," Julia says as Elena slides two fingers into her. The friction coupled with Elena's constant contact on Julia's clit is working, and her first orgasm crashes into her like an avalanche. Only it's not cold; it's hot and *wet* and so fucking amazing. Julia cries out and says Elena's name over and over like a prayer.

Elena looks up. She's holding up Julia, whose legs are like Jell-O. Elena guides Julia's leg down, firmly plants her foot on the ground, and stands. The light catches the glimmer of Julia's wetness on her face, and Julia almost comes again from the sheer sexiness of it all. Elena's eyes seem darker, if that's possible. Elena leans forward and kisses Julia, and she tastes herself on Elena's tongue. "God, Elena," she says into her kisses. "You are amazing."

"Oh, City Girl, that is only the beginning."

Julia can't help but laugh, deep and throaty, as Elena wraps her arms around Julia. "Oh, really?" Julia says against Elena's ear.

Elena takes Julia's hand and leads her into the bedroom. The room has a dim glow from the outside lights, but it's just enough for Julia to make out every curve of Elena's body. Aside from Julia's own heartbeat, she can hear the music from the party, low, with a small amount of bass.

Elena undresses herself quickly. Almost too quickly. Julia wanted to do it…wanted to take her time doing it…but Elena clearly has no patience. Julia isn't disappointed, though. She knows she'll eventually get her chance to undress Elena, one article of clothing at a time. Now, the only thing Julia gets to take off is Elena's panties, and *holy shit*, they're black and a thong, and Julia's mouth goes dry when she finally sees how gorgeous Elena's body is. Julia reaches forward and slides her fingertips over Elena's C-section scar, over the soft, trimmed hair on her center. Elena moans, and the sound makes Julia instantly wet again. Julia catches Elena's eyes in the soft glow of the lights. It hits Julia hard in that moment that she is so in love with Elena. She can feel the emotion bubbling in her throat, and she has to swallow to keep from crying. Julia breaks eye contact, bends her head, and takes in the sight of Elena's full breasts. Her areolas are a shade or two darker than her skin, and her nipples are so hard. Julia smiles. Not because it's funny, but because she honestly never thought she would get to see Elena like this, and she is so excited and happy.

"What are you smiling at?" Elena asks, her voice low, throaty, amazing. *Fuck, her voice.* How can a voice be so fucking perfect and sexy?

Julia reaches forward and ever so lightly runs a finger around one of Elena's nipples. "I'm smiling because I'm happy," she says before she leans forward and captures that same nipple in her mouth. Elena's sharp intake of air spurs Julia on, and she gently starts to massage both of Elena's breasts. She tweaks one nipple between her forefinger and thumb, pulls on it as she sucks and bites gently on the other. Elena is moaning, and her hips are rocking.

"Oh my God, Julia," she says, and it's followed by a groan, and then her body starts to quiver. Julia's eyes widen as she looks up at Elena, who instantly starts laughing.

"What…"

"Yeah," Elena says while continuing to laugh. She smooths her hands over her face, and Julia can tell Elena is embarrassed.

"Are you okay?"

Another laugh and she finally looks at Julia. "Yes. I just fucking came from you playing with my nipples."

A smile spreads across Julia's lips, and she's sure it's a blind smile because she has never done that to a woman before. "Wow."

"Yeah. That's a first for me."

"God," Julia says quietly. "Think I can make you come with my mouth now?"

Elena guides Julia toward the bed, her hands on Julia's shoulders. "Please, yes." And she pushes Julia back onto the bed, and she lands with a thud. Julia can't take her eyes off Elena as she easily straddles Julia's hips. Julia lifts her center until it's touching Elena's, and she's so wet against Julia. She wants to fuck her so bad. She has never wanted another person like she wants Elena Bennett. It's consuming every inch of her.

"Ride my face," Julia says, and Elena does as instructed. She places her knees on either side of Julia's face and within seconds, Julia is licking Elena's folds, sucking Elena into her mouth, dipping her tongue into Elena's center. And Elena has found her rhythm, moving her hips, rubbing her wetness on Julia's mouth and chin. She looks up at Elena, at her hands as they grip the headboard. She is so goddamn sexy, and her voice is so amazing as she says Julia's name, moans so loud, and says "fuck" more times than Julia has ever heard from her.

Julia has Elena's clit in her mouth now, and her hands are on Elena's ass.

Elena looks down at Julia, bites her lip, and moans before she says, "Put your fingers inside me."

Julia does as she's asked when Elena leans forward more. She fills Elena with two fingers. Julia isn't sure how she contorts herself, but she is successful, and Elena starts grinding even more. Julia can tell Elena is close. She has never understood a body more than she has with Elena, and she can sense it as Elena's orgasm approaches. And then, as if on command, Elena clenches around Julia's fingers, and it happens. Elena comes, and Julia feels Elena's wetness dripping down her chin. Julia looks up at her as she sags against the headboard. Her ass is on Julia's chest, her knees bent, her stomach moving in and out with her heavy breathing. Her hair is hanging around her face. Julia is so enamored watching her as she comes down.

Elena starts to laugh, and it shakes Julia's entire body. "I'm sorry," she says finally.

"For what?" Julia's fingers slide from Elena's wetness as she dismounts from Julia's chest and face. Elena leans against the headboard. Her breasts look so perfect, and Julia wants to suck and bite her nipples again. Julia wants to laugh at herself because she is so hot for Elena. It's ridiculous.

"I came all over your face."

"Are you kidding me?" Julia asks as she rolls toward Elena. "That was the hottest thing that has ever happened to me."

"Julia," she says in a whisper. She runs her fingertips over Julia's cheek, down her jawline to Julia's chin. "*You* are the hottest thing that has ever happened to me."

Julia rolls her eyes and goes to sit up, but Elena makes a move and somehow tops her. Julia's on her stomach, though, and Elena is in between her legs. Elena leans down against Julia's back, presses her breasts into Julia, gets insanely close to her ear and says, "Are you ready to be fucked?"

Julia swears that it's a primal need that makes her legs open wider. Elena chuckles against Julia's ear, and dammit if Julia isn't soaked again. Elena moves down Julia's back, her breasts touching Julia the entire time. Julia can feel Elena's nipples against her lower back, the dimples that she has above her ass, then as hard pebbles dancing across her ass cheeks. She runs her nails up the backs of Julia's legs. She places her lips on Julia's right ass cheek and bites down hard. Julia groans and pushes her ass into Elena until she finally feels Elena's fingers slip inside her. Julia slides up onto her knees, backing into Elena, giving her access to everything, her heart, her soul, her entire world. Elena starts out slow, then starts to thrust harder and faster, with so much intensity that Julia feels herself start to cry. It doesn't hurt. No. It feels *so good.* Julia has never felt this good before. She didn't know she could ever feel this good. And then Elena reaches around with her free hand and starts to massage Julia's clit.

And oh, God, Julia was wrong before.

This is the best she has ever felt.

"Kneel," Elena says, and Julia doesn't argue. She would literally do anything Elena asked. Julia would die if Elena asked her to. Elena latches onto Julia's earlobe again. *Fuck, why does that feel so fucking good?* When Elena lets go, she says, "Are you going to come for me?"

Julia turns her head and kisses Elena as her orgasm builds. It's so close, dancing on the precipice, ready to free-fall into the abyss. Elena knows it's close, too, because Julia can feel her smiling into the kiss. "Elena," Julia says against her lips. And her gentle *mm-hmm* reverberates into Julia's mouth. "Please don't stop fucking me."

"I'll never stop," she whispers.

And that's the moment when Julia's entire world shatters. Her orgasm rips through her body, throwing her forward, and she braces herself against the mattress. It's literally the best orgasm Julia has ever had. Elena continues to thrust gently, and Julia is still so very open for her. Another orgasm builds and hits Julia like a runaway train. She finally collapses onto the bed, completely spent. Elena stills inside Julia, whose entire body is pulsating. *Every* muscle. Every fiber of her being. Elena wiggles her fingers, and Julia can't help it when she shouts, "Please stop!" Elena laughs against Julia's ass before she ever so slowly slides her fingers out of Julia's wetness. "Not funny."

Elena rolls to the side, pushes Julia's hair away from her face, and runs a damp finger across Julia's cheek. "You okay?"

"Yes," Julia says. Then she breathes out and corrects herself. "No." She smiles. "Maybe?"

"I told you I was going to fuck you hard," Elena says before she leans forward and kisses Julia's forehead.

"You weren't lying."

Elena laughs as she snuggles down next to Julia. She pulls a blanket from the end of the bed up around them. "Go to sleep," she says. "City Girl."

❖

Julia's eyes slide open. She blinks, then looks around the bedroom. She realizes she's alone in bed. She squints at the red numbers on the digital clock on the bedside table.

2:37 a.m.

She slides out of bed, taking the sheet with her as she pads down the hallway into the kitchen. The light over the sink is on, and Elena is leaning against the countertop wearing a very loose AC/DC T-shirt. She's holding a glass of water, her hair is a mess, and the entire scene makes Julia's heart race.

"You okay?" Julia asks when Elena smiles before downing the rest of the water.

Elena nods, wiping her mouth with the back of her hand nonchalantly. She takes a couple steps toward Julia. "I was thirsty," she says softly. "And really hot."

"Mmm, you are definitely hot," Julia responds, her voice low. "My T-shirt looks good on you."

"You think so?"

Julia runs her hand up under the material to Elena's bare ass. "Yes," she says, pulling Elena toward her. "Come back to bed with me."

Elena pulls the sheet up and up until Julia's legs are exposed. She then moves her hand under the sheet and slips it between Julia's thighs. "We could christen this room," Elena says.

"That isn't a bad idea." Julia moves her hand from Elena's ass to between her thighs and mimics Elena's movements. And within seconds, Julia is pressing Elena's back to the wall of the small kitchen, and Elena is moaning Julia's name over and over again. "That was far too easy," Julia says as she adjusts the sheet still wrapped around her body.

Elena breathes out, then with one smooth movement, pulls the sheet from Julia and drops it on the floor. "Well, I guess it's my turn now."

Julia pulls Elena toward her and kisses her deeply, all too excited to let Elena have her turn.

Chapter Seventeen

As Julia wakes up in the morning, she feels a jolt course through her body when she remembers that she isn't alone. She looks over at Elena, who is on her stomach, and her hair is wild, and all Julia wants at that moment is to start their night before all over again.

Julia tears her eyes away from Elena's sleeping figure and looks up at the ceiling, flashbacks flooding her memory. She in't a stranger to good sex, but last night? Is it a cliché to say it was *mind-blowing*? Oh well if it is, because that is the only way to describe it. And Elena. *Elena...* She was perfection wrapped in the body of a goddess.

"What are you doing awake?"

A smile spreads across Julia's lips as she turns her head to look at Elena. "Couldn't sleep." Julia rolls closer and runs her fingertips down Elena's bare back.

Elena sighs. "That feels nice."

Julia leans over and places her lips on the bare skin in front of her. "Last night was fun," she whispers between kisses.

"It was more than fun," Elena says before she adjusts herself. "It was—"

"Perfect? Incredible? Everything I never knew I wanted?"

"All of the above."

"Spend the day with me." Julia runs a finger down the length of Elena's arm, crossing the faint tan line on her bicep. "Spend the day *naked* with me," she corrects herself.

Elena nods and smiles before she pulls Julia into a kiss.

❖

The two women spend most of the morning finding new ways to make each other moan.

And scream.

And curse.

And take the Lord's name in vain.

Julia learns quickly that Elena comes harder when she has Julia's tongue inside her, and when she alternates between sucking and biting at Elena's clit. The way Elena's breath hitches in her throat and her back arches, and her muscles in her neck tighten; Julia is now an addict, and making Elena come is her drug.

They climax together more than once, and Julia realizes that coming together, with their fingers inside the other, their mouths busy kissing each other, is the most intense and real feeling she has ever felt. It's only when they are both completely spent that they peel themselves out of bed and shower together, where the sex is only intensified by the water and the feel of cold tiles pressed against warm bodies. Julia leaves a mark on Elena's inner thigh, and Elena smiles when she sees it, says she feels like a teenager again. And when Julia rakes her fingers down Elena's back, she is instantly turned on by the sight of the dark red marks that remain.

It's late afternoon when they finally emerge from their sex-induced haze. Elena starts to rummage through Julia's fridge. "Your food supply is laughable, Miss Finch."

A warmth fills Julia's chest as she turns and looks at Elena. She is wearing a pair of Julia's running shorts and a Star Wars T-shirt. It's quite possibly the best sight Julia has ever seen. She walks toward her and runs her hands up the back of Elena's bare thighs. "I know what we could eat," she whispers, reaching around to cup Elena's still warm center.

Elena turns and instantly starts kissing Julia. "How do you do that to me?" she asks between kisses.

Julia shrugs before she slips her hand under the waistband of the shorts Elena is wearing *without* panties. She can feel that Elena is already damp, and just touching the wetness makes Julia feel the same way. "Elena?"

"Yes?" she says, panting, looking at Julia.

"I want to fuck you again," Julia says quietly as she slides her fingers through Elena's wetness.

"Do it," Elena replies. "Please." Julia backs her up against the countertop before she slides in two fingers. Elena leans her head back, spreads her legs a little wider, allowing Julia to go deeper. Julia's thumb starts to brush against her clit. "Julia, I'm going to come," Elena says.

"Come for me," Julia whispers. She repeats herself, adding Elena's name. She watches as Elena's orgasm hits. Her hands are gripping the countertop, her breathing is ragged, and she looks so *fucking* incredible.

Elena starts to laugh after Julia slowly slides her fingers from Elena's center. "Dammit," she says quietly. "I was all clean."

"Not anymore," Julia says as she looks at Elena and takes in a deep breath. "Do you realize how beautiful you are?"

"Julia," Elena whispers. She leans forward and places her lips on Julia's, kissing her deeply. She wraps her arms around Julia's slender frame and holds on tight.

❖

Elena manages to find enough ingredients to throw together a pasta dish with tomatoes, garlic, and basil. Julia is thankful that Elena started filling her fridge with supplies; otherwise, they'd be eating crackers and beer.

"You know this basil keeps much better if you put it in water and place a bag over it?"

"You're kidding me, right? I didn't even realize you put that in there, let alone know how to keep the stuff *fresh*."

Elena rolls her eyes and continues to stir the tomatoes and garlic. Julia watches as Elena adds a pinch of red pepper flakes. "Gives it a kick," Elena says when she glances at Julia.

"You think we need more heat between us?" Julia asks as she raises her glass of water to her lips.

"Heat isn't bad," Elena says. She dips a clean spoon into the sauce and raises it to her lips. When she tastes it, she looks at Julia.

"Jesus," Julia mumbles from her spot where she's seated on the counter, white knuckling the countertop. Her entire body tingles at the sight of Elena with the spoon in her mouth. "You're a tease."

"Maybe." A smile spreads across Elena's lips. "Would you rather I not tease?"

"You're joking, right?" She doesn't wait for a response when she says, "You could tease me all day, every day, if you really wanted to." She takes another drink of her water. "Of course," she says as she sets the glass on the countertop, "I'll have to pay you back eventually."

"Oh, you think so, huh?" Elena discards the spoon and takes the couple steps toward Julia. She places both hands on Julia's bare thighs, a look of pure desire on her face. "I feel like I'll always win with the teasing."

"Why do you think that?" Julia asks, her response broken up by her labored breathing.

Elena smiles as she heads back to the stove. She takes the pasta from the colander and then mixes it into the sauce. "I just have a feeling."

After the two eat dinner and Julia tells Elena over and over again how awesome it all tastes, Julia starts to feel their evening and morning activities catching up with her. Both women retire to the couch, the glow from the lamp illuminating Elena while Julia relaxes at the other end. There's a knock at the screen door, which is followed by Cole's voice. "Mom? Jules?"

Elena picks her head up from the book she's reading. "Cole?"

"I just wanted to tell you that I'm home," Cole says after he lets himself into the cabin. He flips his boots off at the door and makes his way over to his mom on the couch. After he leans over and kisses Elena on the cheek, he waves a hand at Julia. She smiles at him, at the way his hair is sticking up all over the place and the sheen of sweat still on his skin.

"How was your night, dear? I hope you didn't get into any trouble," Elena says.

Cole sits cross-legged on the floor in front of the couch and snorts quietly. He's still in his dark blue jeans from the night before, but he has on a white undershirt. "No, no trouble," he says, his voice deep. "But it was a super fun night."

Julia smiles. "Hey," she says, "did you get to hang out with Allison?"

The blush that fills Cole's cheeks is reminiscent of his mother's. His eyes are wide when he says Julia's name in a voice that is laced with worry and embarrassment.

"Cole, I know about your crush on Allison," Elena says.

"You *do?*"

"Yes, I do."

"*How?*"

"Because I'm your mother, and I know everything. And besides, you are about as subtle as a freight train." Elena purses her lips. "You light up like the Fourth of July around her."

"I do not!" he says as he looks at Julia. "Jules, back me up. *Please.*"

"Not the Fourth of July, Elena," Julia says, and Cole beams. "See?"

"I'd say more like a five-alarm fire."

"Julia!" Cole says. "That is *not* true!"

"I think that's a perfect description." Elena grins as she looks over at Julia and winks. "So, did you hang out all night with this girl?"

"Ugh, *Mom,*" he says, elongating the *O.* "I really can't talk to you about this stuff."

"Why not?" Elena asks, followed by a huff. "I am a great person to talk to about this."

Cole leans back and props himself up with his hands. "Fine," he says. He sounds as if he can barely control his excitement. "She asked me out on a date."

Julia's fist shoots up in the air, a smile plastered on her face. "Cole! That's great!"

"Yeah, she said she really loved my vest, too." He nods at Julia. "I owe you for telling me to ditch the jacket."

"I'm telling you, I know my stuff."

"So, what did you guys do today?" Cole asks. He looks from Julia to his mom.

They exchange a look, then say, "Nothing."

Cole cocks an eyebrow and tilts his head. Julia wonders how perceptive he really is. "Ah, a lazy day," he says, eyebrow still raised.

Both women nod, again in unison.

Cole motions to Elena's shirt. "Nice shirt," he says with a grin.

"I just borrowed it," she says quickly.

"*Sure,*" Cole says.

Julia cannot get over how much Cole resembles his mother at times, and now, with his eyebrow arched and that little smirk on his face, he looks exactly like her. Julia doesn't speak for fear of blowing their "lazy day" cover. Although, clearly, this kid is a regular Sherlock Holmes and is already putting together the puzzle of his mother and the ranch hand.

Cole gets to his feet, brushes off his pants, then bends down to kiss his mom on the cheek. He says good-bye to Julia, and when he picks up his cowboy boots, he turns to say, "You know there's no sense in hiding *this*"—he motions back and forth between Julia and his mom—"from me." He smiles. "I'm *totally* okay with it."

Julia looks at Elena, her mouth hanging open slightly. "Um," she manages to get out, and then she hears Cole chuckle before he leaves, the screen door banging shut behind him. "What just happened?"

"I have no idea."

"I think your son just outed us."

"I think you're right," Elena says. She places her hand on Julia's leg, which is still stretched out over her lap. "Are you okay with that?"

Surprisingly, yes, she's really okay with it. She didn't give a shit about people knowing the night before. So of course she's okay with Cole knowing. And when other people start to find out, she won't let it ruin everything. But she can feel it in her bones. Her emotions are running rampant, pulling her in a dozen different directions. The need to run, to flee, to get the hell out of there, followed by the need to stay, to love, to *be loved*. She smiles, tries to remain calm and says, "I am." Because after she pushes that need to hate herself that is always bubbling below the surface, she really is okay…At least for the time being.

CHAPTER EIGHTEEN

It's three weeks after Julia has finally settled completely into the ranch. Elena and Julia spend so much time together that it's no longer a secret. Even Penn knows, and Julia is clearly a thorn in her side. Julia doesn't care, though. She is happy. Maybe the first time in her life, she feels at peace. And she feels free.

The best part? Aside from the amazing nights (and sometimes mornings and afternoons) she has with Elena?

Julia has repaid her debt to Elijah.

When he drops her off at the front of the auto body shop, Elijah smiles. "You ever think this day would come?"

Julia laughs. Her hand is on the door handle. She notices that her palms are sticky with sweat. She's nervous, and she knows it's because they're picking up her car. "No, actually. I thought you'd own my ass forever." Julia opens the door, climbs out of the truck, and slams the door.

"City Girl?"

Julia turns and looks into the passenger window of the truck. "Yeah?"

"You know this doesn't mean you have to leave the ranch, right?"

Julia doesn't want to leave, but this car is like cocaine to a cocaine addict, and the thought of having it back frightens her. "I know," she says.

"I think Leia would be pretty sad to see you go."

"Had to mention that, didn't you?"

Elijah shrugs. "Go on. Get your car."

Julia watches Elijah drive away before she makes her way to the door of the auto body shop. When she enters, she sees Ray standing behind the counter. He looks up, a dopey grin on his weathered face. "Ray, how are ya?" She glides toward the counter, presses her palms against the glass top, and studies the old man.

"Oh, City Girl, I thought you weren't comin' back for your baby. I was all ready to take her off yer hands for ya." Ray's eyes twinkle. "She's runnin' like a beast now."

"I knew you'd be able to fix her. I'm sorry that it's taken so long for me to get back to pick her up. It's been crazy up at the ranch."

He looks her up and down. "Ranch life seems to be treatin' ya well there. You're not thinkin' 'bout gettin' into this car and drivin' off toward that sunset you were so tore up about before, are ya? I know ol' Elijah would be sad to see ya go."

Julia smiles. "Oh, he would now, would he? That's not how he acts."

"He hides it well," Ray says, followed by a deep, gravelly chuckle. "Come on now. Let's go get you set up."

Julia follows Ray through the back office that is piled high with papers and old car parts, then through another room that has even more car parts, some in new, clean boxes, some just gathering dust. Ray pushes the back door to the building, and it swings open and hits the outside wall with a clang. She sees her car immediately, shining in the sun. She looks at Ray, then the car. "She looks great! What'd you do to her?"

"Well, she got a wash, and I waxed her myself. When was the last time you did that? She was pretty bad. And the rust. Jesus Christ, the rust."

Julia laughs. "I'm from Chicago. Our cars rust."

"Take care of her." Ray grins, showing off his gnarly teeth as he drops the keys into Julia's hand. "And come back in three thousand miles for an oil change."

Julia climbs in, sits in the driver's seat, and slides the key into the ignition. The gas pedal feels strange under the sole of her boot. It's a weird sensation, sitting in this beast and not being eager to get the fuck out of town. When she turns the car over and it roars to life, the urge to run washes over her. *Ah, there it is.* She wondered when that old nagging fear of commitment and love would finally smack into her.

It's fitting that it is happening in the very tool she uses to fulfill the addiction to flee. She's not sure what to do with the emotion other than dismiss it as fast as it hit her, but the lingering urge is still sitting above her heart, even after all these months. Now that she has the car, what should she do?

She pulls around the corner of the building and looks right. That direction is where she came from, the way out of this town, away from everything that has become familiar. If she turns that way, she'll break Elena's heart, her spirit, her soul. Hell, she'll break her *own* spirit and soul if she leaves, and she knows that.

She closes her eyes and turns her head to the left. When she opens them, it hits her. Home is that way. Home is to the left. And it's the only way she should be going. She checks her rearview mirror. Ray has been watching the whole time, his arms folded across his chest, his dirty boot tapping the pavement. She revs the engine, fixes her eyes back on the road, and turns the wheel to the left, pulling onto the road that will take her home.

❖

Driving onto the dirt road to the ranch in her own car is refreshing. After driving around and exploring for a couple hours, Julia feels complete again. It'd be funny to say that to someone who has never felt a connection to a car, but this car has been with her through everything. It's the most reliable relationship she's ever had. Well, except, of course, until now.

She pulls in next to the old Ford trucks and turns the engine off. "Ah," she says, running her hand over the steering wheel. "Home at last."

"City Girl, you're back! I thought for sure that was the last we'd see of you."

Julia shakes her head. "Thanks, Elijah, for, y'know, paying for her."

"You're welcome," he says. He walks over, dust surrounding him. "She good now?"

"She's never run this good," Julia admits when she looks at the car. "It's pretty awesome, actually." She looks back at Elijah. "Did you really think I would leave?"

He smiles. "Kinda?"

"Man, still not trusted, I see."

"You were gone for a good three hours."

"I was out driving around. Testing her out. Letting the wind blow through my hair."

"Well, we were worried."

"We? Who's we?"

"Me, Caroline, Cole." Elijah clears his throat. "Elena."

"Shit." Julia feels her heart fall. "I gotta go find her. Where is she?"

Elijah motions to the horses. "She took off on Samwise about two hours ago. It's getting late, though. You shouldn't go after her."

"Hell yes, I should. I don't want her to think I left!" Julia sprints into the barn and over to Leia. "Wanna go for a ride, beautiful?" The horse's ears perk, and the gentle neigh that follows warms Julia's heart. "Let's go."

❖

Julia clicks her tongue, and Leia takes off into a gallop around the bend, into the clearing, and just past the aspen trees that surround the property. She adjusts the reins in her hand, feels the sturdy hoofbeats underneath her, and knows for the first time in forever that she's actually at peace. It's been a long time coming, this whole settling down thing, but she's starting to enjoy it. After the last couple weeks, she and Elena seem really good. They have so much fun together. And the sex? The sex is amazing! She's not sure what the hesitancy is with Elena, though. She can feel it in her kisses and the way her happiness seems to not quite reach her eyes, but Julia is trying to not worry. She's a worrier by trade, and it's starting to affect her the more she holds it in. Happiness has never lasted for Julia. So, why should this last? But there's no way she's going to let Elena think she took off. No way. Not this time. She's not going anywhere, and Elena needs to know.

When Julia cuts through the grazing field. She vividly remembers the spot where Sully and Scout were hanging out when she and Elijah found them. It's hard to believe that was almost two months ago. The way Elena had helped her up onto Samwise still causes chills to course through her body.

Julia sees Penn standing next to Sully. She, *of course*, looks like a picture-perfect cowgirl: hat, jeans, button-down shirt with the sleeves rolled up to the elbows, the whole package. Julia wants to vomit. Why does this woman have to be so threatening in all her beauty?

Penn takes her hat off and waves it at Julia from across the field. *When the hell is that asshole leaving?* Penn has already worn out her welcome, but she just keeps sticking around like a bad case of lice. Julia has asked Elena about it a couple times now, and she always gets the same answer: "She's helping out. We need the help, Julia." She wants to tell Elena to hire someone else, but it really isn't her business. She's so sick and tired of seeing Penn, though. And seeing Elena around Penn. It makes her skin crawl. Their interactions are always so cordial and kind. Penn's always putting a hand on Elena's shoulder or the small of her back, and it scares Julia to death because what if Elena isn't being honest? What if Elena is still in love with Penn? What if this whole thing between Julia and Elena has been a scam? The thoughts themselves make Julia want to scream.

Julia finally mimics the gesture with her ball cap. She still hasn't relented on the cowboy hat, and at this rate, she's not sure if she ever will. After she secures the hat back on her head, over her French-braided hair, she steers Leia over toward where Penn is with Sully. She's getting ready to ask if she's seen Elena, when out of the brush comes Elena mounted atop Samwise. "Elena!"

Elena's head jerks up. "Julia! Oh my God. I thought…" Her cheeks are flushed, and she looks utterly miserable.

"No, I didn't leave. I'm here!" Julia steers Leia toward Elena, and her eyes move from Elena to Penn and back to Elena before she opens her mouth to say, "What's going on?"

"Nothing," comes Elena's too-quick response. She won't even look at Julia now, which is making Julia's stomach churn.

"Elena," Julia says. "What the hell is going on?" She reaches out with her free hand as Elena moves past her on Samwise. She touches Elena's arm, but still Elena doesn't look. Julia looks at Penn, her eyes on fire. "Care to enlighten me?"

"We were just talking. Things got…" Penn pauses as she slides her foot into the stirrup on Sully, bounces once, then twice, and mounts the horse. After situating herself, she looks at Julia. "Things got heated."

"Heated?"

"Yes, *heated*."

"What the *fuck* does 'heated' mean?"

"It means there was some unresolved tension between us," Penn says. She pulls on a pair of leather riding gloves, and all Julia can do is roll her eyes. Riding gloves? *Really*? Of course, this bitch has riding gloves. What a fucking asshole.

"Penn, I swear to God—"

"Oh, please," Penn says. "I told you I'd find a way to get you to run, little girl. You're not winning this one." Her blue eyes look like glass, and her maniacal smile is making Julia want to punch her. Of all the times Julia wished she had learned a thing or two from her hard-ass cellmates, now is it.

Julia turns Leia around smoothly and takes off after Elena. She catches up to her with ease, and surprisingly, Elena stops Samwise. "What the hell is going on, Elena?"

"Penn kissed me." Elena spits the words out, and Julia almost feels as if she needs to duck so they don't hit her in the face.

Julia looks at Elena, her eyes, her lips, back to her eyes. "Did you kiss her back?"

"No!"

"Why did she try, then?"

"What do you mean?"

"Why did she try to kiss you? There had to have been a reason." Julia watches as Elena's facial expression goes from scared and embarrassed to sad and worried. "Did you give her the idea that it was something she should do?"

"Julia, listen to me. There's a lot of history—"

"No, Elena. Answer the *fucking* question." Julia is seething now. And Elena's expression is exactly why Julia never stays, and she always runs. "Did you give her reason to think she had a chance?" Again, Elena's eyes tell the whole story. "I was gone for a few hours, and you automatically assume that I'm gone for good? Don't you trust me? Don't you trust this? *Us?*"

"Julia, yes! I trust you! I thought you left! Just like she had—"

"Why would I run from you? From us?"

"I don't know," Elena whispers.

"Elena, you are everything I want. Why would I run?"

"I was scared."

"So am I!" Julia shouts. "I shared things with you that I have never shared before. And now this? Penn? You know how I feel about her and you. I've never trusted her with you."

"Penn isn't who I want! You have to believe me!"

"So, I'm supposed to believe you, but you don't even trust everything I've shared with you, everything I've done with you. None of that is enough for you? Now you have to break my heart on top of that? Don't you understand that this right here," she motions between where Penn is still perched atop Sully and Elena, "this is exactly the reason I didn't want to open up to you!"

"Julia, wait!"

But it's too late. Julia has taken off on Leia toward the clearing, past it now, over the hills, into the meadow, away from the house, the corral, everything. She's riding like crazy, and Leia lets her. The beautiful horse is carrying Julia with the ease and speed of a racehorse. The sound of her hooves is beating in time with Julia's heart, and she is so upset. So *very* upset.

It's not until they get about a hundred yards from the edge of Miller's Gap that Julia finally slows Leia down. They walk up to the edge of the ravine, and Julia instantly starts to cry. Her face is in her hands, and the world around her is spinning; she can feel everything and nothing all at once. This is it. This is why. This is why she always runs. All of these emotions and drama.

Trust is the worst of the human conditions. Why did she let herself do it? Why did she let herself get to the point where she trusted Elena Bennett? She knew it was only going to end in heartache. She fucking knew it!

Yet, she fell for the woman. For her spirit and beautiful soul…

And now this?

Julia leans forward and wraps her arms around Leia's neck. "I can't stay here, Leia," she says against her buckskin fur. Leia sniffs as if she understands, which makes Julia cry even harder. Her stomach is in knots. "Why did I get so attached to you?"

And she knows she really means why did she get so attached to Elena.

Oh, no. *And Cole*. Her heart almost breaks in half when she thinks about never seeing him again.

And Elijah!

"Goddammit," Julia says as she sits upright and pulls her ball cap down on her head. These fucking feelings! She wipes at her eyes and nose, smearing tears and snot across her face. She absolutely hates that she has let herself get to this point where she actually has feelings for anyone on this stupid ranch. Especially Elena. She knew she was going to get hurt. She just knew it.

Of course, Penn had to have the last laugh, didn't she? She had to be the one to finally win Elena back. Julia shakes her head, closes her eyes, and fights back the tears that are on the verge of reappearing. "I am not going to let this place get the best of me."

She cannot stay at the ranch, not when she doesn't feel welcome anymore. She's going to have to leave everything that has become familiar and safe. For the first time ever, she's going to run away from a place she doesn't want to leave. Her heart aches knowing that she was right about everything, though. Elena didn't really want something real with her. The thought that everything Julia went through with Elena was built on a lie makes Julia want to vomit. Every single time she opens up, this happens. But that's the last time she allows it to happen. She's not going to sit around and wait for her heart to get broken any more than it already is! No way! No how!

❖

The sun is low in the sky when Julia slows Leia to a trot as they approach the pasture before the house. The air is cooler, which is strange, but apparently, August gets that way in Colorado. Everything about the way the air feels is weird, though. Julia's hair is standing up on the back of her neck, and she wonders if maybe she's getting sick. Just what she needs. *A fucking cold.*

She keeps thinking about what her next move is going to be. It's been so wonderful not having to think like that. She's been planning her next move since she was a kid, moving from foster home to foster home. And then jail and now this? She got comfortable. She let Elena break her walls down. Now she has to start building them back up. The idea of reconstructing all those years and years of now blown apart rubble makes her stomach twist.

Julia shakes her head. It doesn't matter how much it hurts. It hurts more to *be* hurt by someone else. Leaving is her only option. Should she just pack her bags and her couple of boxes and hightail it out of there? Not tell a soul good-bye? Should she actually make a point to tell Cole that she'll miss him? And Elijah? Should she slug Penn in the jaw on the way out?

Her mind is going wild. She honestly has no idea what to do.

Julia hates the idea of leaving, though. She doesn't want to go anywhere! She finally admitted to herself that this, all of this, is her *home*. She loves her little cabin with the creaky, uneven floorboards and the wonderful lighting and the fireplace she hasn't been able to use yet. She even loves that damn bed with the mattress that is God only knows how old. She loathes the idea of packing her belongings back into those two sad little boxes, starting up the old Dart, and driving down the dusty road. She doesn't want to watch this place disappear into her rearview mirror. She wants to stay and be in love with Elena and live happily ever after. Isn't that what was supposed to happen?

Julia smooths her hand down Leia's neck. "What should I do, girl? Hmm?" she asks the horse, when all of a sudden, the horse stops in her tracks. Her ears are flat against her head, and Julia can feel the tension in her muscles.

"Leia, what's wrong?" Julia asks and starts to scan the area. She can hear Leia's nervous hoofbeats on the hard ground. She knows she needs to get the hell out of there. It's not safe.

And as soon as those words pass through her mind, she hears a low growl on her right-hand side. "Oh, Jesus," Julia whispers. She doesn't know what to do; everything feels as if it's moving in slow motion. And before she knows it, she's being bucked off the horse. Her back hits the ground with a horrible thud. She can barely breathe, her eyes slide closed, and she has no idea if this is the end or not.

Chapter Nineteen

When Julia opens her eyes, she has no idea where she is. The room is dark, the blinds are pulled, and the small lamp across the room isn't providing enough light to make anything discernable. She tries to lift her head but is met with a horrible, throbbing headache. And when she tries to move her body, she feels as if she's been hit by a Mack truck. Even her toes hurt. She looks around through squinted eyelids and sees Elena sitting next to the bed in a chair. She's sleeping, her head is leaned back on the back of the chair, and she has her hands clasped across her stomach.

Julia reaches to pull the covers from her body, and it's so hard to move. What the hell happened to her? Why is she so sore? All she can remember is riding Leia through the pasture. It was peaceful and cool, and everything was fine.

And then she remembers the low growl and the flash of fur and teeth and claws.

She clenches her eyes tight and tries to pull a deep breath into her lungs, but a coughing spell stops her.

"Hey," Elena says, her hands moving to Julia's shoulders, then down her arms. "Are you okay?" She's holding a glass with a straw. "Here. Water."

Julia is peering through one open eyelid, and she's not sure whether she should loathe her or love her right now because all she can remember is the hurt she had felt, but dammit, she really is thirsty. She takes the straw and sucks two gulps into her mouth. The water feels amazing as it fills her mouth and rushes down her dry throat.

"How are you feeling?"

Julia doesn't answer the question. Not just because she doesn't want to talk to Elena, ever again if possible, but also because she really doesn't know how she is feeling. Aside from being sore, she has no idea what really happened. Why is she in this bed? How long has she been here? What the hell happened?

"Julia, please. I need to know." Elena places her hand on Julia's forehead. It feels as if she's checking Julia's temperature, but Julia can't be positive.

"What happened?" Julia finally asks with a scratchy voice. She's surprised by how scared she sounds.

"A bear attacked." Elena's hand is held to her chest, clutching at her heart. "You know we've been seeing that one female around, but something must have spooked her, and she attacked."

Julia feels absolute fear flood her veins. "Leia," she says. "What happened to Leia?"

"She saved you, Julia." Elena's voice is so soft and sincere. "I don't know exactly how or what happened, but you were hardly harmed. The bear was dead, trampled, and Leia only has a few marks on her left side. Some pretty deep scratches and the vet came and gave her stitches, but..." Elena pauses. "Do you really not remember anything?"

Julia shakes her head, too afraid to answer.

"She carried you home, so you were semiconscious. I don't even know how she...how did she know to kneel down to you? How did she know? Were you conscious? You really don't remember?"

"No," Julia whispers. She closes her eyes, searches her memory bank, but sees nothing after her back hit the ground.

"Maybe it'll return as time goes on," Elena says. And Julia kind of hates her for how beautiful she looks right now in the lighting with her hair hanging loose over her shoulders and the baggy Denver Broncos sweatshirt on.

"Where am I?"

"My room." Elena leans back in the chair next to the bed and crosses her left leg over her right. "You have a couple broken ribs, and you're bruised up. I needed you close to me."

Julia rolls her eyes, and even that hurts. She breathes out, but all it does is cause her to start coughing, which hurts the rest of her muscles. "Don't think this changes anything," Julia finally is able to say after her coughing fit. "I'm still leaving."

"You mean you're running away?"

A wave of rage washes over Julia. It reminds her of the waves crashing into her when she would swim at the beach in Chicago when she was a kid, the cold Lake Michigan water with the undertow and the current and the inability to ever truly feel in control. She has no idea what to say to Elena to defend herself, which she knows only means she has no defense, and that pisses her off even more.

Elena leans forward, props her elbows on her knees, and looks down at her hands. "Listen, Julia—"

"I do not want to talk to you about whatever you're going to bring up." Julia raises her hand and stops Elena. "I really don't."

"Can you please let me just explain? I think I deserve that."

"Yeah, well, I didn't deserve to be treated like that, yet here we are." Julia watches as Elena's eyes fill with tears. It's hard to be a spectator right now because it's taking everything in Julia to stay strong. And she wants to stay strong. She does. But Elena's eyes and that damn quiver of her lip makes Julia's heart flutter. "Tell me, then. Explain."

Elena wipes away tears that have made their way from her eyes onto her cheeks. "You know, Julia, I like you a lot, but you can be real pain in the ass when you want to be." Elena wipes at her nose with a Kleenex. "You think any of this has been easy? I'd be lying if I said Penn being here didn't throw me for a loop. It did. I loved her. She came into my life at a time when I really needed it…needed her."

"You can have her," Julia says. "I really don't care anymore, Elena."

"Would you let me finish, please?" Elena looks at Julia, shakes her head, and sighs. "You act like this has been a cakewalk for me. You think you coming in here with that chip on your shoulder was something I bargained for? I did not want, nor did I need, another woman in my life. Especially one with the ability to break down my walls. Yet you showed up with that smile that took my breath away, and those green eyes that saw into my soul. And the horses…You're so good with them. So, so good with them." Elena smiles. "And don't even get me started on Cole. And the way he bonded with you. He loves you. And him opening up to you made his relationship with me better. It's been forever since he's laughed or genuinely smiled. As a mother, seeing your child smile after not seeing it in forever…I can't explain it to you." Elena pauses, looks down at her hands, then back at Julia. "So, I could not stop myself."

Dammit. Julia feels herself getting ready to crack.

"I don't want Penn, Julia," Elena says, her voice so quiet in the dimly lit room.

Julia tries to push herself up onto her elbows in the bed. It's hard, and all of her muscles are straining, but she finally manages to adjust herself. She's looking at Elena, at her sad eyes, and all she wants to do is kiss her. She's crumbling like a cookie.

"Mom?" comes Cole's voice, followed by a knock on the closed bedroom door.

Elena's head drops, and she can't help but chuckle. "He always interrupts us, doesn't he?" she whispers.

Julia shakes her head and shares in the soft laughter. "He really does."

"Yes, Cole?" Elena says, and the door swings open.

Cole's eyes light up when he looks at Julia. "Oh, Jules, you're awake!"

"Easy, Cole, easy!" Elena says as Cole leaps onto the bed to hug Julia.

Julia's *ows* and *oh my Gods* are enough for Cole to get the hint, though, and he quickly stops the hug and starts apologizing. "I'm so sorry, Jules. Are you okay? Oh God, man, we were so worried. You've been out of it for like, what's it been now, Mom? A week?"

Elena nods. "Well, five days, but yeah."

Julia holds her hand out and looks at Elena. "Will you help me? I want to get up."

"Why? You're not leaving yet."

Julia knows Elena's words are meant to be icy, but they're just sarcastic and sad enough that Julia has to fight to hold back a smile.

"Y'know, I have half a mind to—"

"To what?" Elena stares for one beat, then another before she takes Julia's hand. Elena's skin is so soft, and Julia curses at herself for even noticing. The whole process is slow going at first, but after Elena gets Julia situated on the bed, she helps Julia stand.

They're looking into each other's eyes. Julia's head feels a little better after standing, and even though she's uneasy on her feet and very worn out, it feels really good to stand. "Will you take me to see Leia?" Julia asks.

"Cole? Is Leia ready?"

He clears his throat. "She's been a little antsy today. It's like she knew or something."

"Knew what?" Julia asks as she looks back at Cole.

"That you were going to wake up." Cole's answer is matter-of-fact, and he shrugs, his hands shoved into his front pockets. He looks so young, yet so mature at the same time.

"Take me to her."

❖

Julia is leaning very heavily on Cole as they approach the barn. It is probably way too soon for Julia to be out and about or to even consider seeing Leia, but she can't help it. She feels as if she needs to see her, make sure everything is really okay.

When they turn the corner into the barn, Julia stops in her tracks. Penn is standing there, pitchfork in hand, dirt and grime covering her, drinking from a water bottle. Cole huffs and urges Julia to keep walking. "She's been helping with the horses. She's leaving at the end of August, according to Mom."

Julia rolls her eyes. "I'll believe it when I see it."

"Jules…Mom needs you. I need you."

"Cole, don't, please." She moves with Cole, slowly but surely, toward Leia's stall. She can hear the horse before she sees her.

"Jules, wait," Cole says as he stops them before they get to Leia's stall. He looks back. "Leia was really upset at first. I don't think she's back to normal yet. She's settled down tremendously, but she's real skittish. I don't want you to think it's you."

"What do you mean?"

"I mean, she was scared, Jules. She wouldn't let anyone near her at first. Even the vet had issues. She got banged up pretty bad. Not just her body but her spirit. I don't know, Jules, sometimes trauma like that does stuff to a horse. It's gonna take time." Cole squeezes Julia's forearm. "So, leaving? Right now? Running away like I think you want to do and must always do, according to Mom and Elijah?" Cole purses his lips, runs a hand through his black shaggy hair. "You just can't do it. Not even because Mom and I need you. But because you can't leave your horse like that."

Julia studies Cole while he stands there. He's so tall and so handsome. He looks so much like his mother; even her dark skin tone was passed down. She wonders when in the time she's been here did this kid grow up and mature because everything he's saying is so wise. Julia finally nods, gathers all of her courage, and motions for Cole to keep walking. They get to the stall door, and Julia peers over the top as she uses the frame of the door to steady herself. She can see the scratches that Elena was talking about earlier on Leia's right side. They must have been deep because there are stitches, about fifty or so. A muscle twitch runs through Leia's body, and it makes Julia's heart hurt. "Leia?" Immediately, Leia looks at the stall door. Her ears start to perk up, her eyes lose the crazed look, and she takes a few steps toward the door. "Hi, girl. I heard you saved me?" Julia cannot even describe the feeling that washes over her when Leia's snout nudges her hand. It's almost as if she can see the stress leaving Leia's body.

"How is it going?"

Julia glances back when she hears Penn ask the question. She watches Cole motion toward her and Leia. "Have you ever seen something like this before?" Cole asks Penn. Julia looks back at Leia and tries not to care what Penn has to say.

"Once," Julia hears Penn say. "It was my daddy's horse. But never again since then."

And for the first time since meeting Penn, Julia wishes she didn't hate her so much, because she'd love to hear more about a horse saving a person's life.

❖

The bruises on Julia's rib cage are still a very deep purple. There's yellowing around the edges, but they are sore to the touch. Julia turns and looks over her shoulder into the mirror in the bathroom. The bright light makes her squint a bit when she sees the bruise along her shoulder blade. It's the darkest and hurts the most out of all of them. She picks up her towel and secures it around her body, looks into the mirror at herself, at her wet hair, at her dark tan lines on her biceps. Everything about her condition right now makes her angry.

And *confused.*

She needs to have Elena help her rub the liniment on the bruises on her back, but she's also so nervous to have Elena near her right now. Julia is still mad at Elena, still doesn't want her around, still feels the constant desire to kiss her even though she wants to cry in her presence. It's infuriating.

Julia opens the door to Elena's master bathroom and sees Elena sitting on the bed. "Can you help me?"

"The liniment?"

"Yes. I can't reach the bruises on my back."

"Those bruises are the worst."

No shit, those are the worst. She almost got eaten alive by a fucking bear. Julia doesn't respond, though. It's not worth the sarcasm.

Elena is in the bathroom now, unscrewing the cap on the liniment the doctor suggested to help speed up the healing. "You need to, um, move your towel down," she says, whispering the last part.

Julia listens, loosens her towel, moves her hair, and tries really hard to not watch Elena in the condensation-covered mirror. Her efforts are futile, though, as she sneaks a peek at Elena in her gray Colorado T-shirt and flannel pajama pants. She feels Elena's strong fingers land on her skin. The ointment is cool, but Elena works it in small circular motions, and Julia feels everything in that area start to warm. "What is this stuff that you are putting on me?"

"You wouldn't believe me if I told you."

"Try me."

"Tiger Balm."

"Are you fucking kidding me? I almost get killed by a bear, and you're putting something on me called *Tiger* Balm?"

Elena runs her fingers up the length of both of Julia's shoulder blades and over her shoulders. "The irony is ridiculous, isn't it?" She glances at Julia in the mirror, and their eyes lock. "Do you want me to rub this on your other bruises?"

"On my rib cage?"

Elena groans. "I've been doing it since it happened. It's not like I've never seen you naked before."

"I mean, you don't have to. I can handle it."

"Stop being an ass. Turn around, hold the towel up, and stand there."

"I almost forgot what a jerk you could be," Julia says, barely above a whisper. She still does as she's told, though, and is standing holding the towel up under her arms when she feels Elena's hand slip under the terry cloth and land on her rib cage so very gently. Julia's heart leaps into her throat when Elena's soft fingers smooth over the bruised skin. It shouldn't be turning Julia on, but it is. It really, *really is.* And when she looks at Elena, at her full lips and her beautiful eyes, all she can feel, besides the intense heat growing between her thighs, is the need to kiss her.

"There," Elena whispers as she pulls her hand away. "All done."

Julia's eyes slide closed, and she draws a deep breath into her lungs. There's not a bone in her body that doesn't want to drop the towel and beg Elena to take her on the bathroom counter right now.

But then she remembers riding back to the ranch on Leia and why she was even out there in the first place and why the fucking bruises are there.

And the moment is fleeting. Even though she can still feel everything in between her legs.

Chapter Twenty

It's been two weeks since Julia woke up, and every day she feels better and better. She moves back into her cabin four days after she wakes up, away from Elena, away from her eyes, where she feels as if she can breathe. Being around Elena was wonderful and horrifying all at the same time because Elena is all the things that Julia needs and wants. She's comfort and love and beauty, and she's *home*. Julia wasn't sure if she was ready to forgive her yet, so seeing her in the mornings drinking coffee, reading the newspaper, making Julia eggs or pancakes and bacon…It was all just too much.

Julia came to terms with the fact that she was in love with Elena after the hoedown, after their night together, after everything that the two shared. And every time she looked at Elena in the dimly lit bedroom with the really amazing, plum-colored sheets, she knew it was only a matter of time before she cracked and let Elena back over her poorly reconstructed walls.

So she moved back to the cabin.

Alone.

And everything is the same. The bed is too small, and the sheets are too rough, and the lights are too harsh. All she can think about is how much she misses Elena's smile and her cooking and her fingertips as she massages her bruises.

But Julia is going to stay at the ranch. She's not running. She promised Leia and Cole, *dear sweet Cole.*

And Leia's getting so much stronger, too. Every day, they go for a walk together. Never to the pasture. Not yet. But they still walk; Julia leads, and Leia follows, and Julia talks to Leia like she would a best friend. She tells Leia about her day, about her struggles, about how all she wants is things to go back to normal. She tells Leia about her foster life, about her biological parents, about jail time and relationships that went wrong. It makes Julia sad some days that Leia can't just answer. It'd be so much easier.

Julia is walking back to the barn with Leia when she hears boot steps approaching. She glances over her shoulder and sees that it's Penn. Her heart isn't ready for this altercation. Truthfully, she isn't sure if she'll ever be ready.

"Julia?"

She stops in her tracks, doesn't look back, doesn't really move other than rolling her eyes. "What?"

"I'm really sorry."

Julia stands still, stoic, unwavering.

"I just wanted to make sure we, me and Elena, make sure we were done. And we are. So, that's all. You gotta understand."

She still doesn't move.

"I feel *real* bad for how this all shook out."

"You should feel bad." Julia's answer is mean, and she hopes it stung as much as it was supposed to.

"Well, I do," Penn says; her voice is forceful but unsure and shaking, and it's a side of her that Julia has never seen. "You know Elena found you and Leia. As Leia was bringing you home. I was locking up and heard Elena shouting. Leia was carrying you on her back, and you were gripping her mane." Penn pauses. "It's my fault you were out there."

Julia cannot stop herself from turning around now to look at Penn standing there, her blue eyes sparkling with tears. There's a part of her that wants to tell Penn she's right. That it is her fault. But Julia knows that's not true. It's not Penn's fault that Julia is so broken that she can't handle anything emotional anymore. It's no one's fault but her own. "Penn, it wasn't your fault," Julia says calmly.

"Yes, it was. I'm the asshole that tried to pull Elena away from being happy with you."

"I'm not going to disagree with you about being an asshole." Julia shrugs. "You kinda deserve that. But," she pauses, takes a few steps toward where Penn is standing on the dirt path, "I'm fucked up. And that is not your fault."

Penn loops her thumbs into the front pockets of her jeans. She ducks her head, then glances back up at Julia. "I should have never tried again with Elena, though. And I'm really sorry about that."

Julia looks away from Penn out across the property toward where the sun is setting and sighs.

"You need to forgive her. She was hysterical when she saw the state you were in."

"I do *not* need your advice about love." Julia huffs, her spine stiffening almost on command.

"Love, eh?"

"I just meant, like, matters of the heart or whatever."

Penn chuckles. "Ya know, Julia, your 'stubborn ass' routine is pretty cute. But let me give you a piece of advice, since I got about ten years on ya." Penn stops and looks straight at Julia. "Sometimes, you just gotta say, 'fuck it' and go with what your heart wants. And we all know what Elena's heart wants." She starts to walk away from Julia but turns around and finishes with, "Don't spend your life running from everyone. It's gonna get tiring."

Julia watches Penn tip her cowboy hat, turn around smoothly, and walk away. She hates to admit it, but Penn is right. That thought alone makes her want to scream. *And* run. Straight for the hills and not look back.

It really is good advice, though. She knows she should listen. She needs to listen to someone for once in her life. Why not listen to the one person she wants out of her life?

❖

Elijah is waiting for Julia on the porch steps of the cabin after she has put Leia away. She has hardly talked to him since everything happened, and seeing him makes her throat sort of ache in a way she doesn't know how to handle. Is this what missing a friend feels like?

"City Girl," he says, his voice filled with sincerity. "Figured I'd come see you since you've been avoiding me like the plague."

Julia's mouth falls open. "Are you kidding me? You've barely said three words to me since the accident. What the hell am I supposed to do? Chase you around?"

"Well, yeah."

"You're crazy."

"Well, *yeah*." Elijah raises his eyebrows and flashes his teeth, and Julia starts to laugh. "I knew you'd laugh eventually." He pats the open spot on the step. Julia sits, looks at him, then back out across the field. "You doin' okay?"

"I think so?"

"Is that a question?"

"Yeah," she says with a soft snort. "I don't know if I'm doing okay. I'm feeling better. That's for sure."

"Then? What's goin' on in that head of yours?"

"Oh, Jesus. That's a loaded question."

"I'm all ears."

"Penn just apologized for everything."

"Did something happen there?"

Julia looks at Elijah, her eyebrow arched, her lips pursed. "Don't be a dick. You know what happened."

He raises his hands in mock surrender. "Okay, okay. I didn't want you to think we gossip about you." He leans into her shoulder. "How'd the convo go? Do I need to rough her up again?"

"*Again?* What do you mean?"

Elijah's face falls after his admission. He shrugs and rests his elbows on his knees. "I sort of," he pauses, "got into a little bit of a, um, what do you call it? A 'scuffle'?"

"With Penn?"

Elijah nods.

"What the hell? She's a woman."

"Fuck that. She fuckin' kissed Elena and pissed you off, and she's not even *welcome* here anymore."

Julia can't fight the smile that appears on her lips. "What'd you do?"

"Well, I didn't hit her. But I went and talked to her and well, when she got pushy with me, she sort of stumbled and fell and landed in some fresh manure."

A giggle bubbles out of Julia's mouth, and for the first time in a while, she's actually *laughing*. Full on laughing. With Elijah. And it feels so very good. Even though her ribs are hurting, it still feels good. "I cannot believe that. Seriously?" He nods, and she leans into him a little harder. "I love ya, Elijah."

"I love ya, too, Jules. I'm glad you didn't run away."

This is the first moment she's actually glad she didn't run away, too.

❖

It's not long before there's a knock at Julia's door while she's eating popcorn on the couch, occupying herself so she doesn't do something stupid like march over to Elena's so she doesn't have to be alone any longer. She wants to act as if she's not home, but she knows that won't work. She turns her head and shouts, "Come in," over her shoulder, prays it isn't Elena, and cringes when she hears the familiar footsteps and even more familiar exasperated sigh.

"Seriously?"

"What?" Julia asks, not moving from her spot or making eye contact.

"You have got some nerve."

"What the hell are you talking about?" Julia cranes her neck and looks at Elena. Her arms are crossed, her skin is flushed, and her hair is a mess. She looks as if she's going crazy. Or maybe that she's already arrived at crazy. "What is going on?"

"Oh, you know damn well what's going on."

"Um—"

"Uh, no, you just shut your mouth."

Elena's tone makes Julia's spine straighten. Julia wants to protest, but she's learned a lot about Elena in the past months, and it's best to just listen when told.

Elena takes a couple steps into the house, her hand in the air. "You come here, to *my ranch*, and you disrupt *my life*, and you get close to *my child*, who absolutely thinks you're the best thing since sliced bread, and…and…you make me *fall in love* with you, and then fine, I screwed it up, but I have been practically begging you to forgive me. Begging! You know everything that happened wasn't just me. You know that was Penn, too! And yet, nothing. You still won't budge. You sit in here, in *my* cabin, using *my* electricity, on *my* couch, reading." Elena lunges at

Julia and snatches the book out of her hands. "What the hell book is this anyway? *The Horse Whisperer*? Are you *fucking* kidding me!" She tosses the book up in the air and screams, her hands in fists, raised to the ceiling. "I cannot believe you, Julia Finch!"

Julia cannot move. She's paralyzed. She doesn't even know what to say to defend herself because honestly, she's not sure she wants to even try right now.

"Are you even going to say anything?"

Julia shakes her head.

"I swear to Christ."

Julia watches Elena start to pace. She walks from the entryway to the window to the couch to the chair to the wall and then starts the loop all over again. Julia has never seen Elena like this in all the times she's been around her. In a different setting, it might be comical. Right now? It's freaking her out.

"All I want is for you to realize that I'm sorry. I am so sorry. I never meant to hurt you. I never meant for this to happen. I never meant for you to get hurt. I never meant for Leia to get hurt. I just wanted to—"

Julia is standing now, and she's positioned herself in front of Elena on one of her passes to the window. Elena stops abruptly, her breath audibly hitching in her throat. Julia can feel the electricity in the room surrounding them. "You fell in love with me?" Her question is so quiet, so smooth and gentle, that she barely feels as if she said it herself. But when she sees Elena's eyes, the way the tears that have been threatening to fall since the moment she burst through the door, relinquish their rights to the territory, she knows she said it.

"Yes," Elena whispers. "I fell in love with you. I fell in love with you the moment you met Leia. I knew. In that instant...I knew."

"Elena." Julia's voice is caught in her throat.

"I can't keep doing this, Julia."

"Can't keep doing what?"

"This." Elena motions to herself and then Julia. "Us. This back and forth thing. We don't even do it well."

A smile starts to tug at the corner of Julia's lips.

"I don't want you to be here in this cabin. I want you there." Elena points at the house. "I want you with me. I need you with me. Please, come home with me."

"And Cole? He's okay with this?"

"Cole?" Elena raises her voice, and the screen door opens, slams shut, and in walks Cole. His ball cap is on backward, his hands are shoved into his jean pockets, and he's all legs and arms.

"Hi, Jules," he says sheepishly. "I'm better than okay with this. You need to come home." He picks his head up and looks at Julia square in the eyes. "You're the first person I've wanted Mom to be with in a long time. Shit, you're the first person that's understood me in a long time."

"Cole, language," Elena says, followed by a groan.

"Ma, come on." Cole sighs. "I just mean, Jules, you're like, part of us now. And who's going to be there for Mom when I go to college?"

Julia's mouth falls open. "Whoa, what?" She looks at Cole, then at Elena, and then back at Cole. "Seriously? You got in?"

Cole can no longer hide his smile when he turns his ball cap around and shows off a University of Illinois Chicago emblem. "I'm going to Chicago, Jules. In December. I start in January. I got in!"

Julia rushes over to Cole and throws her arms around him. "I am so proud of you! I told you that you could do it. I knew it. I just knew it!" When she feels him hug her back, she realizes that she's crying. She's full on, tears streaming down her face, crying. She pulls away from him and wipes at her eyes with the sleeves of her T-shirt. "You're going to love it so much."

"For the record, I wish you two would have consulted me about this," Elena says as she walks up behind Julia and Cole.

Julia spins around and runs her hand through her hair. "Well, yeah, I mean, that was all Cole's fault."

"Jules, what the hell?"

Elena just shakes her head.

Julia laughs when Cole puts his arm over Julia's shoulder. "Thanks for letting me do this, though, Mom. I know you'll be okay since Julia will be with you." He looks down at Julia and smiles. "Right?"

Julia looks up at him, his glowing smile, his dark eyes that are so much like his mother's, and his expression that is so filled with excitement that it really is contagious. "Right," she says before looking at Elena. She reaches forward and intertwines her fingers with Elena's. "So, I need to come home, eh?"

Elena nods, her eyes filled with tears.

"Can we move my stuff tomorrow?"

Another nod from Elena, and tears are falling from her eyes.

Julia moves closer to her and slides her arms around Elena. When she pulls Elena into a hug, she can feel her body start to relax, and it makes everything in her heart feel lighter.

For the first time in forever, she finally has a home. And people that want her. And to think she almost didn't let any of them break down her walls.

Epilogue

It's been a little over a year since Julia drove into town with a sturdily built wall and a chip on her shoulder. Things are good now. They're really, *really* good. Even Cole is doing well. He has a straight A average, he has a new girlfriend, and he even made a group of friends that seem really awesome. And they were all super outgoing and fun when Elena and Julia visited him during spring break. It was so great to see him in his element, settling into big-city living in Chicago and actually doing what he wanted to do. It makes Julia happy that she was able to have a hand in that.

Julia looks over at Elena as they stand on the edge of the mountain where they watched the stars almost a year ago. "Thank you," she says and reaches over to hold Elena's hand.

"For what?" Elena's cocked head and small smile indicate that she knows what Julia means, but Julia humors her.

"For this." She motions to their surroundings, to the mountains and sky. "For giving me a place that actually feels like home."

Elena squeezes Julia's hand. "Thank *you* for not running away."

"I'm really glad I didn't."

"Me, too."

The two stand again in silence, the June sun shining on them, and look out over the valley below them. Julia breathes in deep and remembers the first time she pulled Colorado air into her lungs. So much has happened since then. So many amazing moments that have helped her get to this moment. Julia looks over at Elena. *To get to this woman...*

"Should we go back?"

"Do we have to?" Julia asks as she pulls her gaze away from Elena's beautiful features and looks across the valley one more time.

"You're nervous, aren't you?"

"Yes. Insanely."

"You didn't have to do this, you know?"

Julia takes a deep breath and lets it out. "I know, but I wanted to respond. Getting the letter from my parents was…almost too much to handle." She looks at Elena. "I felt like I owed it to myself to accept their apology."

"I know, my love."

"I just hope inviting them here wasn't a mistake."

Elena pulls Julia closer to her. "I am here if it turns out to be one. But," she says as she kisses Julia's cheek and leans her forehead against Julia's temple. "I have a feeling it's going to turn out exactly how you want."

"You really think so?"

"Yes," Elena whispers. She reaches up and turns Julia's face toward hers. "I love you, Julia Finch."

It's amazing how many times she's heard that in the past year, but it never fails to take her breath away. This time is no different. "I love you, too," she whispers.

❖

When Elena and Julia come galloping into the field before the house, she places her hand on the side of Leia's neck. It seems to help calm the horse when they pass the area where it all happened. It took a lot longer than she thought it would to even get a leg over Leia again, but once it did happen, it was as if no time had passed. She knows that it created a bond between them that can never be broken, though, and even though it was a lot of trauma, she wouldn't trade the bond she and Leia share for anything.

"You know it does get easier. Every day, right?"

Julia shrugs. "I know. I still dream about it, though. The bear, the claws, how hard the ground felt when I slammed into it."

"You've fallen a lot more since then," Elena says. "And you always get back up."

A smile spreads across Julia's lips, and she nods. Elena's right; she does get back up. But it's hard to explain the memory to anyone, even Elena. The post-traumatic stress she went through was enough to drive a sane person crazy. Thankfully, Elena was patient. So, so patient. And kind…or Julia isn't sure she would have survived the months following the attack.

When they round the bend, and the log home and barn come into view, she sees Elijah leaning against the barn, his arms crossed, his left leg crossed over his right, and a grin on his face.

"What are you all smiles about?" Elena asks when they approach. Both women dismount their horses and hand Elijah the reins to hold.

"I just heard that Penn is engaged."

"Well, that's great news." Julia keeps her eyes on Elena's facial features the entire time to gauge her reaction.

"Who did you hear this from?" Elena asks with her hands on her hips. "Because I heard something, but I don't know if it was a reliable source."

Julia lets out a laugh. "Oh, really? And when were you going to share this information? Enquiring minds want to know!" She's smiling, and so is Elena, and it's nice that the mention of Penn's name doesn't cause either of their spines to stiffen or lips to purse.

"Elijah? Who is it?"

"None other than, drum roll please." Elijah starts patting his belly rapidly to create a drum roll.

"Get on with it!" Julia says.

"Antoinette Carson."

"Toni? Shut the front door!" Julia shouts.

Elena laughs a hearty laugh and shakes her head. "That's what I heard, too."

"Holy shit! I haven't heard from Toni in weeks. When she said she was leaving town, I didn't believe her…and now this? How crazy!"

"Yeah, well," Elena says. "Until you, Toni was always the free bird of our little town, so I'm not surprised."

"Benjamin ain't happy about this news. He's been licking his wounds something fierce. Now it's even worse. I can barely have a drink down there anymore."

Julia chuckles at Elijah's forlorn expression. "Oh, buddy, I can't imagine how hard that must be for you." They all laugh, then abruptly stop when they hear a car pulling up the road.

"Is that them?" Elijah asks.

After the engine turns off, the doors open, and a man and a woman step out of the car. Julia's heart is beating like mad. "Jack, Kelly, hi," she says as she approaches the couple.

Kelly smiles and reaches out with a hand. She places it on Julia's forearm. "Thank you so much for—"

"Inviting us." Jack smiles when Julia looks at him.

"Well, you can't drive through Colorado and not make a pit stop here, I guess." She motions for her parents to walk toward the picnic tables. "Let's, um, let's go catch up," Julia says softly. Elena gives Julia a thumbs-up and smiles. It helps, but Julia is still so nervous.

As soon as Kelly sits down she leans forward and says, "Julia, honey, I just have to get this out of the way. We know what we did was wrong." She sighs. "I never meant for this to happen like this. I just wasn't—"

"Equipped to deal with a daughter who's a convict?" Julia crosses her arms.

Kelly raises her head and straightens her shoulders. "Honestly? Yes. That was it. It was like a punch to the gut to know that what we did, giving you up, was the wrong thing to do. We did it so you'd have a chance. We were young, stupid, mixed up with the wrong crowd. It was for the best."

"We fucked up." Jack shrugs and folds his hands together on top of the wood surface. "But we are so happy that we found you. And we're very thankful that your landlord was so forthcoming with your forwarding address." Jack looks down at his hands. "I would have run, too, after how we treated you."

"We weren't perfect, so why should we judge you?"

Julia looks next to her at Kelly. It is a strange sensation to look at someone that you resemble so much. "So, let's move forward?"

"We would love that, if you're really okay with it, of course…" Jack pauses and reaches across the table, and Kelly takes his hand. "We really would like to be in your life a little. Or a lot. Whatever you want."

Julia's eardrums feel as if there's pressure behind them. She looks from Jack to Kelly and then back to Jack again. "I think I could handle that."

"You're sure?" Kelly asks before Jack even has a chance. "We don't want to overstep any boundaries. I am still sick about what happened. I want you to know that."

"Is it going to change things if I tell you I'm a lesbian?"

"Doesn't matter to us."

"I wanted to say that!" Kelly says as she smacks Jack on the arm. It's playful, and Julia almost finds it cute. *Almost.*

Jack chuckles. "We're serious, Julia."

"Really serious." Kelly places her free hand on Julia's forearm. "What do you say?"

Julia glances up to the house and sees Elena sitting on the porch steps, her elbows propped on her knees, watching everything like a hawk. "What if neither of you like what I have to offer?"

"Oh, honey," Kelly whispers. "I am so sorry we made you ever feel that way."

"You have every reason to not trust us." Jack clears his throat. "But I sure hope we can make you see that we'll never hurt you again."

Julia looks between them. She can see herself in Kelly's facial features, and it's unsettling and comforting at the same time. Jack's skin tone is her skin tone. It makes her heart hurt. "Okay." Julia places her palms on the wooden picnic table. "I think you should probably meet the love of my life, then."

Jack glances behind him where Julia is looking, then back at her. "That's her, hmm?"

"Yes, it is."

"She's beautiful," Kelly says while smiling. "Really, really beautiful."

"She saved my life."

"Oh? Really?"

"How'd she do that?" Kelly asks as the three stand to walk toward Elena.

Julia smiles. "She took away my running shoes."

About the Author

Erin Zak grew up on the Western Slope of Colorado in a town with a population of 2,500, a solitary Subway, and one stoplight. She started writing at a young age and has always had a very active imagination. Erin later transplanted to Indiana, where she attended college, started writing a book, and had dreams of one day actually finding the courage to try to get it published.

Erin now resides in Florida, away from the snow and cold, near the Gulf Coast with her family. She enjoys the sun, sand, writing, and spoiling her cocker spaniel, Hanna. When she's not writing, she's obsessively collecting Star Wars memorabilia, planning the next trip to Disney World, or whipping up something delicious to eat in the kitchen.